"Cyne." It was a breathless sound, nothing like how she had meant to say it. Her fingers moved of their own accord, skimming his side.

He put his hands over hers, laughing, and she realized she had tickled him. She laughed herself, only it wasn't a happy sound. To her mind it sounded as if someone was torturing her.

And he was.

Trailing his finger behind her ear and down her jaw, he leaned toward her, kissing her cheek lightly, his full lips warm against her skin. She trembled, her hands reaching up to curl around his forearms.

Truly, Aleene could not believe her luck in finding Cyne in her forest. He was the key to everything she wanted, and yet she yearned for more. A more she didn't understand.

Another feather-light kiss teased the corner of her mouth. Holding tightly to Cyne's arms, she moaned, relaxing toward her husband. She wanted to surrender to him, have him comfort her, take care of her.

The next kiss came down on her li...

A deep kiss.

"Save me, Cyne," s...

Other **AVON ROMANCES**

HER NORMAN CONQUEROR

Malia Martin

AVON BOOKS ◆ NEW YORK

AVON BOOKS, INC.
1350 Avenue of the Americas
New York, New York 10019

Copyright © 1998 by Malia B. Nahas
Inside cover author photo by Jerry Cauchi
Published by arrangement with the author
Visit our website at **http://www.AvonBooks.com**
Library of Congress Catalog Card Number: 97-94939
ISBN: 0-380-79896-4

First Avon Books Printing: August 1998

AVON TRADEMARK REG. U.S. PAT. OFF. AND IN OTHER COUNTRIES, MARCA REGISTRADA, HECHO EN U.S.A.

Printed in the U.S.A.

WCD   10 9 8 7 6 5 4 3 2 1

*To Steve, for always knowing
that it would happen and for
doing dishes, changing diapers and
eating take out along the way.*

*And to Cindy, Justine and Kay:
how will I ever do it again without you?*

Part I

Chapter 1

"**S**hall we have the prisoner killed, milady?"

Aleene kept her back turned toward her steward. "No." She fingered the heavy tapestry that hung on the wall of her chamber.

"Surely you don't wish him tortured."

"Of a sort, Cuthebert." She brushed the pads of her fingertips against the silk threads, knowing she shouldn't handle the beautiful piece so. "I shall marry him."

"Marry?" Her steward's voice cracked in the middle of the word. "But, milady, Aethregard and the king . . ."

"Will not succeed in their quest to control me." She turned slowly, keeping her shoulders squared, her spine straight. "Bring the priest and collect the prisoner, Cuthebert. We must do this before Aethregard returns." Her steward swallowed, his Adam's apple bobbing in his

3

throat. She waited a full second, then blinked once. Her gaze, she knew, was icy.

"Milady, he is but a lowly poacher. A simpleton at that!" Cuthebert's face had turned a mottled red.

"Cuthebert," she said, "I have not asked you to expound on my decision. Bring the prisoner and the priest."

Her steward shook his head. "You cannot, milady! Your betrothal has been accepted by the king. And Aethregard will expect . . ."

Aleene cut off his words with a slice of her hand. "Now!" She did not yell, but Cuthebert stopped in midsentence, his eyes bulging.

"You shall incur the wrath of powerful men, milady," he said, anger straining his voice. He turned on his heel and left.

Aleene waited until she could no longer hear Cuthebert's retreating footsteps before she allowed herself to let the air out of her lungs. Clenching her fists, she stilled the tremor that radiated down her arms. There was always that split second before her servants obeyed her when Aleene was sure that they wouldn't. And what would she do then?

She went to the massive chair that had been her father's and sank into it. She hated the doubt that ate at her tenuous self-esteem. She hated it so she hid it from all. Now, alone, Aleene dropped her head into her hands, as the shaking she thought she had mastered overtook her. Her entire body trembled as if she had just come from a sound dunking in the icy waves that splashed against the cliffs below. She did not allow tears, though. Never tears. Others would never know she had succumbed to her fears for a few still moments just so long as she didn't cry.

Her thoughts turned to the dirt-encrusted prisoner she had seen being led from the forest that morning, and she felt her stomach heave. She must do this! It was her only hope. She had hired professional soldiers, house-carls, which usually only earls had, she had bought ships and readied her coveted castle for attack. All this to show King Harold that she needed no man, yet still he wanted to wed her to Aethregard. Still he felt the jewel that sat at the mouth of Pevensey Harbor would be better controlled by a man.

When the knock at her door sounded, she had once again found control. She stood facing the massive doors of what had once been her father's bedchamber and bid Cuthebert enter.

He did, looking twenty years older than he had when he left. The priest followed him, clutching his book of prayers like a lifeline. Behind this sorry troupe came the prisoner, shackled and dirty. The entire room suddenly reeked of manure. Aleene did not allow herself even to wrinkle her brow.

She turned to the priest. "You may proceed, quickly."

He stared at her, misgivings written clearly in his lamblike eyes. Aleene put every ounce of disdain she could in the look she settled upon him. He did not speak his discontent.

He motioned for Cuthebert to bring the prisoner forward. The man shuffled in deference to the chains about his feet. Or, perhaps, that was how he walked normally. Aleene could not have known. She had seen him only once before, when her men had brought him from her forests where he had been caught poaching. He had been trussed up and ready for the dungeon then as well. He looked at her now as he had then, blankly. He blinked once, then twice. He scratched himself and stared.

Aleene turned toward the priest and nodded.

The priest opened his prayer book quickly, his fingers clumsily going through the pages.

"Dispense with the trivialities, Father Bartholomew, get this thing done quickly," Aleene ordered in her haughtiest voice.

The priest nodded, his eyes darting from her to the book in his hands. He gulped loudly and began to read. Aleene watched as fat beads of perspiration emerged from the edge of the priest's tonsure and slid down his pale, rounded cheeks. His girth jiggled beneath the coarse robes he wore, as he shifted his weight from one foot to the other.

Aleene stood erect, not allowing herself to blink.

Cuthebert breathed heavily behind her.

The prisoner stood a sword's length away from her, staring blankly out the window. She would lie with him this night, and through every night that stood between now and Aethregard's return. The thought of allowing another to touch her brought terror, but she pushed it aside. She would not allow her stepbrother to annul this marriage, and so she had to be with child, soon. Aleene controlled the shudder that stirred at the base of her spine.

"Milady?" Father Bartholomew looked at her, his brows raised in hopeful question.

Aleene berated herself for letting her thoughts wander. She tried to think of what the priest might have asked, then understood suddenly. "I will," she said.

The priest's brows dropped in a crestfallen expression. He continued.

Aleene clenched her hands in the fabric of her gown, only then realizing that she wore one of her oldest kirtles, and it covered an equally old tunic. Her mind reached back to memories of her early childhood. She had dreamed often of her wedding. She would wear silk and jewels. She would sing and be merry. Her husband would be tall and strong.

An almost unbearable sweep of longing crushed through her defenses. She might have even let out a small gasp. The priest looked up quickly, but Aleene saved herself. She immediately stiffened, and stared down her nose at the short, fat man.

He averted his eyes, and continued.

Aleene stole a glance at the flesh and blood husband beside her. Even with his shoulders hunched forward he was tall, taller than her, which made him taller than most men. His straggly, long hair, so matted with dirt and who knew what else she could not tell what color it was, hid most of his face. His blank stare turned to her then, and she studied him in return.

His eyes were blue. They might have actually been a startling feature had any intelligence glowed there.

Aleene looked away, the longing for her childhood dreams of happiness that had crushed her before now threatened to bring her low, but she stood straighter and gritted her teeth together. There was no avoiding what she must do.

The priest moved suddenly, and Aleene realized it was over. She had married the half-wit poacher. Cuthebert's breathing had escalated to an alarming rate. She feared he might succumb to a faint. As she turned, she had a hysterical need to laugh. Life really was quite hilarious in a sick kind of way.

"Bathe him and return him," she managed to instruct Cuthebert. "I will have an heir growing in my belly before Aethregard's shadow darkens Seabreeze Castle."

Cuthebert looked as if he might be ill. Aleene knew how he felt, but retained her regal bearing still. "Now, Cuthebert."

The steward grabbed her husband's arm and dragged him toward the door.

"And shave that beard from his face. It looks to be crawling with vermin."

Cuthebert stopped, nodded, then cleared his throat. "Shall we shave his hair as well?"

Aleene looked at the prisoner's mass of tangled hair and suddenly she needed everyone gone. She was going to lose control. She felt she might even cry. "No!" she cried a bit too vehemently. Taking a deep breath she managed to say again, "No, just kill anything that moves in that mess. Now, Cuthebert, go."

Cuthebert looked at her strangely, but grunted an assent and left with the prisoner.

The priest looked as if he wanted to counsel her, but Aleene turned her back on him. "Be gone!" she demanded, barely keeping her voice steady, and only staying calm until she heard the heavy door close behind him.

This time the shaking came quickly, almost knocking Aleene from her feet before she had gained the chair. She dropped her head against her hands, her dark hair falling forward. She had done it. She was married to some half-wit poacher unknown to her until this very day.

Unknown to her even now, truly. Aethregard would be furious. Her king would surely seek to annul the marriage. Her people would look on her with even more suspicion and abhorrence.

A tiny laugh escaped her throat. It was a terrible sound that echoed in the cavernous room.

A knock at the door interrupted her musings, but this time she was not ready. She jumped quickly from the chair and clutched her hands together behind her back. She took a deep breath and closed her eyes for a moment.

"Enter," she said finally.

Berthilde, her maid, bustled in, an army of servants behind her.

Aleene blinked and stepped backward at the invasion. "Berthilde, send these people away."

"I have ordered ye a bath, milady." Without looking at Aleene, the woman directed the servants to put the deep, wooden bath in a corner and begin filling it with steaming buckets of water.

Aleene watched the activity in silence. Berthilde was one of the people Aleene loathed to contradict. She knew the serving woman to have a will of steel, and she did not wish to be challenged before the others. These past six months since her stepfather, Tosig, had finally left his earthly bounds, Aleene had tried her hardest to gain the respect of her people. She wanted them to look upon her as the ruler of

Seabreeze Castle. They would not. They wanted Aethregard, Tosig's son, as their liege.

Seabreeze was a dower estate, handed down through the female line of Aleene's family. Always, the women had been supported as the rulers of the estate. But Aleene's mother had made the terrible mistake of marrying a foreigner, a Spaniard. He had built a large castle in the new French style where before there had been a traditional Saxon Hall.

The people of Pevensey feared the dark man on the hill and were happy when he died, and Aleene's mother married Tosig. They knew Aleene had never gotten along with Tosig, and they now feared Aleene would be as treacherous to Seabreeze's stability as her mother. Aleene knew of their feelings. She knew she must fight for the respect of her people. So she fought the only way she knew how, by covering up her insecurities and showing them a strength she could only hope to have.

Finally the room emptied except for Berthilde, who came forward and helped Aleene from her kirtle. The maid turned away then as Aleene undressed completely and slid beneath the water.

Berthilde handed her a pot of soap without turning around. It was a routine they had perfected over the years. Other servants would have thought such manners strange, and whispered among themselves and to others of the strange lady at Seabreeze Castle. And so she allowed only Berthilde to assist her, for she knew the woman would keep her own counsel.

"So ye have married a half-wit poacher, milady." Unfortunately, the woman would not keep her mouth closed in Aleene's presence.

"Yes." She soaped herself ruthlessly, scrubbing between her toes and fingers.

"King Harold will not be amused, I'm sure." She clicked her tongue against her teeth. "Neither will Aethregard."

Aleene rinsed herself, then lowered her head beneath the water. It took two good dunkings to get her long, thick hair completely wet. "I am the heiress of Seabreeze," she said as she flipped her hair over the side of the tub. "Aethregard has no right to anything." She lowered herself until her chin just grazed the water. "I am ready, Berthilde."

The woman turned. She pushed the crinkly gray hair that had escaped its moorings away from her face with pudgy fingers. "I hope you are."

Aleene wasn't sure what the woman meant, and wasn't sure she wanted to know. She covered herself with her hands even though the murky water now hid her from sight as Berthilde soaped her hair. "I am finally rid of Tosig. I will no longer be controlled by anyone."

Berthilde's fingers stopped moving and silence pulsed between them.

"Do not say that if others are around, milady," Berthilde finally said.

Aleene pulled away from her maid's hands and turned carefully to face her. "What, Berthilde, what must I not say?"

Berthilde held her soapy hands above the water and stared at Aleene with sad, old eyes. "Do not say you are rid of Tosig."

"But why? I am rid of him, and I am happy of it."

"Turn around and let me finish your hair." When Aleene did what the maid asked, Berthilde gently resumed massaging the soap into Aleene's scalp. " 'Tis just that I've heard people talk. There would be some who believe you are responsible for Tosig's death."

Aleene huffed a disgusted sound. "If I had been brave enough to kill him, I would have done it many years before this."

"Do not play with fire."

Aleene sighed.

"You say you wish not to be controlled by anyone, and yet with this rash marriage, you put yourself in jeopardy of being controlled by the Bastard Duke."

"All these dire warnings, Berthilde, are too dramatic. It is nearly winter; the threat of invasion from William's Normans is over until next summer, surely."

"Ye have put yourself in jeopardy," the

woman repeated, and Aleene bit the edge of her tongue this time and said nothing.

"I'll not be saying anything more, milady."

"Good."

Berthilde pushed Aleene forward and dumped a bucket of clean water over her head. The water had become chilled and it shocked Aleene into a small cry.

"But perhaps there are those around with your best interests at heart." The woman defied her earlier statement and said something more. "Perhaps there are those who do not wish to control but to protect and help." Berthilde stood still for a moment over Aleene.

Aleene remained huddled in the large tub. She pulled her knees to her chest and bent her head. "Be gone, Berthilde," she said into the water. Her breath sent small ripples out in a circle. She could see her eyes, large and dark staring back at her, screaming at her that she didn't belong, that she, a dark-eyed, dark-skinned daughter of a Spaniard, didn't belong among the fair-haired people she ruled.

Berthilde sighed, a long sad sound. "Yes, milady." She turned, but Aleene waited for her to leave before moving. "Ye intend to couple with this new husband of yours, milady?"

Aleene breathed in strongly and gripped the sides of the tub. A mind-numbing feeling of ugliness, of vulnerability, shook her entire body. A darkness almost swallowed her, but it was not completely black. There was something there, someone, coming ... Aleene pushed it away quickly. She closed her eyes and shoved it back. She would not allow Tosig to rule over her again. She had success within her grasp. With the half-wit poacher and a babe in her belly, she would be able to oust the ghost of Tosig and his arrogant son forever from her life. "Aye, Berthilde, I shall. I will be ruler of Seabreeze as was meant when King Aelfred himself made this a dowry holding to be ruled by the women of my line."

"Ye will need more knowledge than you have now of the mating process, milady."

Aleene laughed, she threw back her head and guffawed. "Tis nothing I need less than to have more knowledge of the mating process."

"Ye shall have to make him ready, milady, for I do not think he will know what to do." Berthilde ignored Aleene's outburst. "Let him touch your breast, that would be easiest."

Aleene almost choked on the fear that clutched at her throat, but she remained silent.

"He will become hard then. I shall leave the sheep grease."

Aleene closed her eyes hard. Sheep grease. The stuff smelled vile. She was not sure she could put it on again without vomiting.

Aleene closed her eyes and hugged herself tightly against the waves of terror that coursed through her. Still she remained silent.

"It will be different this time, so perhaps you can rub yourself against him and not need the sheep grease."

Aleene shook her head. "Different? Is it not always abhorrent?"

"No, milady 'tis not always abhorrent." She closed her eyes and shook her head. "Still, I do not like this."

Aleene nearly laughed again, but she choked on the sound and it sounded more like a gurgle.

Silence stretched between them for a long moment, and Aleene finally looked up at her maid.

"I will never forgive myself for not saving you from that monster." It was a rare burst of emotion from Berthilde. Rare because Aleene had spurned such intimacy for so long. She stiffened.

"I didn't realize. For so many years, I didn't realize. And then it was too late."

"Enough, Berthilde, be gone." Aleene turned her head, staring at the wall. It *was* too late.

She heard the door close behind her maid. Aleene surged from the tub, fumbling for the large drying sheet. She wrapped it around her shaking limbs and stood in the middle of the room. It was too late to save the naïve trust of a young girl, but it was not too late to banish her captors and give to her, finally, ultimate control of her life.

The room was completely dark when Cuth-

ebert returned with the prisoner, her husband.
Aleene stood as far from the door as possible
and bade Cuthebert to leave the man near the
large bed.

"Shall I post a watch by the door, milady?"
His words were tinged with sarcasm, hatred.
"He has been docile, but he is still a thief."

"A thief no longer, Cuthebert." She trained a
steady glare on her steward. "But my husband,
your lord."

Cuthebert blinked slowly, his chest moving
quickly with his heightened breathing. "We
shall see."

"You see now, Cuthebert." Aleene struggled
to breathe normally. "Aethregard has no hope
to rule this castle as of tonight." She turned
away from the man. "I will not need a watch."

"The prisoner has not spoken, milady, he
seems to be mute. He is of lowly birth, I should
say. Gobbles his food like a pig. I cannot vow
he will not give you trouble if left alone with
you."

"He is no prisoner, but my husband. His
name is Cynewulf, Lord Cynewulf," she said,
remembering the poems her mother had sung
to her many years before by that bard. "I shall
handle him." With clenched fists she turned to
Cuthebert. "Be gone, steward, I wish no more
of your presence."

The steward stared at her for a long moment.
She could see the war waging within him as he

gritted his teeth, making a small muscle in his
jaw jump. Aleene waited, inwardly terrified
that Cuthebert would defy her, call in the castle
men, have the prisoner taken away, have her
bound until Aethregard could return and claim
her as his wife, claim her castle as his own, give
Tosig the final victory.

The man turned and left without another
word.

Aleene sagged against the wall and closed
her eyes. She had won again. Another battle behind her, but still so many before her. She
would now have to prove completely her ability to rule her own holding, be lady to her people. For they would surely revolt once it was
widely known that Aethregard had been ousted
from the position of control he had taken since
his father's unfortunate demise.

Aleene sighed heavily and opened her eyes.
She was not alone. She stared at the dark outline of the newly named Cynewulf. She had forgotten him in the moment of turmoil and fear.

Aleene swallowed against the new surge of
terror that shook her. She must now commit the
final act that would bring her out of the clutches
of Aethregard, Tosig, or any man who would
wish to rule her or her holding, make her do
things against her wishes, humiliate her. She
conjured up the feelings of awful vulnerability
she had felt at Tosig's hands. Those were the
feelings she would banish now, by doing this

disgusting act. The air Aleene took into her lungs raked against her throat, filling her ears with harsh sounds.

Taking this man, one so malleable within her hands, would make her master, finally. Yet, still, the ever-present fear kept her leaning against the wall, her legs inert beneath her.

She did not move for a long time, unsure of what to do and not liking that feeling. The man, Cynewulf, did not move either. She watched the shadowy image closely. Because she stared so, the darkness began to play tricks with her eyes. She thought he had moved, thought he was near her, then she couldn't find him. When her breathing calmed, she realized he still stood by the bed, exactly where Cuthebert had left him.

"Come, husband," she said finally, startling herself with the harshness of her tone.

Cynewulf did not move.

She strode across the room. The night seemed overly warm and the room close. She wanted to be alone, to peel away the layers of clothes for relief. Instead she must share her chamber with the dark, shadowy figure that stood hunched near her bed.

She came close. He had shed his malodorous aroma and now smelled musky, male. She halted, fear gripping her heart. He smelled like a man ought to smell.

He shuffled a bit then, his feet moving slightly in the rushes.

"Lie down." She pointed toward the bed. Aleene saw her husband's head move, his gaze following her gesture.

He did not move.

Aleene did not like to touch or be touched, but she knew she would have to guide her new husband. She put her hand tentatively around his arm. Fear blossomed anew and froze her limbs.

He was strong. She could feel the muscles beneath his tunic. They bunched when she touched him, as if he might swing at her. And then they relaxed, quickly, against her fingers.

She pulled her hand away, unbalanced by the strange intimacy of the fleeting touch in the dark, scared by the hidden strength that touch revealed to her.

They stood still, the quiet in the room pulsing with its own life. She could feel her husband's breath fan against her cheek. It smelled of dark ale and fennel. She had expected to endure the stench of rotting teeth and old food. This man surprised her.

She did not like to be surprised. Aleene stepped backward and clenched her hands at her side. "Lie down, Lord Cynewulf." She jerked her head toward the bed. "Now."

The man cocked his head to the side. She couldn't see his expression, but felt that perhaps he looked confused. It would be a nice change from the blank, stupid look that never seemed to change. "I have named you, since you cannot tell us your name. You shall be Cynewulf, Lord Cynewulf of Seabreeze Castle." She turned from him and moved further away. "A great honor. You have been blessed with luck this day, Lord Cynewulf." She spoke to him without looking at him. She heard his feet move among the rushes again. "You are the lord of a rich castle, one of only a few in this land."

Aleene went to the small, high window and looked out. The night was dark. Clouds covered the silver moon, keeping the landscape shrouded in shadows. "Kings juggle for control of this castle, Cynewulf." She found comfort in speaking, a comfort she hadn't felt in many years. "But they shall not have it." She could hear the waves crashing against the cliffs. She sighed and laid her cheek against the rough wooden wall. Cool against her skin, it was a welcome reprieve from the stifling heat of the room. It felt so good to put distance between herself and the intruder in her life. Closing her eyes, Aleene willed herself to be strong. Walking away from him, speaking to him as if he understood, only delayed what she must do. She nearly laughed again as she considered the irony of her goal here tonight, an act she had once fought so often she would now have to initiate with another.

The ropes of her bed creaked in protest, and Aleene realized her husband must have finally done her bidding. She did not move. The pounding surf became a dull roar in her head. A bead of sweat trickled down her neck, and she pressed her tunic against herself to stop its descent. Her fingers rested against the swell of her breast, and she remembered. He would touch her there.

Aleene squeezed her eyes shut against the terrifying images that catapulted through her mind: darkness, heat, hands, groping, fear, crying. Her breathing came fast, making her feel dizzy.

Gripping the edge of the window, Aleene fought to banish the memories. She must do this. Better to bed this half-wit than a true, whole man. A man sired by Tosig. She shuddered, then stiffening her back and thrusting out her chin, Aleene pushed away from the wall.

Chapter 2

S he turned, her heart falling in on itself, her breathing labored. A break in the clouds must have come, for a streak of silvery moonlight suddenly lit a small path along the floor and across her bed. She saw gold.

She stopped, startled.

His hair was gold, a soft, wavy mass of sunburnished gold. He sat at the edge of her bed, his face towards her, but still in shadow. Only his hair lay in the path of the fickle moon.

Aleene wrung her hands together and prayed. She prayed for the strength and courage to do what she must do. She prayed for this man before her to stay docile. She prayed for the moon to go back behind a dark cloud.

A low sound came from the direction of her new husband. Aleene blinked. It was a grunt, like that of a pig. She froze.

Cynewulf stood, the moonlight revealing his rather formidable height and the horrifying breadth of his shoulders. She blinked again, sure that the light played tricks with her eyes. He hunched, then, and she knew she must have been mistaken.

Her fear did not abate, though, for he moved. A need to scream clawed at her throat. A panic-born thought brushed at her conscious. *Could she scream?* She remembered the filthy hand clamped across her mouth those first few awful times, and then the nights afterward when the hand was no longer needed. She never screamed. Who would listen? What if, now that she might need to, she found out that she couldn't? What if she opened her mouth and nothing came out, no matter how hard she tried?

He shuffled across the floor, away from her. Aleene gripped her hands together as her entire body trembled. He grunted again, and she nearly ran. As he leaned over, she could see his outline, faint and shadowy now that he had moved away from that treacherous moonbeam. He straightened again and heaved upwards. Breathing in sharply, Aleene drew her hand to her throat. His arms came down and with it the tunic that he had worn.

He was undressing.

Aleene backed away, terrified now that he had taken the lead. Would he rape her? Did he know how? When she felt her trunk pressing against the backs of her knees, she stopped her retreat.

He moved again, and she opened her mouth, ready to attempt the scream she wasn't sure she could accomplish. He shuffled along the floor, then sat down on the bed with another grunt. The silence that descended over the room seemed deafening. After a moment of stillness, she relaxed slightly.

He turned his back to her and put his head on the pillow, curling into a fetal position. Aleene stood motionless. A secret, intimate part of her felt terribly violated as this man lay upon her bed, his body against her bedclothes, his hair against her pillow.

Another part of her, deep, deep down, felt a slight frission of connection with this man. He seemed so alone, the moonlight now gilding the muscled planes of his back. He was alone in his silence, alone in the dull wit of his mind. Aleene knew how it felt to be alone. To feel as if her body was a huge prison, and her soul a small, useless creature inhabiting a tiny corner.

The man on the bed made another sound, this time a snorting, snuffling sound. He slept. Just like that he had fallen asleep. Aleene frowned. How dare he fall asleep! She had stood, pressed up against her trunk, scared, while the man she married went to sleep.

Resolve straightened her spine and determination filled her chest with a deep, cleansing breath. She must get herself with child, now, before Aethregard came back from his audience with the king and tried to annul this hasty marriage. Quickly, before fear could stop her, Aleene pulled her soft blue kirtle over her head, and dropped it over the chest on the floor.

For a moment she hesitated, everything within her fought this. She curled her fingers around the cloth of her tunic, needing to remove the clothing, but unable to. Her breathing quickened, making her feel faint. She smelled the tangy scent of her own fear. Gritting her teeth, Aleene finally jerked the tunic over her head, rushing so she would not have time to balk.

When she finally stood naked in the dark room, terror wrenched through her. Squeezing her eyes shut, she chased it away, locking it back in that dark place inside of her.

She went to the bed, quickly, her arms brushing against her breasts and awakening new panic. Standing near the bed, she stared at her husband's back for a long quiet moment. His side rose and fell with the slow intake and gentle exhale of his breath. He was well made, this husband of hers.

She frowned, this stupid poacher had the breadth of shoulder and muscles of one who swung a heavy sword in battle. The thought brought new fear, but Aleene pushed it away, knowing that she only tried to delay the inevitable with silly wanderings. He was no soldier, but a simpleton. Obviously, he had been taking care of himself for many years, chopping wood and fending off men who would hurt him.

Berthilde's words ran through her mind. This man must touch her breast. Disgust roiled through Aleene with a power that nearly brought her to her knees, but she wiped her mind free of any thought except her goal. Freedom.

Seabreeze would be hers, completely. She would have no man hurting her, humiliating her. Aleene stared down at her new husband, a man unable to hurt her in any way. But she must get with his babe, and make the marriage unbreakable first before she could banish Aethregard forever from her sight and her mind.

Aleene reached down and took the man's hand. It was large, strong. Hard calluses scraped against her own soft skin. What had this man done to obtain such work-hardened hands? She shook her head, dislodging the thought. She did not care about the man. She only cared what he could do for her.

With a violent shudder, Aleene turned her husband's hand toward her, spreading the long fingers wide and fitting the palm over the mound of her breast. Closing her eyes, she let go of his hand.

It flopped back to his side.

Aleene's eyes flew open. She stared down at

the listless form of her husband. The fear and terror that lingered just beyond her control slithered away. Grabbing the man's hand again, Aleene pressed it hard against her.

He did not move, did not grunt, did not snort, nothing. She rubbed his palm back and forth across her nipple. It hardened, puckering against the male hand in her grasp. She breathed in sharply at the unsettling jolt of feeling that snaked its way from her breast to her belly.

Biting her lip, she let go of Cynewulf's hand, and pushed her chest forward. Again, his traitorous limb dropped uselessly to the bed. Aleene let out a frustrated sigh as she stood naked beside her husband.

Anger now replaced any trace of fear. "Cynewulf!" She used her most commanding voice.

Lord Cynewulf did not stir.

"By the gods, man, you would sleep through your own death!" Obviously he agreed, for he did not move. Aleene made a disgusted sound and stalked around the bed, crossing through the ever-shining moonbeam and climbing onto the bed next to her slumbering lord.

"Perhaps this shall be better. I do not think you must be awake, anyway," Aleene muttered as she knelt in front of Cynewulf and sat back on her heels. "I must only get your member hard." She grimaced.

And then she must put it inside of her, which

meant she must touch it. With a long-suffering
sigh, Aleene closed her eyes and reached out.
Her hand encountered the hard ridges of a
well-muscled stomach. With a startled cry, she
jerked her hand back and peeked between her
lashes. The man had not moved. Well, she *had*
prayed for God to make him docile.

Squeezing her eyes shut again, Aleene
reached out, this time a bit lower. Her hand encountered a wiry brush of hair. Her belly quivered strangely. Curling her outstretched fingers
into a fist, she said another quick prayer for
courage and slowly reached out. Again, the
wiry hair tickled her fingertips. Aleene forced
herself to bury her fingers deeper until she felt
heated flesh. She let her hand rest there for a
moment and opened her eyes. The dim light
revealed a trail of hair that swirled from Cynewulf's navel, beneath her fingers, and down.
Her hand drifted and encountered hard silk.
Aleene jumped, her eyes squinting in the darkness. And she saw it, huge and hard, laying stiff
against his belly.

With a shocked cry, she pulled her hand
away and covered her mouth. It was damaged!
Once she had peeked between her lashes as Tosig left her, and seen his shriveled member
hanging between his thighs. It had not stuck up
toward his nose.

Aleene knit her brows in thought. Perhaps,
though, it did when he had slept? She had no

idea, but could only hope that this man she had taken to husband was not disfigured. He must give her an heir.

Berthilde had said it would be hard. She hadn't said which way it must point. Taking heart at this thought, Aleene dredged up her flagging courage and touched her husband's manhood once more. It was hot against her fingers, hot and smooth. She curled her hand around it. And hard, yes, definitely, hard.

In relief she relaxed her shoulders, realizing only then that she had hunched them around her ears. Leaning backward slightly, Aleene peered through the murky light at what she now held. It was overwhelmingly strange. So soft, like the underside of a baby's bottom, yet so hard. She stroked it and it moved, lurching against her grasp.

Cynewulf made a noise, a strangled sound. Aleene snatched her hand back, watching him steadily, waiting. Still, he didn't move. Aleene watched his eyes closely, but they didn't even flutter.

Sitting back again, she crossed her arms over her breasts and felt her nipples, puckered and sensitive against the inside of her arms. Aleene shuddered. A dark, yawning hole seemed to open up low in her stomach. Her fingernails bit harshly into her arms. Closing her eyes, she thought she could feel the beat of her heart in the very core of her being. Her throat went dry, her skin wet, her breathing harsh in the quiet. Fear was only partly responsible for such peculiar symptoms, though. She knew, for she knew fear intimately. There was something else making her feel as if the air she took into her lungs was not enough to sustain her life. Aleene stared down at her husband.

She must do it now. She had let him feel her breast. His member was hard. Now she must put it inside of her. Quickly, before she could think of what she did, Aleene pushed her husband onto his back. He flopped over, his arms spread wide.

She would have to get atop him. With a deep breath Aleene swung her leg over his and straddled his hips. She felt the hair on his legs brush at the inside of her thighs. Her breath came more rapidly.

Cynewulf's eyes remained closed. At least they looked closed. Aleene strained to see him better, but shadows shrouded his form. Her back now blocked the moonlight from revealing anything. Staring intently at the darkness that was her husband's face, Aleene lowered herself until her most private place pressed against the length of his hard member. Gritting her teeth and steeling her mind from what she did, she rubbed up and down as Berthilde had said.

His member jerked again, and she stopped. She could not believe that it moved on its own, as if it were an arm or a leg. It was passing strange. Aleene shook her head, took a deep breath, and rubbed against him again.

This was different. Perhaps because he was asleep? Or maybe because she did not lie beneath a rutting boar of a man, but sat atop, with a feeling almost of power? Aleene was not sure, but she knew that this rubbing had actually begun to feel—she stopped, thinking. Nice, it felt nice. And she did not like to stop. Her body wanted more and so she assuaged that want.

Aleene arched her head back. Her hair swung rhythmically around her shoulders, and she knew that it dragged along her husband's legs. The image summoned a strange moan from deep within her chest and, suddenly, she felt herself convulse. That dark hidden place of her seemed to clench.

Aleene gasped at the tremors that traveled along the inside of her skin. She shook her head and couldn't help but smile in the dark. She was learning much this evening. Men's members danced of their own accord and her own private place seemed to want to grab hold.

And it was not abhorrent.

She stopped suddenly. But she was not done. She must put his member inside of her. Aleene closed her eyes, swallowing hard. She looked down. Cynewulf's member still pointed toward his chin, trapped between their bodies

Aleene pushed herself up slowly on her knees. Her hand stroked down Cynewulf's glistening chest almost as if she caressed him. It happened without her thinking, and now she curled her fingers into her palm and pressed her balled fist against her own belly.

Invasion. She was going to be invaded. Only this time she invited it, needed it. She could hear her own breathing, sharp and tense in the silent room. She did not want it, though. She could not want this. She closed her eyes, willing herself to be strong, and smoothed her hand against her husband's chest once again.

She found his member and closed her hand around it. Then she lifted it, holding it against her woman's place. Aleene gasped, her chest heaving with the breath that she had been holding. Fear made her tense, but still something strangely compelling made her legs feel like melted wax.

She made herself lower down onto her husband's shaft. The tip moved easily against her, taking her breath, and then slowly it began to penetrate.

"God's teeth!" she said heavily between breaths.

And then brutal memories crashed against her mind like the fall of a heavy sword cleaving through flesh. She convulsed with the fear and ugliness of it, her hands coming up to cover her face. It was terrifying and dark and came from deep inside her.

A cry of sheer agony pierced her ears, and

she realized it came from her. She dropped forward, only then remembering that her husband lay beneath her. Her forehead encountered his hard chest, her hands slid down his sides.

She cried out again, but strong warm arms wrapped around her and pulled her down. She fought against it, terror welling again in her throat, threatening to spill over. She stopped fighting as the dark memories overcame her again, stilling her very heart with their intensity. She felt ugly, dirty, and terribly afraid. Her body quivered violently and she squeezed her eyes shut and rocked. Only she wasn't rocking herself. Strong arms held her, a crooning sound thrummed in her ears and another body rocked hers.

Her mind let go and she sank into the safety, pulled away from the terror. She heard a song, a child's song, a lullaby. "Mother," she wailed, but she knew it was her own voice singing. Her mother was gone. The song came again and she let it, her mind shaping the long-forgotten curve of her mother's cheek and softness of her mother's breast.

Chapter 3

◯◯

Aleene awoke slowly. For a few sweet moments she remembered nothing. The only thought that skittered through her head was that it had been an unusual summer, uncommon northerly winds making it much warmer than usual. And then she remembered what had happened the night before. Her chest tightened painfully, and she sat up, trying desperately to drag air into her lungs.

With a pitiful whimper, she rolled off the bed and tried to stand. She must run, leave. Her legs would not support her, though, and she leaned against the bed.

She saw her new husband then, staring at her with wide blue eyes. Terror gripped her and she squeezed her eyes shut against it. The darkness flooded her mind. "No!" she cried, trying to stop them. But they came at her like arrows from a conquering army. She could only put her arms across her face and crumple to the floor

35

for protection. But nothing could protect her. She was young again, and Tosig was there, her mother's new husband, hurting her, making her feel so lonely and sad, and completely vulnerable.

Aleene leaned her chest against her knees and her forehead to the rushes that littered the floor. She breathed in the heavy scent of herbs and crushed flowers. Her stomach rolled violently.

The darkness opened and took her inside. It was ugly and deep, terrifying and lonely. Her head whirled with the broken visions of earlier years, the good safe times when both her parents lived, combining with those evil days her stepfather ruled over her. Her heart thumped a broken, terrible beat against her chest.

She felt a hand, large and warm against the back of her head, but didn't move. She knew. He was there. Gathering all of the strength she had, Aleene straightened and then pushed up from the floor.

She was naked. The realization took her breath and her dredged up courage. With a sick groan, Aleene wrapped her arms around herself and bowed her head.

Rough wool scratched her shoulders. She jumped, but one large hand held her still as the other wrapped a blanket around her. Those hands, those large, work-roughened hands, had touched her body. They had touched her where other, smaller, slack, beringed hands had been. With a violent shudder, Aleene clutched at the edges of the woolen blanket.

A sob rose in her chest, but Aleene swallowed it. She had not cried then, and she would not now. As if tears would ever bring back her innocence, bring back the naïve days before all those she loved had betrayed her.

The thought brought a memory of her mother. The woman who was supposed to protect her. Her frail little mother, sitting in a rocking chair in her chamber, the sound of the wood creaking and echoing in the room. The memory brought more bitterness than those of Tosig, for she had trusted in her mother, not Tosig.

Again, she felt her husband's hand against the back of her head. She stilled, breathing deeply, trying to find her control. Closing her eyes, she saw what she must look like in her mind's eye, naked, trembling, and on her knees.

She could not allow herself to be like this, to show her weakness so blatantly. He would use it to hurt her as everyone else had. Clenching her fists, she fought the memories and the hurt that came with them.

She pushed herself up from the ground, opened her eyes, and took a deep breath. She must remember the woman she had forced herself to be. The strong woman she showed to all, who could not be defeated.

And now she must face her husband. She faltered. He had seen her weak and cowed. She hadn't let anyone see her thus since . . . Aleene stopped the thought quickly and straightened her shoulders, then she turned toward her husband.

His beauty hit her like a blow to her stomach. She blinked, fear and something else making her blood move crazily in her veins. The little girl she had been long, long ago clutched at his beauty. She remembered dreaming, running through green fields, lying among the flowers and staring at a clear, summer sky. His eyes were that sky. The clearest, bluest of blues. It hurt her heart to look at them. His golden hair, so opposite her own, shone in the sunlight like molten honey. And his face was strong, his jaw chiseled; he was godlike.

He dipped his chin to his chest, breaking the brief eye contact, and shuffled his feet in the rushes. Aleene caught herself wishing he would look at her again.

She gritted her teeth against the useless wandering of her thoughts. His actions brought back to her in full force exactly how stupid it was of her to regret the weakness her new husband had witnessed. He would not know, could not know, what he had seen. And he certainly could not tell anyone.

Still the newly relived memories of her stepfather's abuses against her made the floor beneath her feel unstable, her knees weak, and her need to be alone acute. "I must wash." Her voice caught on the last word and she turned sharply away from her husband just as a knock sounded at the door.

"Enter."

"Milady," Berthilde opened the door slightly and peeked in. "Would ye have me bring food on a tray for ye to break your fast?"

"No, Berthilde." Aleene hugged the blanket tighter around herself. "I need to bathe, now."

"Yes, milady." The maid backed away.

"Take Cynewulf." Her voice had a distinct hint of desperation. Aleene breathed slowly and battled for control. "Take my husband with you, Berthilde."

Berthilde nodded and came all the way into the room. Snaring Cynewulf's arm, she smiled at the tall man. "The children are playing in the yard, Lord Cynewulf. It is delightful to sit and watch their silly games."

Aleene turned away and closed her eyes.

Another knock heralded Berthilde's return. Quickly, Aleene went to stand at the other side of the room, staring out the window before she bade the maid enter. Aleene listened as the servants filled the old tub and left.

"Leave Berthilde. I shall bathe myself."

"But, milady . . ."

"Be gone!"

The maid was silent for several moments, then Aleene heard the door close. With a relieved sigh, she realized she was alone. Dropping the rough blanket to the floor, Aleene went to the deep, wooden tub and stepped into the water. It was tepid and refreshing after huddling beneath the warm blanket.

Aleene dipped her hand in the scented bowl of soap and began to scrub herself. She washed every inch of her body, ruthlessly. While she bathed, Aleene allowed herself only to think of the security she would find when she knew no other would take Seabreeze away from her. Her thoughts turned then, inevitably, to her father.

She had been seven when he had died, so sheltered with love that she had not even realized how very different she was from the people around her. How those people looked upon her dark Spanish looks with suspicion and hatred. Those people had rejoiced when her Anglo-Saxon mother married again, this time to one of their own.

And Aleene had mourned. She had mourned right up until Tosig had fallen from one of the jagged cliffs that surrounded Seabreeze. And now she would mourn no more. For she was the lady of Seabreeze. None controlled it or her. She would be able to live as she once had so many years before, when her father had protected her.

Only this time, she must protect herself.

When she finished her bath, Aleene dressed in a clean white tunic and covered it with a light green kirtle. Once, long ago, her mother had told her she looked pretty in green. Aleene hooked a gold-link girdle around her slim hips, took a deep, steadying breath, and went in search of her husband.

Loud, raucous laughter greeted Aleene as she entered the large deserted hall. She followed the sound outside to the yard and saw that the children were playing. A deep yearning stole through Aleene, for the innocence of being a child. With a slight smile she remembered her childhood, having the security of love, the ability to play with all her heart, and the freedom to dream and believe.

Another shriek of laughter grabbed Aleene's attention from her musings.

In a doorway opposite her, she noticed Berthilde. The maid stood wiping her weathered hands on a piece of linen tucked at her waist. They stared at one another for a long moment, time receding. Berthilde had been with her from the beginning. She alone, among the many people at Seabreeze, knew of the trusting girl Aleene had been once.

She could remember many times laughing and amusing herself in this very spot under the ever-watchful eye of Berthilde. Aleene could not help the small chuckle that tickled her throat as she also remembered the many times she had run into Berthilde's warm embrace when the dogs became too playful or a bee came too near.

Her old maid smiled tentatively at her now, but Aleene only sighed and turned away. She squinted against the harsh sun and scanned the yard for her husband.

He rushed about, picking up children and setting them down. Aleene frowned at his antics, wondering what game he played. One of the smaller children pulled a cloth from over his head and jumped up and down. "Here I am!" the boy cried.

Cynewulf twirled around and thrust his arms into the air, acknowledging the found child. The others laughed uproariously. The child covered his head with the cloth, and Cynewulf again assumed a confused expression, running around the yard and mocking a thorough search for the lost boy.

Or, perhaps, he did not mock the search. Aleene smiled as she watched the young boy again reveal himself.

Her husband saw her then and a wide grin broke over his face.

Shocked surprise made her stare. She could not remember when anyone had smiled at her, and with such a total lack of guile. And with such beauty.

With a nervous gesture, she flipped her veil off her shoulder shifting her weight on her feet. "Cyne, we must break our fast." The children

moaned, and then stopped, as if suddenly remembering that she were some sort of ogre to
be afraid of. Stiffening, Aleene turned away and
moved back through the door of the hall.
"Quickly, Cyne," she said over her shoulder,
"you must wash your hands."

When she felt him behind her, she relaxed a
bit. She had to yank on his hand to get him to
sit, but once prodded, he did so without balk-
ing. Her confidence strengthened. This would
not be so difficult.

Aleene showed her husband how to wash his
hands with the rosewater brought to the table,
and then their trencher was set before them and
Cynewulf lived up to his name. He tore at the
bread as a wolf would tear at a captured rabbit.
Aleene winced and wrinkled her nose as her
husband sloshed ale over her sleeve and got
more food on the floor than in his mouth.

She sighed and put a hand on his arm. Again,
the strength there surprised her, but she firmly
got his attention, and pulled her hand away. He
stopped mauling his food, his eyes staring
blankly at her.

"He seems in need of table lessons. Perhaps
we should find a nursemaid for him."

Stifling the gasp of surprise that leaped from
her throat, Aleene looked up to see Aethregard,
her stepbrother, standing before her. His leanly
muscled arms were crossed over his chest, and

his small, beady gray eyes stared at her with complete hatred.

"You have returned," she managed to say without showing any of the hidden panic that caused her fingers to tremble.

"Aye, the king is happy with our decision to move our marriage ceremony up. He, as well as I, did not understand my father's wish to stay the marriage until your twenty-first birthday." He strolled to the table and picked up a chunk of cheese. "He will be here to celebrate with us."

Aleene stood, knowing that her height intimidated her smaller stepbrother. "It was not our decision, 'twas yours." She took a deep breath. "Your father decided on our betrothal, and now you have decided we should marry before my birthday. Nothing has been mine, ever."

"Now, now, Aleene, you mustn't be petulant." He took a bite of cheese and chewed slowly, then patted her hand.

She pulled quickly away. "Much has changed, though." She forced herself to face her stepbrother. "I have finally made my own decision, brother dear." Aleene gestured toward Cyne. "I have married."

Aethregard did not even bother to look at Cyne. He quirked one sandy-colored brow. "Yes," he hissed. "Cuthebert has informed me of this strange act of rebellion, Aleene." His eyes seemed like the dull steel of a deadly sword. "And I've heard that you have already had the wedding night."

"Yes." She knew this information would soon reach the king, he would probably send for her or come to Seabreeze himself. Taking a deep breath, Aleene tilted up her chin, eyeing her stepbrother down the length of her nose. "And I thank you not to be disrespectful to the new lord of Seabreeze Castle."

"New lord indeed." Aethregard spit on the ground at her feet. "You shall not get away with this, you cold-hearted bitch."

When his gray eyes turned dark with anger, she saw only her stepfather staring at her. Fear writhed up Aleene's spine, but she stood fast. "It is done, Aethregard."

"It is not, Aleene. I have power here. Your people look to me for guidance, not you. I can force you away from your *husband*," he nearly spat the word.

Aleene cleared her throat and held her stepbrother's gaze. She wished she could make him leave Seabreeze. But now more than ever she needed to keep as much peace as possible with King Harold, and Aethregard and his men were staying at Seabreeze in service of the king. They were in the Fyrd, the king's army of local men watching the beaches for sign of invasion from Normandy.

"You can do nothing of the sort. 'Tis my castle you stand in. By law, 'tis mine. You will never control it, or my people."

He laughed derisively. "And you do?" He snorted like a pig. "It has been eight months since this holding reverted to you, Aleene, eight months since your eighteenth birthday. Have your people ever looked to you for guidance? They looked to my father, and when he was killed they looked to me."

He spoke the truth and it frightened her. Still, she would not allow that fear to put her right back where she had been since the day her mother married Tosig, in the hands of one who would hurt her. "I will not let you win, Aethregard, you cannot."

"No, *you* will not!" He threw down the rest of the cheese in his hand. It hit the table, bounced up, and glanced off Cyne's forehead. "Your marriage to this lowlife will be annulled, and you *will* live up to your betrothal agreement." With those venomous words, Aethregard turned away from her swiftly.

"Aethregard!"

His back stiff, the man stopped and turned around.

She was beyond caring about King Harold any longer. "You have given your two months in the Fyrd to the king. I wish you and your men to leave!"

A big chunk of hard cheese flew through the air and hit Aethregard squarely between his eyes. "Aaaagghh," he cried, staggering backwards, his hand against his forehead.

Shocked, Aleene could only stare as Aethregard found his footing and glared with gleaming hatred just beyond her shoulder.

She turned. Her husband stood behind her, grinning.

"That lackwit!" Aethregard shouted. "He brained me with the cheese!" Her stepbrother surged forward, his hands outstretched towards Cyne.

"Hold!" Taking a step forward, Aleene put herself between her smiling husband and her menacing stepbrother. "He is lord of this castle, Aethregard. If he chooses to throw rotten tomatoes at you, it is his right."

Aethregard stopped, his hands clenched in fists at his sides. Aleene could hear his breath heaving through his nostrils.

"Be gone, Aethregard, we will speak later."

Anger burned behind his beady eyes as he stared first at her then her husband. "Yes, my dear," he said in a low, shaking whisper, "we shall speak later." Turning on his heel, Aethregard left the hall.

She watched his back as he departed, trying to school her features into a frown, then turned to her husband. "Husband mine, you must not throw food at people."

He blinked at her.

She bit at the inside of her cheek and closed

her eyes. A picture of the small red mark between Aethregard's brows flashed through her mind. She bit harder. Opening her eyes, she addressed the culprit again. "That was not nice, Cyne." Now she had to purse her lips tightly to subdue her mirth.

If possible, Cyne's eyes became even more innocent. He blinked again and then slowly pointed to where Aethregard had once been and then at himself.

Aleene nodded. "Yes, I realize he did it to you first, but he is not always a nice man, so you must not follow his example."

Cyne only stared.

Aleene sighed, her mirth fleeing in the face of the large responsibility she had taken upon herself by wedding this man. When she did produce a child from him, she would have to train them together.

"Sit, Cyne, and finish your food," she said finally as she went to sit next to her husband. "I believe we were just about to have a lesson on proper eating habits when we were sadly interrupted." She tried to smile, but knew the attempt was quite dismal.

Cyne sat slowly on the bench and looked down at his food, then back at her, his expression that of a newborn babe. Aleene purposefully tore off a piece of dry bread, keeping her eyes on Cyne as she chewed slowly and swallowed.

Mimicking her actions, Cyne took the bread and tore off a piece. He bit into it, baring strong white teeth, then chewed slowly just as she did. When he finished, his tongue flashed out and caught a bit of bread that clung to his full lips.

Aleene found herself staring and quickly looked up from her husband's mouth, only to encounter his eyes. She stood quickly. "Cyne, come with me. I will show you my castle."

Her husband blinked in confusion.

Aleene knew he was probably still hungry. Her own stomach growled with the need to be filled, but suddenly eating bread and cheese seemed such an intimate act, she could not continue. "Please, Cyne, come."

He stood slowly, his eyes on his food. Aleene walked away and motioned for him to follow. With a sad look back at the table, he did.

"My father built Seabreeze Castle." Aleene led her husband out of the hall and across the busy yard. In her mind she pictured her father as she remembered him, tall and lean, laughing, handsome. She swallowed hard and continued. "He was a wealthy Spaniard who came from Normandy with Edward, the Confessor. He married my mother, the daughter of a Thane, and built a castle here, behind the old Roman Pevensey Castle, to protect Harold's lands from invaders."

They reached the guard tower and Aleene led the way up the narrow stairs. Once at the top,

Aleene stepped aside, sweeping her hand with a flourish toward the glittering expanse of sea. "It is wonderful, is it not?" She smiled, a gust of wind from the sea pulling at the veil that covered her hair and bringing a rush of pride.

"It is mine, a dower land that has gone through the female line of my family for centuries. Before my father built this castle in the new French style, it was a forgotten piece of land." Turning, she glanced at her husband and realized that she could not allow herself to look at him often, he was too uncommonly beautiful. Too uncommonly distracting.

He looked back at her, his forehead crinkled, his eyes confused. She sighed, and turned away again, staring out to sea. "I think it is perfection," she said, knowing he would not understand. Finally, with one last look at the vast ocean, Aleene led her husband down the stairs to the cooking area, and then to the smithy.

Cyne trailed along behind her, stopping when she stopped, looking to where she pointed, his eyes dull, his mouth slack. She wondered if this was an exercise in futility. Would he remember anything she showed him? Did he understand anything she said? They passed the mews and Aleene hesitated. She hardly ever entered the small room that housed her father's falcons. A servant still took care of them, but the thought of the great birds made Aleene think of her father, his laughing smile as he left, with a bird on his arm, to go hunting. Now that memory merely brought loneliness. Aleene simply gestured toward the mews. "My father's falcons," she mumbled, and continued on.

They came to the small garden behind the cooking area, and Aleene reached down, wrenching at a weed that had poked its way through a patch of turnips. The roots of the offending plant held tightly, though, and Aleene gritted her teeth, ready to take out her frustration on the small weed.

A hand, large, callused, and warm, stopped her. For a split second, Aleene felt her husband's large body bent over hers, his breath against her neck, his fingers grazing hers. The strength of him combined with such gentleness seeped the breath from her lungs and caused her legs to tremble.

Her body's reaction to Cyne's closeness scared her, and she jerked her hand from beneath his, taking a hurried step forward before she turned to face him. He looked at her for a moment, something that hinted of intelligence glinting in his eyes, before he quickly averted his gaze and plucked the small yellow flower that adorned the weed. Straightening, Cyne held the flower up so that its nearly translucent petals caught the sunlight and seemed to glow.

Reluctantly, Aleene looked from the flower to

her husband. She knew already that he would look beautiful in the sunlight, and part of her didn't want to see it. Another part of her yearned for it. His hair, like the flower, glinted yellow in the brightness of day. His eyes mirrored the cloudless sky.

Aleene bit at her bottom lip and forced her gaze away. Why did his beauty touch such a deep longing inside of her? Why did it hurt?

"It is a weed. Useless. It kills the vegetables and herbs we are trying to grow." Her voice sounded dead. Aleene sighed and turned away from Cyne.

Again his hand stayed her retreat, and the warmth went through her like the strongest wine she had ever drunk. This time it was a light tap on her shoulder, asking for her to turn. She stopped. He communicated, it seemed, through touch. She wondered if she would ever get used to it.

When she turned toward him, he smiled, and it made her hurt inside.

"What?" she asked sharply.

He took a step towards her, and she automatically backed away. His brow creased in perplexity as he advanced again towards her, holding the flower at arm's length.

Rigid, Aleene did not move. She should not fear this man, he was her husband after all, and totally harmless. Using all of her willpower, she

stayed rooted, her shoulders squared, her eyes
warily assessing.

He smiled again, and she knew that her inner
arguments would not save her. She feared him
because of his innocence. She could handle ugliness, that she knew well; she could not deal
with this clear, innocent beauty before her, it
contrasted with her own darkness too strongly.

Unwilling to show her fear, though, she
waited for whatever her husband had in mind.
He was close enough now that she could smell
the heat of the sun in his leather tunic.

He took her hand in his, lifting it between
their bodies. Aleene could do nothing but
watch as her husband placed the weed in her
palm and closed her fingers around it. She
stared at the small flower for a long moment,
then looked at Cyne.

He nodded at the flower and lifted her hand
toward her face. Cyne bent over the yellow petals and sniffed, his hair tickling her own nose
as he straightened. With wide eyes, he tilted his
head at her. The fear, the calculations, the
thoughts had fled, and in their stead was nothing but the full impact this man had on her
senses. His hands cupping hers, his eyes holding hers, his breath intermingling with hers.
The sun beat warmly through her veil, pollen
motes danced around them and bees buzzed in-
dustriously, but she heard a supreme silence,

saw only her husband, and felt the strength of his presence.

He cocked his head to the side and, again, lifted her hand toward her face, bringing the plant near her nose. She blinked, her heart feeling as if it would break, and sniffed. The small yellow weed smelled of earth, musk, and life.

She looked back at her husband. He nodded and smiled. Aleene had the sudden, yearning need to place her lips on his, feel their softness, their strength, take some of his beauty and innocence into herself.

With a long, strong intake of air, she smelled him, the earth, the sun. Closing her eyes, Aleene remembered her thoughts of only moments before, of her own dark and ugly soul and all that was familiar to her. With a wrenching cry, she crushed the flower in her hands, threw it to the ground, and turned, running from the garden and Cyne.

Chapter 4

❧

What she had believed would be easy had suddenly become a Herculean task. Aleene wiped at the bead of perspiration that slipped from beneath her veil and trailed down her temple. The sun beat mercilessly down on her bent head, making her wish she could wrench the veil off. But she never went bareheaded. She always acted the perfect lady, wearing her veil, spending her morning at prayers, anything to gain the respect of her people. Only it had never worked.

Bending to her task once again, Aleene attacked the weeds that had grown up around her herb garden. As she worked she kept seeing Cyne, his smile bright as he cupped his hands around hers and made her see a weed as a beautiful thing to be cherished. Shaking her head, Aleene tried to shatter the image. But it haunted her.

For days it had haunted her.

And she had thought it would be easy now to get what she wanted. Now that she had married someone who should not have mattered. Someone *she* could control rather than the other way around.

Disgusted, Aleene yanked one of the weeds, breaking the stem and leaving the roots in the soil. She sat back on her heels and wiped her forehead with the back of her hand. She had not seen her husband in three days. Berthilde took care of him, feeding him, finding a place for him to sleep. Aleene hid from him.

A fine way to get a babe in her belly.

Pushing herself up from the ground, Aleene sighed deeply. Why could she not be strong? She tried, with all of her heart she tried. She showed a strong, unbending front to everyone, and yet, always, she quailed within. Afraid of her servants, her stepbrother, herself, and now her husband.

Closing her eyes, Aleene clenched her fists at her side and wished desperately to know complete strength.

"Aleene, I have found you, finally."

Aleene straightened her spine and gritted her teeth. She turned. "Aethregard." She had not forced the issue of Aethregard leaving the castle. He and his men would leave soon; the Fyrd would no longer be needed along the coast with the summer waning and with it, the threat of William's invasion. She was afraid to try and

force Aethregard to leave. She was not entirely
sure she could, and then she would truly look
the fool.

Her stepbrother smiled. Actually, it was more
of a grimace from what she could see through
his dirty beard. "I need to apologize, Aleene,
for my temper of the other morning."

Aleene nodded slightly, her fear abating a bit.
As his father before him, Aethregard had many
different ways of coercion. It seemed he had decided to take a new tack, he was back to trying
to woo her. It was irritating, but much more
manageable than his anger.

"It is good of you to offer an apology."

"Yes." He moved closer, his hand reaching
toward her as if he might touch her. "But really,
Aleene—"

"No!" Aleene interrupted what she was sure
to be a pretty speech and backed away from her
stepbrother. "No, Aethregard. You have apol-
ogized, and I accepted. Please, I am very busy
and wish to be left alone."

Aethregard hesitated. "Aleene," he said finally. "I have noticed the abhorrence you show
to your husband." He moved forward and took
her hands in both of his. "I can only believe that
you have realized what a grave mistake you
have made."

Aleene stared down at her hands in his for a
moment, noting with satisfaction that he had
unwittingly muddied his hands with the dirt

that clung to her fingers. Then, realizing that she had let him hold her for a moment too long, she quickly pulled her hands away. Meeting his gaze, she said, "I have made no mistake, Aethregard. But you do, if you believe Seabreeze shall ever be yours."

She could see the power it took her stepbrother to maintain his calm. "Aleene, why do you fight me so? I wish to wed you, not a castle. And I shall keep you forever from harm."

The honeyed words stank with rot. Aleene eyed Aethregard, saw the underlying hardness in his gray eyes, and knew without a doubt that he was no different from his father. Suddenly Aleene realized that her mother must have been courted in this same way. Constant, never-ending battering of her defenses with sticky-sweet words. But her mother had not seen the menace lurking beneath Tosig's words of love. She had been weak and still mourning her only true love, and had given in.

Aleene would not give in. "I shall keep myself from harm, thank you, Aethregard." Wiping her hands on her apron, Aleene stiffened her back and looked down upon her smaller stepbrother. "Please do not speak of this again. I am married to another man and will remain so. This is in no way appropriate." She coated her words with the frosty tone she had perfected over the years. "I am truly very busy, as I am sure you must be. Excuse me." She turned quickly and left the garden. Though she wished to run, she kept her pace unhurried, her head up and shoulders back.

Never would she fall prey to the power of a man again.

With that thought ringing in her ears, Aleene went in search of Berthilde. The luxury of hiding could no longer be hers. She must find her new husband and face her fears head on.

Aleene took supper in the main hall for the first time in three days. The first sight she had of her husband made her stumble a bit. He was uncommonly beautiful, this man of simple mind.

Taking a deep breath, Aleene sat beside him at the table, keeping her face averted. She reached to tear their trencher in half, but he was there first. Their fingers brushed, and Aleene pulled hers away quickly, lightning tremors pulsing up her arm. She swallowed and watched his hands, large and disturbingly capable, put her half in front of her.

Aethregard sat across from them, watching. Aleene forced herself to look at him. "Good eve, Aethregard." She picked up her cup, turning it deliberately so that her lips did not touch where her husband's had.

"Milady." He mocked her, she knew. She could hear it in his voice, though he bathed his words in false respect.

She wished this awful summer would be done with, that Aethregard would take his men and retreat to his own hall, forever. Looking away from Aethregard, her attention snagged on her husband's hands.

He began to tear his trencher, and without thought, Aleene put her hand over his. It had been three days since she had touched him. She wasn't ready for the reaction she had to him. The strength and warmth of him, her husband, shook her to her very core. She pulled her hand back, and her gaze snapped up to meet his.

He stared at her, his eyes full of confusion.

"No, Cyne," she said softly. "We save the trencher for the poor."

"Until a few days ago that is probably what he was."

Her stepbrother only spoke the truth, but his derision grated against her. "I will warn you only once, Aethregard, not to speak so."

He shook his head, as if speaking to a child. "Really, Aleene—"

"Only once, Aethregard."

He stopped. She knew he wished to say more, she could actually feel the hatred emanating from him. He stayed his tongue, though, taking a long draught of ale.

Aleene watched him, suspicious of his obedience. He was waiting, it seemed, biding his time. She tapped her fingernail against the cup in her hand. He had plans that he seemed to set much confidence in. Her hand shook and she pulled it away from searching eyes, hiding it in her lap. She lowered her gaze, trying desperately to cover the fear she knew emanated from her eyes.

When, again, she knew her face showed nothing of what went on in her head, she glanced up. Her husband stared at her, his eyes intent. It shocked her for a moment, for the understanding that gleamed there made him terrifyingly magnetic.

His blond brows knit, then, above his eyes, confusion dulled his expression. But a hint of something else had been there and it jangled Aleene's nerves. Could there be more to her husband than what he presented? The thought brought a shattering sense of chaos.

She watched him, warily, for the rest of the evening. He ate slowly, chewing with deliberate motions, the wide grin never leaving his face. By the time Aethregard finally rose and took his leave, Aleene was sure she had imagined that small moment in time. With the impending horror of the night, and the strange effect her new husband had on her, her imagination must have taken a flight of fancy.

Obviously finished with his meal, Cyne also stood and made as if to leave. Aleene quickly stood and spoke, not daring to touch him again until it was necessary. "No, Cyne, you will come with me this eve."

The man stopped and stared at her.

"Come, Cyne," she said and turned toward the door that would take her to her room. She knew as she walked that Cyne had not followed. With a deep, steadying breath she stopped and called again, "Cyne, come with me."

She heard his shuffling gate stir the rushes and so she continued on her way. She turned only when she reached the door to her chamber. Cyne had followed behind her, but not closely. It seemed even he balked at what must be done that night. Aleene shook her head as Cyne passed by her into the room. No, he could not really know or understand. He probably had just enjoyed sleeping with the rest of the men in the hall.

A wry smile tugged at her lips as Aleene closed the door and stood for a moment staring at the rough-planked wood. Her husband would rather spend the night with his head resting on the belly of a hound, his back against a hard floor, than be with her. It was funny, really. Still, the smile did not reach her heart. Only a hollow loneliness sat there. She knew it had been there a very long time, but now, for some awful reason, the loneliness seemed incredibly more devastating.

Pushing the feeling away, Aleene turned on her heel. She walked boldly up to Cyne, gathered his hand in hers, and placed it against her breast. Somewhere deep inside of her the child she had once been screamed to yank away from Cyne's hand and run, but the lady of Seabreeze Castle stayed utterly still.

"We must make a babe, my lord." Her voice seemed breathy, and she had meant to sound commanding. She cleared her throat before continuing. "You must touch my breast, become hard and go inside me."

Cyne choked, then coughed, then seemed to do both at once.

Aleene quickly let go of his hand and patted his back. "Are you all right? Did you still have food in your mouth?" Her husband coughed again, staggering backward and sitting down hard on the bed.

Aleene went to sit near him, putting her palm against his forehead. She sighed in relief when she realized he did not burn with fever. Running her fingers through his hair, she tried to soothe her husband. "It's all right, Cyne. Can you understand me, perhaps? Can you understand a bit?" She smoothed his hair again, liking the silky feel against her fingers.

Cyne's coughing lightened and he finally stopped, looking at her from beneath his brows, his expression that of a whipped kitten.

It tore at the coverings around her heart and again, as she had that first night, she felt a connection with this man. Biting the inside of her bottom lip, she reached out and took his hand in hers. It was only when their fingers touched that she realized what she had done. She nearly snatched her hand away, but then took a deep breath and did not break their hold. "Are you afraid, Cyne?"

Her husband dipped his head to his chest, and shame swept through her. She had been so completely self-centered in her quest for freedom, she had not realized the confusion and turmoil she had forced on another human being. Gripping her husband's hand tighter, she brought it to her lips.

"Cyne," she said against his large, weather-beaten hand. "I have been terribly selfish, haven't I?"

His head only dipped further. She knew that he probably did not completely understand her, and suddenly she wanted more than anything else in the world to protect this good-hearted, golden man.

That strange thought gave her pause for a long moment. But then a memory came, a good memory. Her mother stroking her hair, kissing her temple, crooning words of love. Without thinking, Aleene stroked Cyne's hair again. "It will be all right, Cyne. You are safe now." She kissed his temple, tentatively at first, and then when the warmth of his skin caressed her lips, she kissed him again. "You will never be in need again. I will feed you, clothe you." She kissed his cheek. "Never again will you need to be dirty, need to go into someone else's forest and steal food." She kissed the side of his mouth. "You can spend your days playing with the children, and," she kissed the corner where his lips met, "showing me flowers in the weeds." She smiled and kissed him again. "I will try not to run from it."

The words that came from her own mouth shocked her. She hadn't voiced her deepest thoughts in a very long while. But, really, what harm could come of it? Her husband could not tell others her thoughts, he probably did not understand them completely himself. She kissed him again, a tantalizing new feeling of freedom putting wings on her heart.

She wasn't sure if Cyne turned his head, or if she did it on her own, but suddenly she found herself kissing her husband's mouth. And for a few precious moments, nothing came to her mind but a sense of comfort and rightness. Her husband's soft, full lips fit against hers perfectly. She could smell the ale on his breath, taste it and him. His taste finally broke through the comfort and made her feel something else. Something not completely horrible, only different and, as a result, scary.

As if he sensed her fear, his arms went around her, and he pulled her close against him.

He was everywhere. Against her breast, she felt the breadth of his chest, against her thigh she felt the strength of his. He consumed every sense; she could hear him breathing, smell the leather of his tunic, the light fennel on his breath, and another purely male, purely warm scent emanating from his skin. Low in her belly, she felt as if butterflies moved slightly, rippling in the stillness of her body. It was a wholly new feeling that terrified yet excited her.

She tried to focus on the conflicting feelings and with focus came realization. She was not repelled by this man's intimate touch. Slowly, experimentally, she relaxed against him, waiting, still, for disgust to swamp her, for her body to recoil. But no such thing happened. Instead, she found herself enjoying the feel of his lips against hers, the pleasure of his arms around her, holding her as none had before.

She moved her lips against his, wanting to experiment more, feel more. Gripping his arms, she felt the hard muscles flex beneath her fingers and came away from her husband's mouth, only a small space away, so that they still shared breath. She could see his eyes, hazy, unfocused. She licked her lips, tasting where his had been, and his eyes went there also.

He leaned into her, slowly, his gaze where her tongue had been. She held her breath, holding tightly to his arms, then nearly crumpling as her husband put his own tongue to where hers had just been.

Cyne tightened his arms around her and

licked again. With boyish expectancy, he pushed further, breaching her lips with his tongue, touching places only she had touched. She felt him first against her teeth, soft, thrilling, probing slowly, bringing a whole new feeling to their kiss, deepening it, making it something wild rather than gentle.

And then as one they leaned back, lying together on the bed, never interrupting the joining of their lips. And a tiny slice of fear slivered through her. He seemed suddenly to be whole, a masterful, complete man with all of his faculties. Remembering the small moment when she believed she had seen something more than confusion in his eyes that evening, Aleene stiffened and pulled away, peering through the darkness, needing to see his eyes, the vacancy there. Needing desperately to know that he was like no other. That he would not hurt her.

In the blackness she could see nothing, only feel his strength against her and realize that her fingers trembled and something inside of her yearned for his lips against hers once more. And yet she hesitated, hearing only his harsh ragged breathing in the silence.

He waited also, his arms unmoving around her. And then he lowered his head and put it against her breast, just laid it there, moving his arms so they circled her waist. Unsure, a bit afraid, she put her own arms around his neck, holding him against her.

As the night deepened, Cyne's breathing followed, finally lengthening into the rhythm of sleep. Only then did Aleene relax, smoothing her hands through her husband's hair. She enjoyed doing that. It soothed her, released the smell of her own soap from his long, gleaming locks. And when she slept, her dreams were the same golden color as her husband's hair.

She awoke still wrapped in Cyne's arms. In the quiet of the morning, she lay very still, waiting. She knew when he stirred awake. He too, though, did not move immediately. Together they lay, awake, intertwined. When a light rap came at the door, Aleene jumped, holding tightly for a moment to her husband's arm, not wanting to give up the rare peace that had settled in her heart.

"Milady?" Berthilde opened the door, and Aleene shut her eyes to the intrusion.

"I will not need you this morning, Berthilde."

"Milady, I must speak with ye. 'Tis very important."

Finally, she untangled her body from her husband's and sat up. "Yes, Berthilde."

The old maid came further into the room. "I . . ." She wrung her hands before her, flicking a glance at Cyne, who still lay on the bed. "I heard Aethregard last night speaking with his man Ulf."

"Ulf? The big one?"

"Yes, milady, the one with mean eyes."

With a deep sigh, Aleene stood, smoothing her hands down her gown and only then realizing that she had slept fully clothed. "What was said, Berthilde, between Aethregard and Ulf that has upset you?"

"They plan harm for your husband, milady."

Aleene jerked her head up. "Harm?"

"Aethregard wishes for Lord Cynewulf to suffer an accident." The maid shot a frightened look at Cyne. "He cannot protect himself, and ye have left him alone for the past few days." She looked back at Aleene. "I fear for your husband, milady."

Aleene glanced at her husband. He had not moved from his curled position on the bed. "I will take care of this, Berthilde." She dismissed the woman with a flick of her hand.

The maid hesitated, looked as if she might say something more, then with a shake of her head she turned.

"Berthilde." Aleene stopped her impulsively.

She turned. "Yes, milady."

"Thank you."

Berthilde stared at her for a moment, then slowly smiled. Aleene realized it had been a very long time since she had seen her old maid smile.

"Of course, milady." Berthilde turned to leave, then stopped again. "Oh, milady, Cuthebert wishes to speak with you this morning. Some of the tenants are worried about harvest."

"Tell him I will see him after I break my fast, Berthilde."

"Yes, milady." With another tentative glance at Cyne, the maid left.

"Well, you shall have to stay at my side this day, husband mine." Aleene turned to smile at her husband. His own answering smile outshone the sunbeams gleaming through her small bedroom window. A real answering of warmth glowed in his eyes and with a jolt she realized that she had never smiled at him before.

It seemed that the small offering energized him, for he bounded off the bed, gave her a clumsy, childlike hug, and beamed at her again.

She laughed, a true happy sound. Then she stood shocked that she had remembered how. Finally, a touch of self-consciousness made her move away from her husband. Taking up her brush, she went to her small looking glass and worked at the snarls that tangled her hair. "You must stay close, today, Cyne. Do not wander, and do not go near Aethregard or any of the other men in the castle." The brush snared in her hair, and she yanked harder to free it, wincing as it pulled at her scalp.

Her husband's hands covered hers. She jumped and the brush dropped to the rushes between them. Cyne bent quickly and retrieved it, pulling herbs from its boar's hair bristles and releasing a heady fresh scent from the worn rushes as he straightened beside her. He spent a few more moments cleaning the brush, then cocked his head at her.

"Th . . . thank you," Aleene said, reaching for the brush, but her husband did not release it. Instead he reached out and fingered a strand of her hair, then moved closer to her and began to do the task he had just interrupted.

In the wavy looking glass, Aleene could just make out her husband's form behind her as he carefully fingered her hair, then gently pulled the brush through. Aleene stood stiffly for a moment, chewing on her lip and wondering if she should protest. Cyne continued his careful ministrations over her hair, though, and she slowly relaxed her shoulders. Closing her eyes, she allowed Cyne to continue his work. Berthilde often did this for her in the morning, only then she stood rigid, hating the feeling of being at someone's mercy, uncomfortable with the closeness of another human.

But she had slept with the man behind her, his head upon her breast. It seemed silly now to be uncomfortable with his nearness. So she banished her reluctance and reveled in the feel of her husband's fingers against her scalp, in her hair, against the nape of her neck. His fingers strong, yet gentle and warm, so warm. Tipping her chin up, Aleene sighed and relaxed, weaving a bit on her feet. She felt her husband's chest against her back, then his lips against her hair, and she smiled. This would work. It would.

Cyne only knew childlike obedience. The innocence that had so struck fear into her heart a few days before in the garden now proffered freedom to her. With her husband, she could let go of the fear, knowing that he could not hurt her. Knowing that he would never, ever control her, or even try.

And, in no way was this man repugnant to her. She would be able to consummate her marriage, get an heir. Filling her lungs with the cool dew of the morning air, Aleene turned and smiled at Cyne, then went to her trunk and removed one of her veils. She placed it carefully over her hair then used her mother's gold circlet to hold it there.

Her husband had also slept in the clothes he had worn to supper. She straightened his tunic, brushing at a tuft of lint and realizing, again, the breadth of her husband's chest. Her hand came back trembling slightly, but she straightened her shoulders.

"Come, Cyne," she said as she left the room, smiling again as she heard her husband follow. He kneeled silently next to her as she said her prayers in the chapel, then mimicked her again as she washed her hands when they finally sat at the table in the great hall. When he ate his cheese slowly, methodically, and took great care to leave his trencher intact, Aleene realized

with a start that she need not force herself to
sound as a warrior commanding his troops
when she spoke to Cyne. Her husband would
follow her to his death. He knew no other
course than to follow.

That thought brought a burden of shadow to
her light mood. Yes, Cyne gave her a long-
forgotten bit of freedom, but he also weighed
down her responsibilities. As she watched him,
though, his beautiful, blond hair falling against
his cheek as he leaned towards his food, Aleene
knew that she wanted that responsibility,
yearned for it, really. Beside her sat the only
person in her life she did not have to fear or
mistrust.

She kept Cyne at her side when she went to
Cuthebert to speak of her people's fears. Her
husband fingered the rolled parchments in her
steward's chamber, running his hands over the
few rare books with a touch of awe. Aleene
watched him, barely able to keep her attention
on Cuthebert's words.

"Milady?"

"Hm?" Wrenching her gaze from her scru-
tiny of Cyne's jawline, Aleene returned it to her
steward's hunched form.

He arched a brow with just a touch of menace. "Milady, the harvest?"

"Oh, yes." Shaking her head, Aleene tried to
concentrate. "The harvest."

"Most of the men are gone, giving their time

to the Fyrd, and we must begin the harvest."

"The king has promised they may return on the Nativity of St. Mary, Cuthebert, which is only a few days away. By then we may be assured Duke William will not attempt a channel crossing."

"Still, we may not see them for another week as they make their way home. Meanwhile, their crops, and ours, sit ripening in the fields." Cuthebert frowned at Cyne, then pulled a much-treasured tome from his lord's hands.

"The fields will keep for another few days." Aleene scowled at Cuthebert, taking the book from him and returning it to Cyne. "Assure the people that our men will be returning home within the next week. And when they do, I will personally make sure that every family brings in their harvest."

"That is quite a promise, milady." She hated the derision she could hear in her steward's voice, but she knew the only way she was going to wipe it from his tone was to keep her promises to her people, without the help of Aethregard.

Aleene sent an icy look down her nose at Cuthebert. "I have given my word. Pevensey will not go hungry this winter."

Cuthebert averted his gaze and watched Cyne from under heavy brows. "And if the people do not believe even your promise?"

Aleene narrowed her eyes on the small man

in front of her. "They have no reason to doubt it. I have never done anything to give them leave not to believe me."

Cuthebert finally met her gaze full on, his thin lip curling into a sneer. "This castle is without a lord; the people are nervous."

"This castle has a lord now," she snapped, gesturing toward the blank-faced man at her side. "They would do well to remember it."

Her steward settled a disgusted gaze on her husband. "Time will tell," he finally said.

A tremor shook Aleene's hand, but she clenched her skirts within her grasp to hide it. Would she ever find favor in the eyes of her people? Aleene took a deep breath, then smoothed her hands down the front of her kirtle. "I thank you, Cuthebert, for keeping me informed of the people's worries."

Cuthebert blinked, his dark look for a moment broken by surprise. "Well, I . . . you're welcome." His words obviously came automatically, for the man looked as if his own mouth had turned traitor on him. He scowled once again, pursing his lips.

"And I ask you to relay my words of comfort to them."

"Hmmmpf." Cuthebert had regained his sullen demeanor. He turned his attention to his book still in the hands of Cyne. "I shall have the tome now." He put his hand out, lifting it a bit and wiggling his fingers to get Cyne's attention.

Cyne turned his gaze from the book in his hand to the scrawny old man in front of him. He looked from the book to the man's spindly fingers, then back to the book. Cyne smiled finally, nodded, and dropped the book.

Cuthebert made a crashing dive to save his precious volume from hitting the floor and ended up in a bony mass against Cyne's legs.

Aleene's lips twitched, but she bit her lower lip mercilessly and snagged Cyne's arm. "Come Cyne, I must see that dinner is being prepared." Her husband gently stepped over Cuthebert, flashed another beguiling smile at the man, and allowed Aleene to draw him outside across the inner bailey to the kitchen area.

A servant, stripped to his *braies*, hunched over the fire and stirred something in a great pot. Berthilde, her fondness for being in charge showing in each gesture, directed a young girl in the finer points of plucking a chicken. Aleene wrinkled her nose at the several flavors in the air, some not so appetizing, and deduced that blood pudding would be on the menu that day. She had never harbored a liking for blood pudding. "All goes well, Berthilde?"

Berthilde glanced up from her lecture and nodded. "Aye, milady. I have everything in hand."

"Of course." Aleene sidled further away from

the boiling cauldron and its pungent odor. "I would like to lay new rushes, Berthilde. Have Gwen sweep out the Hall and my chambers."

"Yes, milady."

"And the privies need to be cleaned out. Advise Wat to do so as soon as possible." Again, Aleene scrunched up her nose. "I could smell them this morning as I went to chapel."

A slight smile touched Berthilde's lips, the wrinkles around her eyes deepening slightly. "I, also, milady."

"I shall be directing the candle-making until dinner." Aleene stopped when she felt someone nudge her elbow. Looking around, she encountered the wide grin of her husband. Her own lips twitched, wanting to smile back, but she furrowed her brow to keep such a thing from happening. "What is it, Cyne?"

He stood a little straighter and held out his hand. A straw basket hung from his fingers.

"It's a basket, Cyne, to carry things in."

He nodded and put it closer to her face. Inside she saw one of the loaves of bread Berthilde had left cooling, a great hunk of cheese, and some of the dried, salted pork left over from the year before. Aleene blinked at the food, then stared at her husband. "That is one of Berthilde's fresh loaves, Cyne, could you put it back please?"

Impatiently, Cyne shook his head and nod-

ded toward the basket again. Then he pointed
out toward the wall of the castle.

"Cyne, I do not have time . . ."

"He wishes to have a picnic, milady, outside
of the walls."

Aleene glanced at Berthilde. "A picnic?" She
looked back at her husband. "A picnic?"

His smile broadened, and he pointed again.

Aleene shook her head with an exasperated
sigh. "I have no time for this, Cyne. I must get
to the candles, and you cannot go anywhere
without me."

"Milady," Berthilde interrupted. "I can over-
see the candle-making."

"And everything else?" Aleene shook her
head. "No, Berthilde, there is too much to do."
She turned to Cyne. "I cannot spend a day doing nothing."

His smile dimmed, his lower lip pushing out
in a pout.

Aleene rolled her eyes. "Deus, are you to cry
next?"

The lip pushed out further as Aleene heard
Berthilde's disapproving tsk.

"But I shall miss dinner, and I really did need
to speak with Aethregard." Aleene looked at
Berthilde and then to her husband. "I can't, really," she said again.

"It will do you good, milady, to be alone with
your new husband."

"But . . ." Aleene bit her lip, torn between being the hardworking lady of the household of whom none of her people could complain, and giving in to Cyne. She wanted to see those liquid blue eyes of his light from within, wanted to see him happy, because in an odd way that made her, if not happy, at least closer to the elusive emotion than she had been in many, many years.

"Well, the candle-making has waited a day, I guess it can wait another."

"We have plenty of candles to keep us until then, milady."

"Yes, well then, I will be going out this day with my husband on a picnic. Do as I have asked, supervise Wat and Gwen in their chores and tell the women that we shall make candles tomorrow." She turned to leave, then stopped. "Oh, and add a flagon of ale to the basket."

"Yes, milady." Berthilde smiled as she went to get the ale.

Aleene held her hand out to Cyne, and he grasped it enthusiastically.

"You have gotten your way this day, my playful lord, but we must work on the morrow, or winter will find us starving in the dark!"

Pulling her along behind him, Cyne took off toward the gate.

Aleene could not help but to laugh at his exuberance, and she found herself doubling her steps to keep up with his long strides.

"Milady, your ale," Berthilde cried across the bailey.

Aleene yanked at Cyne's hand, and when he didn't stop his mad dash for the gate, laughed and yanked again. "We shall be out soon enough, Cyne, hold for but a moment."

He slowed, allowing Berthilde time to catch up to them and put the ale in the basket. Then, he took off again, whistling a sprightly tune.

Aleene could only laugh at Berthilde's dumbfounded expression, then put all of her concentration to the task of staying abreast of her husband. The gatekeeper smiled at them as he let them out, or rather smiled at Cyne. With a start Aleene realized that nobody smiled at her, at least none had before Cyne's arrival. It was a nice departure, actually, from the grim faces she encountered each day.

Leaving the tall, timbered wall of Seabreeze Castle behind them, Cyne strode purposefully toward the sea. They passed the crumbling, stone walls of the old Roman fort and turned south, following the jagged cliffs that ran along the coastline. Together, hand in hand, they walked, the wet wind whipping at Aleene's veil, wrapping it around her and Cyne as well.

After batting the material away from his face a few times, Cyne stopped, put down the basket and took the veil from Aleene's head. He had it tucked into the basket before Aleene had even registered what he meant to do. She touched her bare head tentatively, a tiny spiral of tension winding through her.

Cyne picked up the basket and recaptured her hand, oblivious to her nervous gesture. Again, a strong whistle came from his lips as he started down the coast, his face upturned toward the sun like the petals of a great yellow sunflower.

Aleene allowed him to tug her along behind him, willing herself to let go of her fear, of her reluctance. She need not fear anything with this man-child. With that thought, she took a great breath, letting the tang of the sea sting her nostrils, and the heavy, wet air fill her lungs.

They passed one of the lookouts, one of the Pevensey villagers who had stayed to protect his own coastline. Aethregard's men stood watch closer to the harbor, where there was more potential for trouble. With a slight shake of her head, Aleene scattered the thoughts of the Fyrd, of Aethregard, and of the king's paranoid ideas of invasion and walked along with her husband, away from the watchful eyes of the villager.

When they reached the edge of the cliff with a steep path winding toward the cove below, Aleene showed it to Cyne. He frowned at the narrow walkway, then carefully started down ahead of her.

"No, Cyne, let me," Aleene protested. "I know the way."

But her husband only frowned again, this time at her, and continued down the path. Worried that he might fall, Aleene hurried down after him, keeping her eyes on his feet. "Be careful, husband." She tugged at her bottom lip with her teeth. "A root in your path, Cyne, beware."

When Cyne halted in his descent, she was so engrossed in watching the path ahead of him, she didn't realize and ran square into his back. A very large, strong back, she noted as she kept her balance by holding onto Cyne's sides. "What is wrong?"

He turned, his eyes alight with mischief, and swung her into his arms.

"Cyne! Put me down! We shall fall!"

He only held her tighter as he carried her the rest of the way down the cliff to the sand. Aleene held tightly to his neck, now equally scared for both of them. So intent on protesting, Aleene did not realize they stood on level ground until Cyne let her slide from his arms. He held her still in the circle of his arms, looking down at her, a smug smile playing about his lips. And then he kissed her.

A light touching of their mouths, his still smiling, hers slightly open from her interrupted tirade. Not a long kiss like the night before, but so unexpected that the intimacy of the act ignited burning fires along Aleene's nerve endings.

She closed her eyes, leaning into Cyne, not understanding the emotions that roiled through her while in this man's presence. And he seemed completely oblivious to them, for he just pressed another kiss to her forehead and started for the shore.

The coolness that replaced the heat of his body shocked her, and she opened her eyes. She watched as he dropped the basket on the sand, sat next to it, and began tugging at the leather shoes on his feet. She yearned for him to be close to her again, kissing her mouth, holding her.

And so she went to him, sat beside him, felt the heat of his body next to hers. She looked up at his face and watched a lock of golden hair fall in his eyes, then reached, herself, to push it back.

He glanced at her, his eyes devoid of anything but the smile that lit his face. He nodded toward the water, then pointed at her feet, still shod in leather slippers. Finally, she realized fully what her husband intended, and she snapped out of her strange reverie.

"No, Cyne, it is too cold." She shook her head, sighed and turned to the basket of food. Her thoughts had taken flight into the clouds, it was as if another woman sat with her husband. For she certainly did not think of people and want to be physically close to them. She took her veil from the basket and spread it on the ground, then sat the food on top of it. "We should have thought to bring a blanket, but with you taking off so quickly, and . . ." Aleene looked up to where her husband had been and saw only sand. She jerked around quickly, searching the shore for Cyne.

A great yell rent the air, bringing Aleene to her feet, her heart beating double time within her breast.

Chapter 5

A loud splash directed her gaze to the water, and Aleene saw her husband. He flung his head, throwing sparkling beads of water through the air, raised his arms and yelled again, loud, deep, and lusty.

Aleene sat stunned. It was the first time she had heard her husband's voice. Unlike his mannerisms, it was not childlike. Aleene stood slowly, her eyes glued to the expanse of Cyne's bare chest. It glistened in the warm sun, a mat of golden hair holding crystals of water. Aleene advanced, her mind overcome, once again, with her husband's beauty.

Finally, she wrenched her gaze from his chest, only to encounter eyes like amethysts. "Wha . . . what in heaven's name are you doing?" She now stood at the edge of the water. A wave rolled onto shore, drenching her shoes. As the water seeped through the leather, she shivered. "It is freezing, Cyne, you will catch your death!"

He laughed, a deep, rich, moving, beautiful sound, more beautiful, even, than himself.

A small wave crashed against his back, and he disappeared. Startled, Aleene froze, her heart shrinking in on itself in fear. Then she moved, quickly, ignoring the shock of cold against her legs as she pulled herself through the water.

"Aha!" He came up again, just in front of her, his smile large, his hair streaming across his shoulders.

"You!" Aleene pushed against his chest, the icy contact chilling her. "You scared me nigh unto death, you beast!" But the anger in her voice quickly dissolved. In fact, she laughed.

And he laughed with her.

Another wave hit them, and Cyne grabbed her, holding her upright. With a tiny screech, Aleene put her arms around Cyne's neck. "It is freezing! And now my clothes are soaking."

He only smiled at her as another wave surged around them, tilting them against each other. Aleene felt the warmth of her husband's great body seep through her wet clothing.

The wave drew back out to sea. She took a deep breath as it left, knowing that another would come, pulsing around them, pushing her against Cyne. And it did come, whirling about her thighs, her clothes swirling up around her hips, her husband's hands imitating the rhythm of the waves against her back.

She closed her eyes and leaned into Cyne's warmth and shivered, but she wasn't cold. For the second time that day Cyne swept her up into his arms. Aleene gasped, opening her eyes quickly and tightening her arms around her husband's neck. Guileless eyes looked into hers, and she realized with a strange, poignant pang that her body had sung a strange new song of desire, alone.

Cyne waded from the water, and Aleene stared over his shoulder at the surging sea, biting her bottom lip and wondering. What was happening inside of her? What happened when Cyne touched her? She hardly noticed when her husband set her down on the sand. She did notice when he began pulling at the ties of her kirtle.

"Oh, no, Cyne, I . . . I can't." Aleene put her own hands over his. "Really, I'll dry."

Cyne shook his head and pulled at the ties again.

"Really, Cyne, it is not necessary. It is a warm day. The clothes will dry soon."

Her husband wasn't listening. He tugged at the now loose kirtle.

"What shall I do? Sit naked on the sand?"

Cyne's fingers stilled, and he ducked his head. It felt almost as if he clenched his hands in the ties of her kirtle. Before she could look,

though, he pulled his hands away and pointed
toward the ocean. When he turned back to her
the benign grin curved his lips. He nodded,
pointed to the ocean and, again, tried to un-
dress her.

"No!" Aleene backed away from him. "I
can't!" She backed away some more, only then
realizing that her husband stood before her
completely unclothed, his glorious, wet body
shining as if made of gold.

"Oh dear!" Aleene quickly put her hand over
her eyes. "Cyne! You are . . . you are . . ." She
swallowed and continued to shield her eyes.
Above anything she wanted to look, see again
her husband's body, but that was wicked,
wasn't it? She let her fingers relax a bit. If she
opened her eyes, she would see, and he would
never know.

Before she could round up enough courage
to look, her husband's large, warm hand covered hers. He pulled her hand away from her
eyes, and she felt his breath against her mouth,
but his lips didn't touch hers. Her entire body
screamed with the nearness of Cyne's, her lips
yearned for the warmth of his. Opening her
eyes, finally, she found Cyne's face near hers.
He leaned in closer, touching the tip of her nose
with his.

She chewed at her bottom lip, knowing that
much more of this turmoil and that lip would
be shredded. With a heart-rending smile, Cyne

backed away from her. When his hands went
to her gown, she did not protest. Deep in her
mind, she wanted to stop him, wanted to keep
her clothes about her, keep her shields in place,
not allow herself to be so vulnerable. But she
didn't move. She did not help him. But she did
not stop him either.

He removed everything but her small, thin
chemise, which reached only to her thighs.
Then, carefully, he stretched her clothing out on
the sand. Aleene watched, keeping her eyes up,
not wanting to see herself. She knew that her
husband could see her body through her trans-
parent chemise, and suddenly she was terribly
ashamed. She did not want him to see her. To
realize fully her darkness compared to his light.
He would see her dark skin, the dark hair at the
junction of her thighs.

But he seemed oblivious to that. For, when
he finally turned to her, his eyes looked only at
her face and he reached for her hand as a young
child might. Burying her shame and reluctance
deep in her mind, Aleene laid her hand in his,
and again felt the connection between them like
something out of a dream.

She followed him, the water not as cold as it
had seemed before, churning up around her ankles, her knees, her thighs. When Cyne pulled
on her hand, she sank down with him, letting
the water lap around her neck.

He looked at her, that mischievous gleam

back in his eyes. She returned his gaze, warily.
When he let go of her hand and disappeared
under the water, Aleene stood. And then she
felt his hands around her ankles and yelled
helplessly as he yanked her feet out from under
her, and she fell backwards.

She came up sputtering, her hair a wet heavy
mass. "Why you . . . oh!"

He laughed, the deep, rich sound sending a
thrill of pure happiness through her heart.
Arching her eyebrows at her husband, she
folded her arms in front of her. "You think you
are the only one with tricks up your sleeves?"

His eyes widened, and he held up his arms,
turning them this way and that, then looking
back at her and shaking his head.

Aleene slitted her eyes at him. "You have no
sleeves, I see that." As she circled her husband,
she smiled, her heart jumping at the idea of
play. She hadn't played in forever. She realized
suddenly that she loved to play. Turning, she
made as if to leave, then swiveled around, cupping her hands and throwing a large spray of
water at her husband.

He jumped backwards, his feet moving faster
than the water would allow, and fell. Laughing,
he emerged, already on the attack as he cupped
his own hands and splashed water on her.

They played for a long time, splashing like
children, dunking each other, laughing always.
When finally they lay sprawled on the sand, the

sun warming the chill from the cool sea, her husband's hand laying against her thigh warming the chill from her heart, Aleene could not stop the smile that curved her lips.

She remembered her father playing in the waves with her when she was young. He had stretched out with her just as Cyne was doing now. Turning her head, Aleene looked at her husband, his eyes closed, face upturned, beads of water rolling slowly across his taut stomach, then quickly plunging over his side and falling to the ground. Childhood memories took flight with the warm breath of wind that teased her husband's drying hair across his forehead.

He felt her gaze, she knew, for he moved his finger slightly against her thigh. And it seemed, for a moment, that he understood. Closing her eyes, Aleene turned her face so that she felt the full force of the sun against her eyelids. She reached down and put her hand on top of his.

"My father swam with me here," she said, then stayed silent for a long time, shocked that she had even said such intimate words. But she found herself continuing after awhile. "The people of the village didn't understand. They believed swimming in such cold water should kill a person. But my father could not stay away from the ocean. It is a warm ocean where he was from. They swim in it often."

Aleene drew in a deep breath and let it out. The warm sun seeped through her skin, the smell of brine tickled her nostrils. "I loved when he would bring me here. I didn't realize how very strange it made us to the people of the village." A dark feeling threatened to crowd out the rare moment of peace she felt. She shook her head as if she could physically dislodge it.

"They still think me strange, have always thought so. They would rather Aethregard be lord of Seabreeze than me, a woman, a woman of foreign blood." Aleene pulled her hand from Cyne's and sat up, wrapping her arms around her bent knees.

From the corner of her eye, she saw Cyne follow her movements. She squinted out at the blue horizon and licked at the salt on her lips. She had never voiced her inner thoughts, her fears. Never. When she had the opportunity, with her father, she hadn't had any fears. It felt strange to hear the words out loud, hear her voice saying them. She found a stick and stabbed the sand with it.

"He was old, my father," she said. "Nearly fifty when my mother had me. But I never thought him old, until he died. My mother said that his heart just quit working. The people blamed it on our ventures out into the icy waters." She waved the stick toward the sea with a sigh. "They were happy he was dead." She had cried then, for days she had cried, her seven-year-old mind not understanding the jubilant spirit of the people. They had never trusted the foreigner among them.

"They rejoiced when my mother married To-sig, the Thane from the north. He was one of them." She broke the stick in half and threw it away from her, staring at nothing, seeing nothing.

Cyne stroked her hair, silently giving her understanding. And, yet, he did not understand. She knew that he did not, not really. He was a boy, a light-hearted, beautiful golden boy in a man's body. She turned to him, forcing her memories away. Cyne leaned quickly over and kissed her cheek. She stiffened and turned toward the sea once more.

Why? Why did this man's body awaken her woman's body as no other had?

It frightened her and it invigorated her at the same time. She did not know how to handle such confusion. She looked at the man to whom she had just bared her soul. He grinned, stroking her hair again, then lowered himself back to the ground and closed his eyes. With a sigh, Aleene fingered her hair, spreading it about her shoulders so that it would dry.

She was confused. But she was happy, too. A wonderous emotion, one she had not felt since her seventh year. She had spoken to another human of feelings deep within her heart, shown another her fear. She should be even more afraid.

And yet, it was liberating. The fears didn't seem as real, as debilitating. A breeze lifted goose pimples on her arms and she shivered. "We should go, Cyne." She pushed herself up from the sand.

She took one more look at the cove as they reached the cliff above it, already missing the bittersweet experience of the day. Cyne held her hand as they walked back to Seabreeze, his step light. She felt as her father must have felt, holding her by the hand as they returned home after a beautiful day of shirking duties and enjoying each other. The gatekeeper allowed their entrance, then tugged his forelock in salute. Aleene nodded, and took Cyne to wash before supper. Fear returned with a little trickle down her spine as she and Cyne readied for bed. She knew she must finish finally the deed of consummating her marriage. Her fingers shook as she loosened the tie of her tunic, but she breathed deeply and pushed the dark feelings away.

Aleene looked over at her husband. He sensed her, surely, for his head came up from his silent task of taking off his shoes. It was dark, and the tiny, sputtering candle only made it harder to see, it seemed. She wanted him to touch her again.

As if she had spoken the need aloud, Cyne stood and came to her, gathering her in his arms. "Cyne," Aleene sighed into his chest. "Do you understand?" He said nothing, of course, only rocked her slightly. "No, you don't, do you? And I am glad. You give me the freedom I have not had in so long. With you I don't have to constantly be on guard."

He moved, picking her up and taking her to the bed. She kept her face buried in his chest as they lay down together. "I am so afraid. And yet, the fear seems conquerable now."

Cyne stroked her back, her hair, rocking her slowly back and forth. "I loved my father so much. He was so strong." Aleene smiled as she thought of her father. "He protected me from everything. It wasn't until he died that I realized I was different, that I didn't belong. And then my mother married Tosig, and . . ." Aleene stopped, her breathing coming in sharp, painful bursts as the image of Tosig emerged from the darkness of her mind. "And the people, they loved him. But I didn't, couldn't. And then . . ." But she stopped there. That part of the story she just could not say aloud.

"I fight for Seabreeze because my father is still here. He built it, and I feel him in the very wood. But I want it to be mine alone. I will not share it with anyone, especially Aethregard." Aleene shook her head as Aethregard's cold gray eyes materialized in her thoughts. "I cannot bear it."

Cyne began to hum. It was a deep sound, reverberating through his chest and warming her own. Aleene blinked, her memories receding at the sound. She was not used to sound from her husband and for a moment fear tickled the back of her neck and made her tremble.

And then she recognized the song. It was the lullaby her mother had sung to her at night. It was the song Aleene had sung that first night of their marriage. She tightened her arms around Cyne, letting herself float on the beautiful tones of her husband's voice, turning away from the dark, ugly memories of her stepfather's abuse.

Aleene fell asleep in her husband's arms, her cheek against the hard wall of his chest, without consummating their marriage. When the light of the morning sun played against her closed lids, Aleene took a deep breath and wondered if she might not mate with her husband now, with the light of day full on them. The wicked thought came, she was sure, from the desperate need to get with child. She did not wish to mate with her husband for any kind of pleasure. No, never that.

She did desire to see him, though, constantly. With a small smile she opened her eyes and turned onto her side, seeking the golden glory of Cyne. Her husband was gone.

In terror, Aleene jumped out of bed and pulled on a gown. She searched the hall, finding only Berthilde. "Cyne." Aleene gulped in air so that she could continue. "Have you seen Cyne?"

The furrow between Berthilde's eyes deepened. "No, milady."

Aleene did not allow the old woman to say anything more. With an agonized groan, she ran for the door and raced across the outer bailey, interrogating everyone she saw. Finally someone pointed to the gates that led outside the walls.

Aleene's heart seemed to stop and she had to close her eyes and take a few deep breaths before she could find the strength to take up her skirts and leave the safe confines of the castle compound. With head bent into the relentless wind, Aleene nearly hollered herself hoarse bellowing Cyne's name.

When she found him on the wall walk of the old Roman fort, she couldn't decide whether to kiss him or kill him.

"Cyne!"

He looked up, surprise registering in his blue eyes before that horrible blankness took its place.

"Cyne, you are never to go anywhere without me!" She took his arms in hers and shook; he barely moved. "Never! Do you understand?"

He blinked, then looked into the air. Aleene sighed and followed his gaze to see a pigeon swoop down, circle over their heads, then head across the cliffs and out to sea. Aleene stared at it, puzzled. "Where on earth does that bird think it is going, France?" She laughed and shook her head, looking back at her husband. He stared at her, warily.

"Cyne, I am sorry for yelling, but you must be careful. Aethregard, the short, ugly man, does not like you." She ran a hand up his arm and cupped his cheek. "He would do you harm, given the chance."

Cyne nodded and turned his face away from her, looking out to sea. The wind whipped his long, blond hair around his head. Aleene sighed.

They stood there together for awhile in silence. And then Cyne laid his hand on the back of her head. She looked up, surprised, but he did not return her gaze, keeping his face turned toward the sea. His hand felt heavy as he cupped her head, then trailed his fingers through her hair and down her back. Taking her hand, Cyne turned down the walk. Aleene followed, wondering at the melancholy way Cyne continued to stare at the sea.

They went back toward Seabreeze Castle, passing a lookout, one of Aethregard's men this time. Aleene frowned at the man, her heart happy that he and Aethregard would be gone soon, that this summer of worry, fear, and endless waiting would be over.

"We shall be happy, this winter, Cyne," she

said aloud, tilting her head to catch the warmth of the sun and letting Cyne lead her along the rocky coast. "The men from the town will be home within a fortnight. Aethregard's men shall be gone. We can bring in the harvest and be secure that the Bastard Duke shall not come from across the sea to claim a crown which is not his."

Cyne stumbled, and Aleene quickly looked at the trail, holding onto her husband. "I'm sorry, Cyne, I am not watching where we are going." She patted his hand, looking then at her castle. There were only a handful of castles in England, most of them belonging to royalty, except this one. She admired the tall, wooden walls closing in the bailey and the tower at the gate; this one belonged to her, a woman.

She smiled again as they passed by the gate-house, then she frowned. "Where are we going?" She tried to stop, tried to turn back to the gate, but Cyne continued past, headed toward the town of Pevensey. "Cyne!"

He didn't stop or turn his head.

"We cannot spend another day playing, Cyne."

He looked at her then, finally, but the grin and mischievous glint in his eye only made Aleene groan. "No, Cyne, I cannot! The candles will never be made if I continue to shirk my duty!" But as she spoke, she walked along beside her husband. "I have not even put on my veil, Cyne." She touched her hair tentatively.

Cyne stopped then, turning to look at her. He smiled, and something in his eyes fanned a fluttering spark deep in her belly. Swallowing, Aleene searched her husband's face. He reached out and fingered her hair, twirling a dark, ebony curl around his large hand. Then he brought it to his mouth, inhaled as if taking in her scent, and kissed.

Aleene felt faint as Cyne, again, took her hand and continued toward the town.

Her head rebelled at the idea of spending another carefree day ignoring necessary preparations for the oncoming winter. Her heart rebelled against her head. And so a war thrived in her breast, until they reached the town and Cyne kissed the tip of her nose. Her heart won.

They spent the morning in town, shopping among the stalls. Aleene selected fish to be sent to the castle, and cloth from a woman who watched her with suspicion, and seemed nearly faint with fear at the look in Cyne's blank eyes. As Aleene browsed among the produce at another man's stall, she could feel the anger building within her. It had abated the day before, with the new experience of speaking to someone of her feelings. But now, she felt it again, the suffocating fear and anger that had lived in her heart for so many years. Would the people ever accept her as lady of Seabreeze?

A shout broke into her thoughts, and Aleene

whipped around, searching for Cyne who had wandered from her side. The shout came again, and she found Cyne.

He was playing with the children, a rousing game of ball. They laughed as they played. The people around them stared. Aleene held her breath. Instead of pulling their children away, though, as Aleene had feared, they let them play. She relaxed a bit, biting at the inside of her lip as she watched Cyne run about. At one point he stopped, cocking his head and bending to inspect some wildflowers. He picked them and carefully arranged them in a pretty bouquet, then handed them to one of the old ladies, who stood gaping at him. She sputtered out her thanks, her face turning a bright shade of red. One of the younger women batted her eyelashes at Cyne as he straightened and went back to playing with the children.

Aleene could only watch in shock. By the time they had bought some bread and cheese and had some supper, the townspeople seemed completely enamored of Cyne. She had spent her life an outcast, not knowing the way in. Cyne had figured it out in a few hours.

In the afternoon, they went exploring in the woods beyond Pevensey. It was as if she were seeing them for the first time in her life. Cyne found flowers with dark, earthy scents to weave into a circlet for her hair, chased after butterflies, scared rabbits from the underbrush, and dropped light kisses on her mouth as they walked. When finally she realized that her feet had grown weary, they had walked nearly all the way around Pevensey Harbor.

"Cyne!" She tried to sound stern, but the laugh in her voice belied any anger. "We have nearly walked to the next town. We must turn back or we will be walking all night."

Ahead of her Cyne stopped. With his hands on his lean hips, he surveyed the countryside, his gaze seeming to drink in everything around him. When she caught up to him, Aleene rested her hand against his arm. The feel of the muscles and strength hidden beneath his clothing reminded her suddenly of the day before when she had watched her naked husband splash about in the sea.

"Cyne." It was a breathless sound, nothing like how she had meant to say it. Her fingers moved of their own accord, skimming his side.

He put his hand over hers, laughing, and she realized she had tickled him. She laughed herself, only it wasn't a happy sound. To her mind it sounded as if someone was torturing her.

And he was.

Something inside of her screamed to touch, to be touched in ways she didn't understand. And, to her ultimate despair, Cyne didn't seem to understand either.

Quickly she dropped her hand back to her side and turned around, away from the beauty and mesmerizing allure of the man beside her. "Really, Cyne, we need to go back."

His arm went about her shoulders, holding her tightly to his side, and he propelled her toward a tree. She glanced up at him, the afternoon sun slicing through the branches of the tree and illuminating his blue eyes so they seemed intelligent. She turned quickly away, a pang of need nearly bending her double.

Truly, Aleene could not believe her luck in finding Cyne. It must have been God that put him in her forest, poaching her game just as her men happened by. He was the key to everything she wanted, and more, for she had found in Cyne someone she could actually talk to and not fear. And yet she yearned for more. A more she didn't understand. Somewhere, deep inside, she wished Cyne did understand so that he could show her. For, he had shown her so much, and she knew he would be able to show her what she needed.

He supported her as she sat at the base of the tree, but she kept her gaze away from him. In silence he sat beside her, his long legs pulled up to his chest, his strong arms around his knees.

Pulling up her own legs, Aleene buried her face in her gown. It was unfair of her to want more from Cyne. He could only give her so much, and, really, wasn't that enough? What he

had given her was much more than she had
ever thought she would have.

She felt his hand against her head, again, just
as he had caressed her that morning at the Roman fort, and closed her eyes tightly, reveling
in the feel of the touch. It felt so very good to
have someone touching her to comfort rather
than hurt. He stroked her hair awhile, then
trailed his finger behind her ear and down her
jaw. She lifted her face then, and he leaned toward her, kissing her cheek lightly, his full lips
warm against her skin. She trembled, her hands
reaching up to curl around his forearms, his
own hands cupping her face.

His lips caressed the skin beneath her eyes,
tenderly, softly. Holding tightly to Cyne's arms,
she moaned, relaxing toward her husband. She
wanted to surrender to him, have him comfort
her, take care of her. And something in the way
he held her face, kissed her cheeks, made her
feel that he could.

Another tender, feather-light kiss teased the
corner of her mouth. Closing her eyes, Aleene
let herself believe Cyne to be a man. A real man,
there to protect her, take care of her. She turned
her face so that the next kiss came down on her
lips, and savored the feel of Cyne's strong lips
against her own. Breathing in the scent of earth,
grass and sweat, she let her husband kiss her
again.

This kiss lasted, a deep kiss, his tongue trailing a hot, sensual path against her lips, inside, against her teeth. Opening to him, she touched his tongue with hers, and felt a sudden, heart-rending need to have Cyne close, against her, in her, around her. She moaned, tightening her arms around her husband and pressing the back of his head with her hand.

He responded, his kiss becoming hard, taking.

And Aleene wanted to give.

She touched him, his arms, shoulders, back, sliding her fingers into openings she found in his clothing. Touching skin: hard, warm skin. Cyne did the same, the callused tips of his fingers scraping against the sensitive skin at the base of her throat, the swell of her breast.

With a deep, startled intake of breath, Aleene arched toward those fingers, wanting them, needing them to touch her, but not understanding where she needed them. She clutched at her husband's back, her fingernails digging into the scratchy wool of his tunic, and moaned, a deep, frustrated sound.

Cyne bit her. Her eyes fluttered open in shock, and he looked back at her with that mischievous glint. For a moment they stared at each other, and then, slowly, he bit her again, softly, his teeth nipping at her bottom lip. He laughed and she melted, holding him to her as if he may suddenly disappear.

His hand brushed down the side of her

breast, his thumb grazing the crest through the layers of her clothing. She gasped as white-hot lightning darted through her at that small touch. Cyne nipped at her earlobe and touched her again, this time lingering, his thumb and forefinger finding her nipple and teasing it.

She stilled, her eyes closed, everything within her focusing on the sensation her husband caused with his hand on her breast. She wanted more.

And then his large, beautiful hand skimmed down her body and pulled at her gown, bringing the material up, caressing her thigh.

Aleene tensed, the new, unknown feelings of ecstasy falling away before an old, familiar feeling. She swallowed, hard, not wanting bad memories to encroach on the beauty. Grabbing her husband's hand she brought it back to her breast. "Please, Cyne, make the good continue," she said, knowing he wouldn't understand.

She kissed him, hard, her tongue seeking his, her mind seeking the excitement she had experienced only moments before.

But the gates that guarded the portals of her memories had been unlocked, and ugly images seeped into her mind.

Tosig, his hand on her thigh.

She fought the memory, clasping Cyne's head, pushing her lips against his.

Darkness, hands pulling up her tunic, fingers against her woman's entrance.

A small sob wrenched through Aleene's lips. She clamped her mouth together, gritting her teeth. She had to couple with her husband, had to force the sickening memories of her stepfather away.

If only. She grabbed at Cyne's hand, pushing it harder against her breast. If only she could capture the new feelings her husband brought: capture the new, expunge the old.

But they were there. The gates were wide open now, and black images of Tosig filled her mind, blocking out everything else. Wrenching away from Cyne, Aleene turned on her side, curling into a tight ball, sobs wracking her body.

And then through the fear, the ugliness, the darkness, she heard the song. Lightly, so faint she thought at first she dreamt it, Aleene heard the lullaby. Her mother's lullaby vibrated in her ear, as arms, strong and large, came around her, holding her, rocking her.

Relaxing, Aleene turned into the arms of her husband as he hummed her mother's lullaby and rocked her fears away.

When he kissed her again, it was a soft, loving kiss that brought a rush of warmth and security. "Save me, Cyne," she said it aloud, because she knew she could. She knew she could show her vulnerability to her husband and he would do nothing with it, save comfort her, hold her, heal her. "Save me from the demons that haunt me."

He held her, humming softly, rocking slowly.

"Save me from me," she said so low she didn't even hear the words herself. And then she put her forehead against her husband's broad chest and let him comfort her.

When finally they stood, the shadows had lengthened and the air had chilled. In silence, hand in hand, they retraced their steps back to the town. And once there, in the gathering dusk, they saw the entire populace in the street, all abuzz at the arrival of King Harold at Seabreeze Castle.

Chapter 6

~~~ೲ~~~

"I am tired, Lady Aleene, so very tired."
The king looked at her with sorrow in
his eyes.

She looked away, her gaze on Cyne, who
stood off in the shadows of the great hall, his
eyes holding her up, supporting her.

"The wedding must, of course, be annulled,"
Aethregard bellowed, his chest thrust out like a
strutting peacock. "She married against your
wishes, your highness. My father, her very own
stepfather, signed our betrothal when she was
sixteen."

Harold's gaze never left Aleene. "Yes, Aethregard, I know. I signed the betrothal also. I
am not an idiot."

"I never ... I mean, I ..." Aethregard stut-
tered. "I would never imply that ..."

"Aethregard!" Harold cut off her stepbrother
with a wave of his hand. "Be gone, man, you
tax my patience!"

"But, your highness . . ." His voice trailed off as King Harold finally looked at him. Aethregard bowed low. "Of course, your highness." He straightened, gave Aleene a scathing look and turned on his heel.

Aleene looked back at King Harold, her mind a cacophony of thoughts: she could not allow her marriage to be annulled. What would happen to Cyne? Did she dare lie to her king?

And then through the agonizing jumble of questions that plagued her, Aleene heard a yell and a hollow-sounding thud. She followed the king's gaze to where Aethregard lay in the rushes, staring at the ceiling.

Cyne, pure innocence radiating from his face, offered Aethregard a hand.

Aleene felt the twitch of a smile tug at her mouth.

"Do you think I did not see your foot?" Aethregard fumed, shoving himself up from the ground on his own and grabbing the front of Cyne's tunic. "You give me that wide-eyed and vacant-brained look as you undermine me and my authority."

"Aethregard, stop this instant," Aleene commanded.

He turned toward her, his fist still clenching Cyne's clothing.

"I demand that you leave Cyne be." Aleene wanted to knock her thick-skulled stepbrother over the head with a chamber pot, but she kept her anger in check. "You should not take out your clumsiness on an innocent bystander."

"Innocent?" Aethregard roared. "He's as innocent as what lies between the legs of a harlot."

"You have forgotten yourself, Aethregard." The voice of Harold, low, soft, but commanding, echoed through the hall.

"I beg pardon, your highness." Aethregard let go of Cyne, pushing the man away. "But I have been forced to suffer the indignities of this ... this half-wit and my ..." His mouth working feverishly, Aethregard turned a menacing gaze on Aleene, "... my ... *stepsister*," he spit the word out between clenched teeth, "for far too long."

"That will be enough, Aethregard."

"But ..."

King Harold lifted his hand. "Go now, I wish to speak to Lady Aleene alone."

Aleene could see her stepbrother wanted to protest further, but he doubled his fists at his sides and turned on his heel. Bits of dried herbs dropped from his clothing and a rather large piece of dry straw, stuck to his backside, bobbed and swayed as he marched out of the room. Aleene twisted her mouth and bit at the inside of her cheek to stop the chuckle that clogged her throat.

"I am not amused, Aleene, lady of Seabreeze Castle."

Sobering immediately, Aleene returned her gaze to her king. Swallowing and clasping her hands before her, she bowed her head.

Harold stood, dismissing the men who waited to assist him. Aleene watched out of the corner of her eye as Cyne turned to leave with the rest.

"Please . . ." Aleene stopped.

"Yes, Lady Aleene?" Something in her king's voice sounded a long-forgotten memory in Aleene. "You wish something?" Soft, yet strong; weary, yet kind, his voice sounded in the silent hall, just as her father's had many years before.

"Please, your highness." She forced herself to look into her king's eyes. "May my husband stay with me?"

Harold blinked, obviously surprised, then he hailed the retreating Cyne. "Stay, lad."

Turning, Cyne smiled hugely and went to stand next to Aleene. His hand, strong and warm, took hers, infusing strength into her very bones. A tiny indefinable thrill traced along her skin, and she clasped her husband's hand and straightened her shoulders.

A weary sigh came from Harold as he turned away, pacing the floor, stopping to examine one of the tapestries, then continuing on.

Aleene waited, preparing herself. She tilted her chin, narrowed her eyes, and stood tall, thanking God for the first time that she was not a small, simpering English maiden.

King Harold stopped before her, his arms crossed over his lean chest. "You went against an edict, Lady Aleene."

Taking note that the top of Harold's head came only to her forehead, Aleene straightened even more and answered, "*I* never agreed to the betrothal. I am eighteen, your highness, of an age to break a betrothal pushed upon me by a man who was not even my father."

Harold glanced at Aleene from under his brows. "Be careful, Lady Aleene. I am weary of intrigues. This long summer has worn on my good nature."

"I realize you have had burdens this summer, your highness. But I have tried not to be one of them. Indeed, I have tried to lighten those burdens."

"Yes, I received the gifts of your ships and trained fighting men, the house-carls." The king began pacing again, turning his back on Aleene. "But they do not buy your right to defy me." He turned again to face her. "I need unity now among my people."

"I support you completely." Aleene tightened her grip on Cyne's hand; she would not let Harold intimidate her. "I have shown you that I can protect Seabreeze Castle and Pevensey. Why can I not marry whom I wish?"

"Because, Lady Aleene, *I* wish you to marry another."

Aleene bit down on her tongue, halting the tirade of angry words that wanted to fly forth.

"Have you slept with him?" King Harold asked abruptly from across the room, nodding toward Cyne.

Silence thundered in the large hall. Closing her eyes, Aleene felt the presence of her husband at her side, strong, caring, loving and knew she could not abide to have him gone.

She lifted her gaze to her king. "Yes." And it was no lie.

His face did not harden in anger as she half-thought it would. Instead, the lines around his eyes and mouth seemed to deepen, his shoulders sagged. He aged in front of her. "Are you with child?"

Her bravado left her quickly, deserting her when she needed it more than ever. "I . . . I cannot say." Her voice shook, as did her hands.

"You cannot say?"

Aleene stayed silent, not able to lie to her king when it finally came to that, but also unable to throw away her only chance at happiness.

Finally Harold nodded, looking away from her as he said, "Ah, I understand. You have not experienced your monthly flow."

King Harold turned back to her, his chest rising and falling slowly as his breaths ticked off the long seconds they stood, silent, assessing each other.

"Guard!" King Harold called loudly, causing Aleene to jump.

A large man entered, probably one of *her* house-carls, and bowed to the king.

The king nodded toward Cyne. "Take him to the dungeon."

"No!" Aleene jumped in front of Cyne. "No, you cannot!"

"Why not, pray tell, Lady Aleene?" Harold raised a questioning brow. "You do have a dungeon as I remember. Very thoughtful of your father to add one."

"Please, your highness." Aleene could hear the desperate tone in her voice, but wasn't sure she could curb it. "I . . . you can't put Cyne, my husband, in the dungeon."

"He will be your husband only until we know for certain that you are not with child." Harold sat with a weary sigh. "Until then you will be separated."

Aleene no longer cared to put on haughty airs or show Harold her strength. "Please don't put him in the dungeon. I will stay away from him, your highness, on my word I will not go near him. But please, please don't put him in that filthy, awful place."

Harold stared at her, then closed his eyes and rubbed at his temples. "Aleene of Seabreeze Castle you are truly an enigma."

Aleene nervously glanced from her silent king to the unmoving guard and back again.

"Put three guards on him," the king finally said, gesturing at Cyne, then looking at Aleene. "I have no faith in your honor, Lady Aleene. You have not earned it."

Aleene winced and bowed her head against the king's hurting words. Next to her she felt Cyne shift, his warmth seeping through her clothing, touching her.

Looking up into his blank eyes, Aleene suddenly realized that he would not understand their separation. He might even think he had done wrong.

Ignoring Harold, Aleene turned her back on the advancing guard and squeezed her husband's hand. "Cyne, I will not let anyone hurt you." She stared at him, tried to make him understand. "We have to be apart for awhile, not long." Her voice seemed thin and far away.

As he looked at her she saw a flash of some emotion, distress perhaps? She tried to soothe him. "It will be all right, Cyne, I won't let anyone hurt you." She kissed his hand, the soft, dusting of hair on his large knuckles, the calluses on his palm.

She felt him move away and looked up quickly. The guard had taken Cyne's other arm. As the man led her husband from the hall, Aleene held onto his hand until it was no longer possible.

*   *   *

The king's minstrels and traveling players sang, tumbled, and laughed with the crowd of men gathered in the large hall at Seabreeze Castle. The revelry grated upon Aleene's nerves. She wished that everyone would leave, wished she could be alone with her husband.

"The Fyrd will be dispersed," the king said, touching her hand lightly to get her attention.

Reluctantly, Aleene dragged her gaze from Cyne, who sat at a lower table. "For the Nativity of St. Mary as was agreed, your highness?"

"Yes." Harold sighed and watched as a juggler strolled by in front of them. "The men are needed at their homes, and with the summer gone we can rest easy that William will not make a move for another year."

"Aethregard and his men will go back to their village?" Aleene said a quick, silent, yet fervent prayer that Aethregard would be returning home with his men.

Harold turned to look at her. "Aethregard is not a bad man."

A huff of air escaped Aleene's lungs. "Yes, your highness." Her words held no conviction.

"He is completely loyal to me."

"As am I." Aleene turned on the bench to face Harold.

"Really, Lady Aleene?" The king stared at her. "Can I trust you to be level-headed in your decisions? Would you obey my commands without question?"

"Of course!" Aleene said quickly, even as she knew with every fiber of her being that she couldn't obey anyone without questioning.

"As you have these past weeks?"

Aleene turned to stare out at the festivity around her. "I . . ."

"If you do not carry a babe in your womb, Lady Aleene, you will marry Aethregard." King Harold cut her off. "He will not leave with his men."

Agony. Her heart wrenched in her chest, but she tired of the verbal sparring. "Very well, your highness," she said quietly.

He patted her hand, a loving, fatherly gesture that made her want to snatch her hand away and run.

Aleene gritted her teeth and folded her arms beneath her breasts, glancing over to check on Cyne.

He was looking at her, his eyes filled with what looked like worry. Could he worry about her? She wished he would, but knew he couldn't. Her heart was playing tricks with her mind. She smiled anyway, a hopeful, promising smile.

"I am going to retire, your highness." Aleene stood.

Harold stood also, as did the others around her, each bidding her a good night. She nodded to the men around her, then curtsied to the king.

"Let your mind be at peace, Lady Aleene," he said. "I will make sure you are taken care of."

Aleene almost laughed in his face. Could he not see that was the last thing she wished from him? But she only nodded.

She moved away from the table, her eyes searching out Cyne. The place he had occupied with his guards was vacant. Worry made her search the hall. If anyone did anything to Cyne, she would personally tear their eyes out. Quickly, Aleene moved to the door, her heart pounding hard in her ears. She peered through the gloom outside of the hall, feeling for the knife she had put back in her girdle after using it during dinner.

And then she saw him, his smile a gleam in the dark. He stepped toward her, his face in shadow, but still she knew it so well now that she could see his eyes in her mind, bright, loving, and kind.

"Cyne!" She rushed forward and took his hands in hers, bringing them to her chest. "Are you all right? Has anyone tried to hurt you? Did the . . ." She stopped as the men who guarded Cyne moved and she realized they were not alone.

Her husband's hands shifted under hers, moving so he held hers. She returned her gaze

to Cyne's shadowed face. "Oh, Cyne." There
was so much she wanted to say. So much that
he wouldn't understand. But still, now, just
touching him seemed to be enough.

She sighed as he squeezed her hands. "We
must . . ." Again her words were cut short. This
time Cyne silenced her, pressing one of his
large, warm fingers against her lips. She
blinked, surprised. And then he threaded his
fingers through the hair at her nape, bringing it
forward and kissing the dark strands.

Aleene watched his fingers in her hair and
felt a pounding need drown out her distress.
Suddenly her body was back in the deep forest,
under the tree, her husband's hands bringing
new and wondrous feelings ringing through
her. She shuddered and spread her hands
against Cyne's chest, her gaze dragging back up
the length of his muscled arm to his darkened
face.

He smiled. She knew he did. She could feel
it wash over her, touch her more deeply than
she had allowed anything to touch her, ever.
His hand cupped the back of her head, holding
her still as his mouth covered hers in a kiss.
Soft, yet possessive; giving yet taking, his lips
moved over hers for a mere moment before
they were broken apart by the guards.

"Here now, man, we'll have none of that."
One of the men chuckled.

"He's more dangerous than he looks," the

man who held Cyne by the arm said, his tone more serious than that of his friend.

"We'll be going back into the hall then." The third guard bowed in Aleene's direction. "I wish you a good night, Aleene, lady of Seabreeze Castle."

Aleene could only stare at her husband as the men led him away from her. She felt as if she had been ripped in half. Still, her heart beat an uneven, quickened rhythm against her breast. She turned away, putting out her hand to steady herself.

She touched the smooth wood of a wall. No pleasure came from feeling the wall, her wall. Her heart did not leap at the sight of it. It did not promise her a lifetime of smiles, of warmth, of love. Aleene pushed away quickly, clenching her hands at her side as she ran for the stairs and her chamber.

Berthilde bustled about Aleene's chamber the next morning, readying the bath.

"Why do you not look at me like the others, Berthilde?" Aleene asked suddenly.

Berthilde straightened, her brows lifted in surprise. "Milady?"

She had spoken on impulse, and now wished she hadn't, but Aleene repeated her question. "The others have always hated me and yet you do not. Why Berthilde?"

"They do not hate you, milady."

Aleene laughed derisively. "They heralded the coming of Tosig as if he were God, they look at me as if I, myself, pushed him from the cliff to his death. And I have fought to be their lady since the day this holding finally passed to me."

"Perhaps you should not fight so hard."

Aleene stared down at her feet, white against the dark rushes that littered the floor. "Why are you not like them, Berthilde?"

"I know you, milady. I bathed you as a babe." They had never spoken thus, and Berthilde now seemed shy. "Now, into the bath, milady." She gestured brusquely and turned her back.

With a sigh, Aleene took off her clothes and lowered herself into the comforting bath water.

"There was a rumor, milady, that you did push Tosig over the cliff," Berthilde said, never turning around.

Aleene stopped in the midst of her ablutions. "But, how could they think . . ." she let the words trail off. "I mean I hated him, but I would never . . ."

"It is only a few who speak against you, milady, but the others listen atimes. You are different from them, and distant."

With a sound of disgust, Aleene slipped quickly down and dunked her head beneath the water. Silence surrounded her for a peaceful moment, the movement of the water making her head bob, the warmth against her skin making her want to stay for a very long time. But she surfaced, finally, breathing in a great lungful of air.

"I am to go picking herbs this noon, milady. Meet me there, we shall speak."

"Speak to me now, Berthilde," Aleene said, a desperate plea in her tone that had never been there before. "I need to talk now."

Berthilde only shook her head slightly, still keeping her back to Aleene. "No, this noon in the forest where no ears are about."

Aleene looked quickly toward the door. "This noon then," she said dipping her hand in the soap on the table at her side.

Immediately following supper, Aleene rushed from the great hall, ready to run the entire way to the forest, but instead she ran straight into a large, unforgiving chest. "Ouch!"

"My dear, sweet stepsister." Aethregard's long fingers wrapped around her upper arms and steadied her. "Where would you be going off to in such a hurry?"

Aleene shook her arms and tried to break free of Aethregard's grasp. He only tightened his hold. With narrowed eyes, Aleene looked up into her stepbrother's slitty gaze. "Let go of me, Aethregard. Now." She put every ounce of disdain she had into her words.

"Ah, my lady of Seabreeze, such modesty."

He released her only to smooth his hands down her arms and quickly grab her hands. "But really we are soon to be husband and wife, can we not, at least, hold hands?"

Aleene yanked her hands away just as Aethregard pulled them up to his lips. "We are to be nothing beyond stepbrother and stepsister, you fiend, and perhaps I will someday find a way to cut even that tie." She wanted to retreat, but she stood firm, chin up, eyes throwing daggers. "If you will excuse me, I have work to do." She stepped around Aethregard and stalked away.

"But, my dear, that is why I'm here." Aethregard's voice so near her ear made Aleene jump. She quickened her gait, but her stepbrother only matched her speed. "I want to see all of the workings of Seabreeze Castle. I have the time now that King Harold has dispensed with the Fyrd. I can spend the entire day with you."

"How delightful." Aleene stopped short, smirking as Aethregard continued on, halting a few feet ahead and looking about as if lost. She smiled, baring her teeth and tilting the corners of her mouth, when her stepbrother turned. "Really, brother mine, I do believe you may be terribly bored to accompany me as I see to the job of a woman." She fluttered her lashes, then raised her hand and hailed Cuthebert, who had just walked into the bailey.

"You shall be much more interested, I'm sure, to spend the day with Cuthebert. He shall show you the books." She knew that Aethregard and Cuthebert were so thick, her steward had probably already shown her stepbrother every book in the castle. A foul taste tinged her tongue as she acknowledged Cuthebert, who stood before her.

"Show Aethregard the books, Cuthebert."

Her steward flashed a startled look at Aethregard. "But, milady, you have asked me not to."

"And now I'm asking you to do it, Cuthebert. Is there a problem?"

"Of course not."

"Good."

"What goes on in that head of yours, Aleene?" Aethregard asked, stepping close to her, so close she could smell his fetid breath and see the black holes that had already began to eat at his dull, yellow teeth.

Aleene grimaced at the sight and gritted her teeth. "Many, many things happen in this head, although I'm sure that is hard for you to believe." It was not in her nature to run, but she did. That voice, those eyes, everything in that moment reminded her of ugly days. Days when she was at the mercy of Aethregard's father, never able to run far enough, never able to wake her mother from her grief long enough to enjoy her protection.

She reached the edge of the forest out of breath and gasping. With her arm across her belly, Aleene leaned over and wretched, heaving when the food was gone and bringing up nothing but small, hiccuping sounds.

"Are you ill, milady?" Berthilde's hands caressed her arms and Aleene quickly shook her head, wiping her mouth with the back of her hand and trying desperately to regain her composure.

Berthilde stepped away from her, clasping her hands before her and wrinkling her brow. They stood silently for a moment, the only sound Aleene's heavy breathing. "Perhaps you could do that for an audience?"

Aleene coughed once more, and straightened. "An audience?"

Berthilde shifted the basket of herbs in her hands, her gaze searching the treetops for a moment. "I fear you are with child, milady."

Aleene smoothed her veil away from her face and shook her head. "Oh, no, Berthilde, you do not understand. I could not be with child, it is just that Aethregard . . ."

"I do not think you understand, milady." Berthilde turned her gaze fully on Aleene. "I fear you are with child."

Aleene blinked, the ramifications of her maid's statement making her head swim.

"We should relay the news to the king."

Aleene bit her lip, anxiety building in her

chest and making it hard to breathe. "Is this what you wished to speak of, Berthilde?"

"I am not your enemy, Aleene. I see the good that Cynewulf has brought with him into this castle of heartache. I want him to stay as you do." She pinched a leaf of one of her herbs between her fingers, releasing a heady perfume of spearmint into the air. "I wish Aethregard gone."

" 'Tis a frightening thing we do, Berthilde. We shall be lying to the king."

Berthilde stopped fiddling with her plants and dragged her palm against her apron. She looked away for a moment. "I shall relay the news of your sickness immediately, milady." Her maid turned away and hurried toward the castle.

Aleene could only stare at Berthilde's back. A tiny ray of hope burned in her chest, but black fear threatened to extinguish it completely.

Chapter 7

~~~⟡⟡~~~

"**N**o!" Aleene cried, feeling as if her world was crumbling out from under her feet. "He is my husband! I am to have his child!"

"And until you have his child, he will stay with me." King Harold turned away from her and stared out one of the large windows that ran the length of the solarium.

Aleene closed her eyes and dropped back into a chair. Why, oh why had she not consummated her marriage when she had the chance? Then perhaps she *would* be with child now. Clenching her fist so hard her fingernails bit into her palm, Aleene cursed her stepfather for hurting her, and cursed herself for being weak enough to let him.

Damn them all. She stood quickly and whirled toward the door.

"Lady Aleene, I have not dismissed you." Again the king's voice sounded weary rather than strong and demanding. But Aleene stopped, bowing her head as she turned back to face her king.

"I do not have to explain myself to you, Aleene." She felt him advance on her, saw his shadow creep closer to her. "But as a friend of your father's I feel I owe it to you." He stopped before her. "Your father built this castle knowing that it would go to you someday. But also, he built it thinking he would be here to make sure you married wisely—"

"But—"

The king held up his hand. "No, Aleene, listen."

Aleene bent her head again.

"This land is strategic, the castle one of a kind," the King continued. "It is important that I know that Seabreeze castle is well defended and loyal to me."

Aleene could feel her anger building. The tiny hairs on the back of her neck stood up straight, her arms trembled, her teeth ground together so hard her jaw hurt. Why? Why could no one see that she could do all of that herself?

"Tosig was loyal to me. We agreed together that your betrothal to Aethregard was a perfect match, although I always thought it strange that he wanted such a late day for your wedding. And now Aethregard wishes to marry you early, and I must agree with him. I find myself having to strengthen all of my strategic holdings. Aethregard is a good man, loyal to me as his father was and smart on the battle field."

Aleene took a breath, ready to interrupt again, ready to defend herself and her abilities and very ready to tell the king that Aethregard was definitely not a good man, but he held up his hand again.

"This man you call your husband cannot be the lord of this castle, Aleene. You shall bear his child and if it is a boy, and if it is clear-headed, I shall allow you to stay here with your husband with Aethregard as your protector until the child is of age to take over."

"But the land is mine, the castle is mine by law," Aleene wanted to yell the words, but she kept her tone controlled, barely. " 'Tis a dower property."

"With this castle and the growing threat from across the channel, this land is too valuable to be a dower property, Aleene."

Aleene stiffened, her breathing slowing. Black dots whirled before her eyes.

"I shall have to force upon you a keeper for this property whom I can trust. A man, Aleene. And beginning with your progeny, Seabreeze Castle will descend through the male line."

Aleene allowed herself a breath of air in relief. She had thought for a terrifying moment that Harold meant to take Seabreeze completely from her and give it to Aethregard. When she had banished any threat of fainting, Aleene began her assault once more. "I do not need a keeper, your highness, you must believe me. I can take care of Seabreeze . . ."

Harold cut her off, holding his hand up as if he could take no more. "I have spoken, it is law." He turned away from her. "You may go now, Lady Aleene. I shall be leaving, returning to Bosham. Your husband shall accompany me."

"But . . ." her voice trailed away as he turned toward her again, his eyes steely, his face hard.

"Aethregard shall remain. We will leave in two days."

Aleene bowed her head and turned to leave. All her strength had left her; she could not fight King Harold. She knew that. Aleene turned down the dark hall and saw Berthilde waiting for her. Their plan had failed. Aleene felt close to complete defeat. What could she possibly do now?

Dinner had already begun when Aleene heard her stepbrother's low voice behind her.

"Whore."

Aleene stiffened, but did not acknowledge Aethregard in any other way. Out of the corner of her eye she saw him move away from her and take a seat further down the table.

She forced steadiness, reaching for her goblet and sipping the dark ale. Servants brought out platters of mutton and set them on the long tables. Wrinkling her nose, Aleene turned her head from the pungent smell of the meat. If it were not impossible, she would think she may be pregnant. Just the thought of putting the dark, oily meat onto her trencher turned her stomach. She quickly broke off a piece of bread and nibbled at it.

In actuality, it was probably her menses. Aleene said a quick prayer that it would not come until the king had left. If he still thought her with child, perhaps she could come up with a plan. She took another gulp of ale. Over the rim, she searched the other tables, finally finding Cyne and his guards.

Beside her King Harold clapped his hands, causing Aleene to jump and spill a bit of ale. "We shall have entertainment this eve," he said, "to celebrate the end of this tedious summer and the end of any threat from across the water!" He sobered a bit. "For another year, at least, we have peace."

The hall echoed with shouts as a bard came forward, lute in hand, and began to pluck out a joyful tune. He sang beautifully, something about a young maiden and lad settling down to prosper on the land. But Aleene was not concentrating on the music; she stared, instead, at her husband.

He turned as if sensing her gaze and their eyes locked. Aleene yearned to go to him, touch his hair, kiss his lips as she had done the night before. His eyes seemed to hold the same yearning. She knew that he could not need her, want her, as she did him. It must truly be beyond his capacity. She clenched her fingers together under the table and told herself not to care. Cyne was everything she needed. He would never hurt her, betray her. He would only hold her, touch her, give her weeds and make her see flowers.

She pushed at the heavy veil that seemed to cling to her neck, wishing she could tear the headpiece off. A stinging in her eyes made her realize that tiny drops of perspiration had beaded along her hairline and now slipped down her face. Wiping the back of her hand against her forehead, Aleene blinked, but kept her gaze on Cyne.

The song of the bard crept into her mind, and she suddenly wondered if perhaps she should run. In her mind she could see herself with Cyne, farming and having children. She would have a family and there would be no fear. No one would want to hurt her, control her. Aleene wiped at her face again, breathing erratically as the hall seemed to close in on her.

No, she could not throw this away. How could she ever run from Seabreeze? It was her life. It embodied a love that would be forever lost if she left. Aleene shook her head and tried to clear her thoughts. The hall seemed to whirl about her. Her stomach felt queasy and she leaned over and bowed her head.

Closing her eyes, she saw a field and Cyne, shoulders bare to the sun as he worked to bring in a harvest. Aleene reached for him, wanting his arms around her. But, as he turned she realized it was not Cyne, but Aethregard.

"Whore!" he screamed, and it thrummed in her ears, reverberating in her head. "Whore!"

Aleene cried out as her stepbrother came for her, his hands rough and angry grasping her arms. "Whore!" And then it was no longer Aethregard, but Tosig who held her, his hands touching her body letting the ugly, black demons loose from the cage in her mind. They raged through her, ripping at her, stomping on her. She writhed, curving her arms around her belly, trying to curl into herself.

But they would not let her retreat. They continued to rip into her, and she saw blood. Blood everywhere, on the demons, on Tosig. She screamed, knowing that it was her blood. Knowing that they were taking her life from her.

Aleene struck out, hitting and scratching anything near. She would not let them take her! She lunged at the black demons, gouging her fingers into their yellow, slanted eyes, screaming and fighting. Finally they retreated and she turned to face Tosig, large, angry, and a hundred times more frightening than any demon.

She cringed, watching her blood pour from her stepfather's stomach. It spouted, draining her life. Aleene weakened, holding her hand in front of her as if to ward off Tosig. But she knew she couldn't. He was so much stronger, bigger, more powerful than her. She could never win against Tosig.

And then she felt a hand in hers. Strong, warm, comforting, it clasped her fingers. She turned to find Cyne standing beside her. She looked into his eyes, loving eyes that held intelligence and knowledge. He tightened his grasp on her hand and said something. Aleene strained to hear, but she could only see his lips moving.

She knew Tosig still stood in front of them, waiting. But she refused to look, instead she let herself be captured in Cyne's gaze. She wanted to go to him, be closer to him than she was, she wanted to be engulfed in his steadiness, his security, his love. She pressed against his body, feeling his hard, muscular thighs against hers, his strong heart beating and thumping at her own chest.

Finally she heard him, his voice low and musical, just as beautiful and golden as the rest of him. "Aleene, you are safe. I will keep you safe, I promise."

With a great relieved sigh, Aleene felt the presence of Tosig vanish. She closed her eyes but did not see darkness, rather a golden light. And she knew with all of her heart that it was Cyne.

*   *   *

"She stirs."

Aleene moved, then groaned as her stomach clenched in pain and her head throbbed.

"Milady?"

Aleene tried to open her eyes, but her lids felt as if they were weighted down with rocks. She groaned again.

"Ah, my poor, poor child." A warm, slight hand stroked Aleene's forehead.

She squinted, trying to open her eyes, wondering where she was.

"Look what they've done to ye," the voice cooed as the hand continued to stroke.

And then another hand took hers. A reassuring warmth spread up her arm and into her body. She opened her eyes.

Blurred images moved over her. She cringed, closing her eyes again as one image came toward her face. She felt the touch of a thin hand against her temple. "Milady? Are ye awake, dear?"

Her eyes fluttered open again. Finally, she focused, seeing the wrinkled visage of her maid. "Berthilde?" The sound from her mouth was cracked and without body.

"There, there, child, don't try to speak just yet." Berthilde moved away. "I shall fetch some water for ye."

Aleene closed her eyes again, realizing then that she still held someone's hand. She turned her head slowly, moaning with the effort, and opened her eyes.

Cyne smiled at her, his loving smile washed over her like the rays of the sun. She tried to speak, but he patted her hand and kissed her mouth lightly. Relaxing, Aleene closed her eyes and held tightly to Cyne's hand. What on earth had happened to her?

Berthilde returned with a bucket of water and a ladle. Cyne tucked a strong arm beneath Aleene's back and supported her as Berthilde ladled life-giving water through Aleene's parched lips.

After the first few drops, Aleene was able to gulp more water. "Slow down, child, ye shall make yourself sick," Berthilde chided.

Aleene slowed down reluctantly, sipping at the water.

"That's it." Berthilde eased the ladle from Aleene's mouth. "We shouldn't overdo."

Cyne laid her gently back and brushed her hair from her face.

She just stared, reveling in his unkempt beauty. A blond curl, displaced from his tousled mane, clung to his forehead. She frowned slightly and looked back at Berthilde. They both looked as if they hadn't slept for a few days. "Wha-at happened?" Aleene was finally able to utter.

Berthilde shook her head and brushed the back of her knuckles against Aleene's arm.

"That bastard stepbrother of yours." A scowl marred her motherly features. "He put ergot in your ale, the pig. 'Tis a poison that rids women of unwanted babes. Fortunately, one of the king's men saw him do it, or we would never have known. When I saw all the blood and vomiting, I knew what it was. Then the housecarl remembered seeing Aethregard lean over and do something with your ale."

Aleene blinked, her hand automatically going to her abdomen.

Berthilde laid her own hand over Aleene's. "Everyone believes you've lost the babe."

Aleene could only stare at Berthilde's hand. It had been many years since her maid touched her with concern. Aleene had not allowed it for that long. She sighed.

"Now, now, dear." Berthilde pulled a blanket higher upon Aleene's chest. "It will be all right." She smiled. "Everything will be all right now."

The look of happiness that lightened Berthilde's weary eyes gave Aleene pause. She turned to look at Cyne, then back at Berthilde. The maid nodded. "Aethregard has been banished!" She laughed then, and Aleene couldn't help but smile.

"Banished?"

"The king himself ordered the boy back to his own land. Said that if he ever heard of Aethregard coming within a hundred paces of this cas-

tle he would have him drawn and quartered!''
Berthilde recounted the events with a singsong
voice, her eyes sparkling and her body swaying.

Closing her eyes, Aleene clutched at Cyne's
hand. She would be with Cyne in Seabreeze!
And all because Aethregard tried to rid her of
a babe that did not exist, yet. Aleene laughed a
bit. The irony was wonderfully humorous.

When she opened her eyes again, Berthilde
stood staring at Aleene's hand clutched in
Cyne's. A look of foreboding had erased the joy
in Berthilde's gaze, but before Aleene could ask
her what was wrong, the woman turned and
bustled away. "I shall find some broth for you.
You must get your strength back.''

Aleene watched the woman's retreating back,
wondering at her maid's sudden soberness. Berthilde opened the door, then looked quickly
over her shoulder at Aleene, before disappear-
ing into the hall. As the door swung shut,
Aleene saw a man in the darkness of the hall.
A large man, with a boiled leather breastplate
protecting his chest and a knife sheathed at his
side.

One of Cyne's guards.

The tranquility that had existed in the room
evaporated, leaving Aleene tense and angry.
The king had sent Aethregard away, but not in
favor of Cyne. Not in favor of her choice.
Aleene squeezed her eyes shut. She would now
face the tyranny of a new man, one she did not

even know. A strong man, of that she was certain.

Cyne smoothed her brow with his hand. She turned toward his caress. She had spent most of her life controlled by a man who hated her. Since his death, she had actually believed she could fight herself free from his influence. Yet still, even with his son gone, she could not grasp onto happiness and keep it.

Aleene clenched her hands together at her sides and breathed in, filling her lungs with the scent of the man beside her. It was a good smell, warm sunshine, fennel, and man. She sighed as Cyne stroked her hair, his fingers tunneling through the long, heavy strands and massaging her scalp.

Why? She had finally found a certain peace, Seabreeze and Cyne. Why could she not keep them? The agony drained her of strength, and she felt the edge of her consciousness blur and knew that sleep haunted her. She allowed it to take her, no longer able to deal with the frustration of reality.

When she awoke next, the room was dark. Moving her head slightly, she saw a tray by her bed with a trencher of cold soup. She knew she had to eat it and regain her strength quickly. With agonizing slowness, she tried to sit up, her head swimming with each new movement. And then suddenly, she felt strength, felt herself lifted. Through the thick haze that seemed to surround her senses, Aleene realized that Berthilde stood beside her, supporting her body. The woman reached for the bowl of broth and brought it to Aleene's lips.

" 'Tis cold now, milady, but still good."

Aleene sipped slowly at the watery liquid. She could feel her maid's breath on her cheek and realized that she had not been this close to the old woman since Aleene had been a child. She swallowed, then said feebly, "Thank you, Berthilde."

"Yes, milady." She tipped the bowl again toward Aleene's lips.

Aleene forced down all the broth. Then, wiping her mouth with the back of her hand, she relaxed onto her bed. Berthilde took the tray away and returned quickly with a wet cloth for Aleene's forehead.

The cloth soothed the ache that throbbed behind Aleene's temples, an ache so constant she hadn't even realized it was there until it began to subside. "Berthilde?" she mumbled through lips gone stiff.

"Shh, dear, you must rest."

Aleene knew she had to protest, knew she should speak to Berthilde, but she could not seem to get the strength to speak. Closing her eyes, she allowed her maid to stroke her hair.

"Why did you frown, Berthilde?" Aleene managed to whisper, already half-asleep.

"Shh, be still."

*   *   *

Two days later Aleene felt much strengthened when the king came to visit her. He stood
quietly by her bedside, his eyes sad and weary.
"We leave on the morrow, Lady Aleene." Before Aleene could even take a breath to ask, the
king continued, "And we take this man, Cynewulf, with us."

Aleene bit her lip to keep from saying anything.

"I concede to your wish not to marry Aethregard." The king stroked his graying beard, then
laid his hand lightly on top of Aleene's. "He
would not do well here."

"He would die here."

"Keep your rebellion to yourself, lady of Seabreeze Castle, for you will want to nurture it."
A tiny smile hovered at the corners of Harold's
mouth. "I shall send another suitor soon."
Again his eyes showed much weariness.

Aleene closed her own, trying not to feel
sorry for the man.

"I have been having problems with some
Thanes in York." The king turned, clasping his
hands behind him. "I shall offer an alliance
with you. They will welcome this wealth," the
king gestured around Aleene's chamber, "I'm
sure."

The only thing that kept Aleene from jumping up and verbally thrashing her king was her
sure knowledge that she would crumple at his

feet from lack of strength. She did not even
think she could argue, not now. She just felt
completely defeated. "Aye."

"That was much too easy."

"To take away everything that a mere
woman has is terribly easy," she couldn't help
biting back, her words reeking with bitterness.

"Ah, there is the lady of Seabreeze Castle. As
you get better, I'm sure your claws will sharpen
and by the time your poor bridegroom arrives,
he will give serious thought to whether this castle and its wealth is worth it." The smile in Harold's eyes belied his hurtful words. "Do not
worry, Aleene, I shall choose more carefully this
time. You shall have a strong man to rule you
in fairness."

Aleene closed her eyes again, letting the silence drag on long enough that finally the king
left, probably believing that she slept. As the
door shut behind him, Aleene clenched the soft
linen sheet between her hands, nearly ripping
it with the strength of her anger.

A strong man to rule her in fairness! As if such
a thing existed! Strong men did not know the
meaning of fairness, especially when it came to
ruling people weaker than they. Especially
when it came to ruling women.

And why should they be given that right? With
all of her strength, Aleene threw off her covers
and pushed herself from her bed. Her knees
threatened to buckle beneath her, but she

pulled on a kirtle and crept over to the door.
Her head swam a bit, but she supported herself
with the wall and opened the heavy door. *Her*
heavy door. This was her castle, her body, her
life. And nobody had the right to rule them, fair
or otherwise. With the added strength of her
anger, Aleene got the door open and went into
the darkened hallway.

"Milady!" Berthilde rushed forward. "Ye
shouldn't be about."

"Berthilde, I must." Aleene pushed ineffec-
tually at the maid's hovering hands. "I must do
something."

"What, milady?"

Aleene looked wildly about. "I . . . you must
help me, Berthilde, I need a plan. The king is to
take Cyne with him. He is going to send another suitor." Aleene dropped her face in her
hands. "I must do something."

A commotion clamored from below. Aleene
looked up, frowning at her maid. "What happens below?"

Berthilde's face showed no curiosity, only
concern. "I know not, milady. You must lie
down. I do not think you are well."

A shout echoed up the winding stairwell.

"Something goes on below, Berthilde."
Aleene moved quickly toward the noise.

"Hold, milady, at least allow me to assist
you!" Berthilde took her arm. "That is all we
need, another death in this place."

Aleene allowed her maid to help her to the great hall where she encountered complete chaos. "What happens?" she asked a passing warrior.

"King Hardrada of Norway has invaded in the north," he said quickly. "We leave immediately for London. Everyone!"

Aleene blinked in shock as the man ran from her, barking orders as he went.

"Holy mother of God," Berthilde whispered beside her.

Invasion? But the summer was over, how could an army get to their fair isle now? It was a threat she had not taken seriously because of the problems that faced her personally. But now it was happening. It wasn't only Seabreeze at stake, but the whole country. She swallowed hard, realizing that her entire body shook.

A flash of sun-burnished hair caught her gaze; she rushed toward it automatically and grabbed at her husband's arm. Even in her terror, Aleene realized she had a great opportunity before her. She pulled at Cyne, trying to get to the stairs. "We shall hide you until the men have left."

"No, my dear, I'm afraid Cynewulf will be coming with me."

Aleene heard the hard edge of Harold's words as she felt Cyne resist her retreat. Turning, she realized her king held Cyne's other arm in an iron-fisted grip. Her own hands clenched convulsively around Cyne's strong forearm.

"Shall we rip him in half, Aleene?" One bushy eyebrow crooked over Harold's eye. "Solomon would deem that fair. You may have one half, I the other."

Aleene felt frustrated tears sear the back of her lids, but she would not let them drop. "You cannot take him into battle. He is but a simpleton. He will be killed." As she spoke, Aleene eased her grip on Cyne's arm and trailed her fingers down to wrap around his hand. That strong, warm hand curled around hers, infusing her with strength.

"He shall not go to battle, Aleene." She detected a hint of softness in her king's voice. "He shall be safe."

"Please, your highness, allow him to stay here with me." She dropped her eyes, her bravado slipping. "I will not lie with him. You have my word."

"He will be safe with me, Lady Aleene. You have *my* word." Harold pulled Cyne toward him and Aleene could do nothing but let him go.

She reached out, brushing at a curl that fell against Cyne's forehead. When her fingers touched his skin, she trembled. Aleene clenched her fingers and pulled them away. Something held them together, a bond connected their souls. She did not understand it, but she knew it to be true. He had the mind of a boy, but still she felt as if she would never be whole without him.

She tipped back her head, straightened her spine, and looked into King Harold's eyes. "Keep Cyne safe, your highness." She looked back into Cyne's eyes and had to bite the inside of her lip in order to tear her gaze away again. "I have your word on that."

With a sigh, the king nodded, then turned, taking her husband with him.

Chapter 8

The days dragged by slowly, the nights slower. Aleene could not make herself care for anything besides news of Cyne. She knew she should be working, readying the castle for winter, especially now that the men were gone and the threat of an invasion hung thick in the air. But the only thing she could make herself do was hike the tower each morning and look across the hills, watching and waiting.

So it was ironic that he should come during the night, as she slept, her watchful eyes closed, her waiting heart surrendered to dreams of him.

In her dreams she was free of fear, free of memories and restraints. She could be happy, love with all her heart. She could be as she had been before reality tore joy from her grasp.

In the blissful surrender of sleep, she felt Cyne reach for her, enfold her in his strong arms, and lightly kiss the tender skin at her nape. She reached around him, giving herself to his kisses. And then instead of waking to find no one, she blinked her eyes open to find that his presence didn't filter away with reality.

"Cyne!" She pushed away from him in shock. "What has happened? Why are you here? How?" Then she threw her arms around him and hugged him close to her body. "Oh, I give thanks to God that you live. That you came back to me."

He only held her tighter as if he understood. Aleene could not help the small laugh that escaped her. It was a strange sound, a sigh, a giggle, a sob all wrapped together in a heart-wrenching response.

Aleene burrowed her face into Cyne's broad chest, and he stroked the back of her head, his large hand so strong and assured, Aleene almost believed that he loved her, too.

The thought shocked her, scared her. She loved this man. How strange, how wonderful. Aleene gripped his tunic in her hands. But how could she? She felt his lips against her hair and banished any doubt. It did not matter. She loved, and he could not hurt her. She would not be afraid.

Finally, she pushed away. "Are you with someone? Did the king return?" she asked even though she knew he could not answer. Then she laughed, and it felt good. She felt free. She did not even care if the king was here. Somehow she would keep Cyne with her. She turned to look out the window at the gray sky that spoke of dawn.

"Well, I guess I should go welcome our guests." Aleene jumped up, grabbed the gown she had worn the day before and quickly pulled it over her head.

Grabbing Cyne's hand, she ran from her chamber, down the narrow stairway to the great hall below. The room was silent, as it had been for many days. No men slept on benches or slouched against the walls.

Aleene turned a puzzled gaze to Cyne. "You have come alone?"

He cocked his head to the side, his eyes intently studying her face. It seemed, almost, as if he would speak. Aleene held her breath for a moment, waiting.

And then he bowed his head, saying nothing. When he looked back at her, the familiar vacant, happy look of a puppy shone from his eyes.

Aleene shook her head, dislodging the strange thought that he might actually speak. Of course, he could not. She squeezed his hand. And she did not want him to, after all. She just wanted her Cyne. The innocent man to whom she could open her heart. "You must have come alone." And then a thought struck her like a blow. Aleene ran for the door, peering out into the silent morning. A few servants filtered out of the chapel and some more worked the fires in the kitchen area.

Aleene surveyed the castle grounds quickly and thoroughly, then turned back to her husband. "You got away!" Her heart fluttered lightly in her chest, and she caught her breath. "You got away!"

A corner of his full mouth hooked up into a funny, cocky sort of smile she had never seen on his face. Silently, she drank in his beauty. She suddenly wanted to throw her arms around him and dance him around the yard. He had gotten away. "And you came back to *me*."

His head bowed then, cutting off their eye contact. But she grabbed his chin and forced his gaze back to hers. "Oh, Cyne, I'm so glad you came back to me." She almost didn't get the words out around the dryness of her throat. She laughed again, and impulsively threw her arms around her husband. His arms came around her, holding her so tightly she feared she might not be able to take a breath. "You give me sunshine," she cried into his dirty tunic. "I'm so glad you're back."

The wind changed that morning. Aleene watched as the flag on her tower fluttered, lay slack against the pole, then straightened with a southerly gust. It was what they had watched for all summer. For a southerly wind meant Duke William would be able to push any ships he might have out to sea and make it to their tiny island.

Now Aleene knew they had no fear of that. No one would try to cross the channel so late in the season. They were safe from attack. And then later that day news came of King Harold's victory at Stamford Bridge just beyond York. They had beaten back the invaders from Norway.

Aleene smiled, happy to know that the men of the town would be home soon to care for their farms and families, but sad that she would again have to face her king and fight for her own happiness. She knew, though, that she could perform her duty as a wife now. She had come close in her dreams, surely she could finish the act with her husband. Her fear seemed a part of another person now, Tosig's tyranny over her an act of aggression from a man now dead. He could not reach out to her from the grave, and she would not allow his darkness to cloud her happiness anymore.

She walked through the yard outside the hall, her steps invigorated and her heart anxious to find her husband. Some of the children played with one of the dogs, throwing a stick for it to fetch. They stopped as she neared, all of them quieting and eyeing her warily.

She felt a tiny twinge of self-consciousness that straightened her spine and angled her chin a bit higher. They clustered before her, their towheads close, faces pale. She fingered her own black-as-night tresses, faltering in her steps. "Have you seen Lord Cynewulf?" she asked them.

They murmured amongst themselves, shaking their heads and backing away from her. She stood silently for a moment, her happiness draining away from her.

One of the smaller children stepped forward. "I believe he went to the cliffs, milady, to the fort."

Aleene took in this information and nodded. Even the children hated her. She began to turn away, but stopped. She had spent many years closing herself to others so they could not hurt her, but, really, how badly could this child hurt her? She smiled, tentatively. "Thank you very much," she said, stumbling a bit over the words.

The boy looked back at his friends quickly, then nodded. "Of course, milady."

She felt a bit foolish as he ran back to play. Had she expected the lad to turn on her, scream that she was not one of them, that she didn't belong? With a jolt, she realized that she did believe that. She had been afraid of it all of her life.

She stared for a moment at the children, then quickly left the castle grounds and followed the path along the cliff to the old Roman fort.

Aleene stopped just outside the crumbling ruins. Tilting her head, so that the sun shone brilliantly against her face. She felt rather than saw the shadow that passed over her. Squinting against the brightness of the sun, Aleene opened her eyes and saw a dove circle above her, its wings outstretched as it caught a gust of wind and sailed away over the water. She watched it for a few moments, wondering how it felt to fly.

His touch startled her, for her mind had glided away on the wind with the dove. She jumped and blinked, then realizing it was Cyne standing before her, she laughed lightly and hugged him tightly to her.

She thought of the bird. To learn to fly, the bird had probably just stepped from the nest and trusted its sturdy little wings. Aleene drew in a deep breath, smelling the salt air that clung to Cyne's tunic.

"I love you," she said, testing her wings.

He said nothing, did nothing, and she realized he probably did not truly understand what she said. She remembered the moment in the forest long ago when she had wished for more, wished Cyne a whole man.

She pushed the thought away, ashamed of herself. If he was a whole man, she couldn't love him as she did.

"Shall we return? I came to bring you home for supper." She leaned away and smiled up at her husband. He lowered his lids, hiding his eyes for a moment, then allowed her to break

away and take his hand as they turned back
toward the castle.

Throughout dinner that night, Aleene knew
that she would finally consummate her marriage. She knew she could now, especially with
the newfound knowledge of her love. Once she
and Cyne reached for their goblet at the same
time, their hands colliding. Aleene turned her
fingers quickly and took her husband's hand.
But Cyne did not bestow his golden smile upon
her, and it surprised Aleene for a moment. She
blinked, frowning at Cyne and the dark mood
that seemed to hang over him.

She hadn't really noticed until that moment,
but then she remembered that he had been
rather somber since returning from the fort. He
squeezed her hand beneath the table, and she
realized that all was well. It was only her imagination and the fears that she had tucked away,
but not yet completely conquered, coming back
to haunt the fringes of her happiness.

Aleene banished them away, not wanting to
be slave to those old fears any longer. She even
allowed herself to think of the act that she
would finish that eve, alone in her chamber
with her husband. She thought of the feelings
Cyne ignited in her with his hands, his kisses,
his smiles and touches. And she thought of children. For the first time, she thought of children,
not as a way to hold onto Seabreeze Castle, but

as a way to share the happiness that threatened to burst inside of her. She thought of small blond children with sky-blue eyes and smiles that glowed with joy and love.

She hurried through her meal, clutching her husband's hand whenever she could and beaming at the servants and others around her. When finally she and Cyne were alone in her chamber, Aleene turned to him, cradled his face between her hands, and reached up to softly kiss his lips.

He hesitated for a moment, and that fleeting fear she had felt during supper returned for a moment. But then he kissed her back, his lips moving against hers, his hands trailing up and down her sides, as if he were memorizing the shape of her.

She let her arms twine around his neck, pressing against his body, her softness yielding to his hardness. With a dark, low groan, Cyne deepened their kiss, his tongue flicking at the seam of her lips.

Aleene's heart thumped double-time against her breast, making her feel breathless and dizzy. She held tightly to her husband, opening her mouth, needing to taste him. He plundered her offering, tracing her teeth with his tongue and finally plunging through to tangle with her own.

Backing toward the bed, Aleene pulled Cyne with her, yanking at the strings of her gown as she went. His hands followed hers, helping her, pulling and yanking until she heard ripping. She reached for him, loosening the ties that held his tunic in place. When finally they stood naked, Aleene stared for a moment at her husband.

"You are well made, husband mine." Her words were raspy and breathless, and she laughed a bit. The hollow at the base of his neck throbbed, and she placed her finger there, feeling his quickened pulse. She caressed him, trailing her hand down his chest to his waist and the golden hair that trailed down to his manhood.

His hand covered hers, and she looked up. In the dark room she couldn't see his face, but she knew he was probably confused. Still, she also knew that his eyes would be filled with trust, for her.

She smiled in the night and brought her hand up to cup his cheek. "Ah, Cyne, I shall not hurt you. For I come to you now with only love in my heart for the freedom you have given me." She reached up and kissed his lips lightly. "I shall never hurt you," she said gently against his mouth.

In the silence that followed, Aleene heard a tortured sound escape through her husband's lips. For a moment she truly thought she heard her name, low, broken, and strange. She backed away slightly. "Cyne? Did you speak?"

He moved then, swiftly, taking her off guard. She gasped as he whirled away from her, bending and taking something from the floor.

"Cyne?" She tried to reach for him, but he moved away. He yanked his *braies* on, tying them quickly as he almost ran for the door.

"Cyne!"

He stopped there, his back to her, his shoulders heaving with exertion.

She moved toward him. "Cyne? Please, try and show me what is the matter." She was close enough that she could see that he had the door partway open, his hand on the latch, his forehead leaning against the rough wood.

"Are you afraid?" she asked softly. "There is nothing to be afraid of. I love you."

Another tortured sound came from Cyne, and he flung open the door and ran through.

Aleene stood for a moment, shocked, then moved quickly, grabbing her shift and throwing it over her head as she left her room and ran down the stairs to the hall. She peered through the gloom, trying to catch a glimpse of Cyne, but could see nothing. She searched the hall, then went outside and looked around the yard, the kitchen area, even the smithy. All were quiet and dark, the moon lending an eerie glow to the deserted bailey. She called his name twice, but only managed to rouse a cat and send a chicken squawking.

Finally she went back to her chamber, half-hoping that he had returned in her absence. Her room was empty. She sat on the edge of her bed, staring hard at the door, waiting and praying that he would return soon. She wanted so badly to take away his hurt, his fear, as he had done for her. She could show him, show him how much he meant to her. She knew she could. If only he would return.

She sat that way for a long time, her mind going numb with the whirl of her thoughts, her hands and feet becoming icy cold. Some time during the night she leaned over, letting her head drop to her pillow, and curling her knees into her chest. She did not sleep, but stayed in a half-waking state, waiting, listening, jumping with every tiny sound. When the sky finally lightened to a gray dawn, she felt herself slip into sleep, her last thought of finding Cyne when the day came. For then it would be easy. She would just look for gold.

She awoke to the clamor of yells and shouts. So many, she thought, how could there be so many people about? Then she shot out of bed, icy dread clamping at her heart as she threw a gown over her shift and raced for the hall. The king must have returned!

Berthilde met her on the stairs, her eyes wide, her hands shaking. "Milady! Ships!"

Aleene grabbed at Berthilde's shoulders.

"What are you talking about, Berthilde? What ships?"

"Ships, they've been sighted," the woman barely got the words out in between gulping breaths. "It can be no one but that scoundrel! They have come!"

Aleene shook Berthilde. "What do you speak of, Berthilde? You do not make sense!"

A yell came from the bottom of the stairs. Aleene looked and saw one of the serving wenches, her gown clenched in her hands, her face covered with tears. "They shall ravish me!" she screamed. "They shall kill my babe!" She touched her swollen stomach, then looked up at Aleene. "Help us, milady, do something!"

Aleene could only stand, unmoving at the top of the stair. Her mind whirled with questions, fear, dread. And then she took a deep, strong breath. She had fought all summer to control her own castle. She had told her king she could protect it as well as any man. She must prove herself now.

"Close the gates!" she yelled to no one, rushing past Berthilde and the serving wench. Pushing through the throngs of people crying and wailing in the bailey, Aleene ran for the gate tower. She took the stairs two at a time, to find the top deserted. But the bay was not.

Ships and barges of every size crowded through the opening to the sea, entering Pevensey harbor, her harbor. Aleene gulped down the terrible lump of fear that lodged in her throat and clamped her hands together to stop her shaking. "Oh, Lord God," she prayed quietly, "let us live through this." A terrible thought hit her as she turned to go back to the people. It would be better to die than to live through what may happen.

She faced the townspeople, trying desperately to rid that thought from her mind. She dredged up every ounce of courage she could find and yelled as loud as she could. "Men!" A few people close to her quieted, but still others continued to talk, wail, yell, cry. "All of the men!" she yelled again. This time the people around her took up her cry.

Soon the people stood quiet before her. "All the men here," she said again. "Go to posts around the castle walls. Women and children inside the hall with you."

People looked at each other, fear paralyzing them. "Now!" Aleene screamed, her own fear tingeing her voice with urgency. They began to move, splitting into groups, the men moving toward the castle walls, the women taking children in their arms and going to the hall.

Berthilde came running up to Aleene, her face haggard with fear and worry. "I can't find Cyne, milady, where has he gone?"

Aleene closed her eyes, her heart dropping to her stomach, making her want to heave. Cyne. He was probably out there, at his fort, alone.

She grabbed Berthilde's arm and dragged her toward the gate in the high wooden wall. "Close the gate behind me, Berthilde, close it and bar it. If I return with enough time to spare, let me back in. If I don't, you must keep the gate barred!"

"Milady!" Berthilde's voice held panic. "Where do you go? I will not bar you from the castle!"

"Do as I say, Berthilde!" She reached the gate and shoved it open. Running through before Berthilde could stop her, Aleene yelled over her shoulder. "Bar it! Don't let anyone through."

She ran from the security of the castle, her gaze darting around her, looking for invaders. The grass swayed in the breeze, the cool sun made lazy shadows dance against the ground. All looked peaceful; nothing marred the beauty around her.

But her heart beat a rapid, fearful rhythm against her chest, and her mind conjured up every kind of evil behind every rock. "Cyne," she cried. "Cyne!" Her voice sounded pathetically weak in the magnitude of her surroundings.

"Aleene!"

The harsh, commanding voice stopped Aleene cold. She whipped around, her gaze darting from the castle behind her to the quickly filling harbor, then over to the fort. Who had called her?

And then over the rise in front of her she saw him. His golden head appeared first, then his entire, strong, muscular body was revealed, as he walked up and over the hill. Only his eyes were different. Steely hard intelligence gleamed in his darkened eyes. "Get back to the castle. Put all of your people inside and bar the gates." His voice matched his eyes: hard, edged with steel. "You shall be safe there." His hard look faltered, he blinked, his hand came up as if he were going to touch her, only he didn't. "Please, Aleene, go back. I can promise you will be safe."

"You can promise? How? Who are you?" She asked, her mind reeling with shock.

His long dark lashes fluttered, shuttering his gaze. "I am Norman, Aleene. I am one of William's knights."

Her heart broke at that very moment. First it seemed to suck all of her life blood from her limbs, taking it all into itself, freezing there for a moment. And then it broke and there was nothing left inside of her.

She stared, her mind blank, her hand pressed against her mouth.

"Aleene." He moved forward, his eyes pleading, the lines of his face set in hard ridges.

"You bastard," she whispered, biting the back of her hand until she tasted blood. Her heart remained broken, but now a protective layer of ice shrouded it. "You bastard."

She turned away from him, his winter-sun beauty, his ice-blue eyes, and ran.

Part II

PART II

Chapter 9

He watched Aleene stride away, her back straight, her head up. Shame battled with duty as he forced himself to turn around and go back to the harbor where William and his fleet were landing.

There were battles to be fought and won, a crown to be returned to its rightful owner. Robert knew that he had to focus his strength and mind on those all-important goals. He could not allow any part of himself to worry about Aleene. She would take care of herself, God knew she had done so before he came into her life.

Robert, forcing himself to place one foot in front of the other, put distance between himself and the proud beauty who had come to hold a special place in his heart these last few weeks. Even as he left her, he could feel her anger, her defenses being rebuilt, higher, stronger.

"Damn!" He stopped and turned to watch

her. If William was successful in his conquest, Robert would lay claim to his passionate wife's castle. They would have to live as man and wife until their death. Running his hands savagely through his hair, Robert turned purposefully toward the harbor. He had a feeling that if Aleene had her way, his death would be terribly soon and most probably at her hands. He couldn't help but let out a half-hearted chuckle at that thought.

"Robert!"

Robert's attention was caught by the thundering yell.

"Robert!" A large, barrel-chested man came running up the hill from the harbor. "You've done yourself proud, man. William sings your praises as if you were God himself."

Robert grimaced, knowing full well that no God would have done anything to warrant the shame and guilt that ran rampant in Robert's heart. "Believe me, Duncan, I shan't be sainted anytime soon."

Robert's best friend reached him, and they embraced heartily. "Aw, but it's good to see you, Robert." Duncan hugged him tightly. "When we sent you away in that tiny boat with nothing but birds for friends, I can tell you now, I didn't think to see you again."

"Thanks for believing in me, Dunc." Robert started walking toward the ships that now lined the harbor and Duncan fell into step beside him.

"It's not that I don't think you're indestructible or anything," Duncan said as he playfully punched Robert in the arm.

"Well, it's not over yet, Dunc." Robert's comment sobered Duncan.

"Aye," he said softly. They walked in silence a few steps. "But now, Robert, we're not to face death with frowns now, are we?" Duncan laughed, then flipped a thumb over his shoulder. "So tell me about the fair maid you've wed! William nearly keeled over in shock when that message came in."

"I don't want to talk about it." They had reached the harbor, and Robert had to shout his last remark to be heard over the hubbub. Horses were being taken ashore, knights in battle gear splashed through the water with their pages in tow, and foot soldiers milled about. Despite the clamor, the atmosphere was light. There was no one to oppose the Normans' landing, and due to Robert's reports, they were fully aware of that fact.

"Well now," Duncan sounded a bit hurt. "You're not sounding like the Robert I remember."

With a sigh Robert turned to look at his longtime friend. "I don't believe I am, Dunc." Resting a hand on Duncan's shoulder, Robert scanned the crowd. He spotted William, standing up the beach a bit surrounded by men. "Shall we meet with our leader?" Robert squeezed Duncan's shoulder, wanting to bring back the easy friendship they had enjoyed most of their lives.

"Sure and he is excited to see you, Robert de Guise!"

"De Guise?" Robert frowned.

Duncan laughed heartily. "William named you! Said if you're going to be a great man with a castle you should have a name."

Robert felt a bit sick. "And de Guise seems appropriate."

"Aw, yes, you've proven yourself a great master of disguise! William is proud, man. He keeps telling everyone of how he took you as a fresh-faced boy and turned you into the knight you are now."

Robert nodded, his thoughts turning inward for a moment. *Was he not better as a fresh-faced boy?* Quickly he shook his head, he owed much to William. "Yes, well, Robert de Guise it is, then." He slapped Duncan on the back. "Shall we brave the crowd?" He gestured toward the mass of humanity surrounding William.

"Wouldn't miss it for the world!" Duncan smiled hugely, his craggy face softened for an instant and then he turned and pushed his way through the people huddled around their leader, making a hole large enough for Robert to follow.

* * *

As the heavy wooden gate closed behind Aleene, so did her heart. The door banged shut, the bar dropped with a thud, and Aleene tucked every shred of feeling inside her heart, closed it, and locked it up tight. She kept her chin high as she crossed the yard, covering her impenetrable heart with a protective layer of ice.

Berthilde came running to her side. "What of Cyne, milady? Did you not find him?"

"Do not say that name to me again."

Berthilde blinked in surprise, her jaw dropping, mouth agape.

"Go into the hall; keep the women and children inside. I shall head the defense." Her words came out with a hollow sound. She turned away from Berthilde, cutting off anything the woman may want to say.

"Stay at your posts!" she yelled to the few men left to guard Seabreeze. "We shall not allow the Bastard Duke entry into this castle!" Stating her intent gave her a tiny surge of strength. She strode quickly to the large watchtower at the gate and climbed the stairs. She could not allow herself to care for anyone but herself and her castle. They were the only two constants in her life, and she would have to remember that. From the top step, she scanned the harbor, dread weighing her limbs as she saw the boats that choked the passage to the sea. There were thousands of men, and hundreds of horses. How did she think to defend herself?

Fear caused her to tremble as a cool wind lifted her veil and whipped it around her body. And what did she do this for? She wondered suddenly. For herself, for her castle. What were they, why were they important?

A few weeks ago she had known. A few short weeks ago, she had been driven to do anything for those two things. And now, when she needed that drive more than ever, she couldn't remember why she did this. Why she did anything.

"No!" She yelled into the wind. "No!" Gripping the edge of the spiked wall before her, Aleene pushed away her discouraging thoughts and dredged up new, fortifying ones. She would do this now to revenge herself against the awful, lying man who had taken away her meaning, taken away any small scrap of self-confidence she had once harbored. She peered down toward the sea again, trying to see a flash of gold anywhere, trying to distinguish the person who had infused her with hate like no other.

She could not, of course, see him. Only a mass of movement: men, horses, supplies. She turned and eyed the men who lined the wall of her castle. They were a pitiful few. Most of them were so old she wondered how they had climbed to their posts. There were javelins to throw, mounds of rocks and some spears. Would her secondhand army even be able to pick them up? She didn't want to dwell on the question.

Aleene took a deep breath, closed her eyes for a brief moment, and opened them again, ready to watch and wait.

They waited for what seemed days. But as Aleene checked the sun again, she realized it had only been a few hours. The enemy army, assembled in the town, had ransacked homes and shops to lay out a huge meal for the men. Aleene had watched it all, her anger becoming a potent, tangible thing. The few people of Pevensey that had not made it to the castle had scattered, probably taking news of the invasion to other villages.

A tiny hope sparked to life in Aleene's mind that perhaps someone would come. But in reality she knew that hope was futile. No one would come. She would have to do what she had boasted all summer she could do. She would have to defend Seabreeze by herself.

When a column of men started up the hill toward the castle, Aleene turned quickly, calling for her men to be ready. A few of them had dozed off, and they jumped, nearly falling from their perches.

"They come!" she cried again, taking up one of the long spears that sat beside her. Her hand

shook with such intensity she could barely keep
hold of the wooden handle. How would she
throw it? How would she throw it with enough
strength to pierce chain mail?

Aleene gripped the handle, clenched her
teeth together, and focused on the army making
their way up the hill toward her fortress. She
yelled again, invoking God to help them. She,
herself, didn't believe He would, but perhaps it
would help her men. She breathed deeply, trying to calm herself, focus herself on what she
must do.

As the army came closer, she had to work
harder at concentrating. Her mind whirled with
questions, memories, thoughts, anything but
the great task she had before her. She thought
of Cyne, the love she had imagined, and she
hurt. She remembered her mother, her fall into
complete depression after Aleene's father had
died. She wondered how her life would be different if her father had lived?

Panic. She was in the throes of complete
panic. Aleene bit the inside of her lip so hard
she tasted blood. At least she realized her panic,
that was good. She could control it! With every
ounce of her being, Aleene focused on the standard bearers at the head of the advancing army.
William, the Bastard Duke of Normandy, had
come. He wanted to take away the only thing
left that belonged to her.

And then she focused on the standards held

aloft and felt her stomach churn with shock. William carried the colors of the pope. This terrible thing he did was being supported by the church. Trembling, Aleene blinked and stared hard at the standard. Yes, it was the pope's. If she defended her home, she would be fighting against God.

How could that be?

How could God wish the women in her hall to be raped, the men murdered? With an anguished cry, Aleene threw down her spear and whirled around. Behind her she saw the confused faces of the old men, the fear written in the expressions of the women who peeked through the door of the hall.

She could not let this castle fall to William, even for the love of God.

Turning back, Aleene took her weapon once more and faced her enemy. Whoever came against her was her enemy, even her husband, even her God.

Aleene clutched the spear in her hand harder and watched the oncoming men. She could do this. She had desperation on her side.

As the men came within range of her missiles, Aleene took a deep breath and readied herself for the command to strike. And then, the army coming upon her did the unthinkable.

They turned away.

Aleene blinked, sure that the sun played tricks with her eyes. Were they going to surround the castle? Fear sliced through her, and she checked to make sure that her men still stood their posts. They watched William's men, puzzlement written clearly on their faces.

They were being tricked. Aleene was sure. William would confuse her and her men, then somehow come back at them and destroy them. She yelled at her men again, "Stay ready!" With the median age of her small army being so high, she probably should have yelled stay awake. Aleene allowed herself a reproachful grimace as she watched the Normans turn away from her castle and head for the cliffs that dropped off into the gray English Channel.

Waiting for the inevitable trick, Aleene sat tensely. A large man with reddish-brown hair walked in the middle of the group, the men around him seemed to vie for his attention. Aleene knew it was William. There was an air about him. He commanded without even speaking.

His face turned as he followed the foot soldiers, his gaze on her castle, and then on her. He was too far away for her to see clearly, but she knew he watched her. She trembled slightly, wondering what he was about.

And then the army was gone. She frowned as she watched the last of the men. She noticed now that many of them carried wood. Long, cleanly cut pieces of wood.

"They shall not harm you, Lady Aleene." It

was a deep voice tinged with a French accent.

Aleene dropped her spear and staggered backward, her heart nearly bursting through her breast. She looked to the source of the voice and saw Cyne standing just in front of the gate. Beside him stood a huge man with masses of flaming red hair. And behind them both were about forty or fifty men, all of them carrying swords and wearing armor.

Aleene regained her composure quickly, shooting a venomous look at the men of Pevensey village who stood their posts around her castle. A great army they were, allowing the enemy to just walk right up to the gate.

"We shall defend this castle against attack, sir!" She yelled, brandishing her spear.

"I would that you allow me entrance. My men shall remain outside."

The red-haired giant scowled at this, grabbing Cyne's arm and shaking his head.

"No." Aleene lifted her spear and looked behind her. "Men, be at arms!"

"If one man here is harmed, Aleene, William will come upon you with no mercy," Cyne said just loud enough for her to hear. "If I must force my way in, there shall be bloodshed." He stared at her, the warmth of his gaze gone, the constant smile a grim line. "If you allow me entrance, no one will die here."

Silence settled upon them. Cyne's men watched her warily. A sharp wind buffeted their standard, reaching up to whip her gown about her and send icy trails of foreboding through Aleene. She swallowed hard and looked at the new Cyne standing before her, strength, intelligence, and determination filled the vacancy Aleene was used to seeing in his eyes. She glanced quickly at the men behind her, knowing full well they would not be able to fight Cyne and his men, much less the army that now set up camp in the old Roman fort.

"How do I know you will not charge the castle if I open the gate?" she asked finally.

"You do not."

Her men murmured lowly at this answer.

"You will have to trust me."

Aleene laughed outright at this, a loud, hollow laugh. "Trust you?" she yelled. Pain pierced her heart. But Aleene took a deep breath and pushed the pain away. Nothing would get through to her heart again, nothing. "Trust you, the half-wit poacher?"

"Yes."

Aleene wanted to turn and run. She felt an edge of panic quicken her pulse as she realized she couldn't do this. How could she defend her castle with no men against the one person she had opened herself up to, the one person she had allowed herself to love? If only the man before her was some foreign unknown, some dirty, ugly human she had not touched, kissed, loved.

"Fine!" she screamed, turning quickly and yanking at the rope to pull up the locking bar. "Fine, I will trust you to enter without your men." She fought furiously with the rope, twining it about the winch and turning. She could see a few people rushing to the gate, opening it slightly.

Dropping his sword in the dirt, Cyne entered. His friend seemed inclined to follow, but Cyne held up his hand and said something in French. The red-headed man stopped, his face set in harsh lines, his eyes darting from her to the men who still sat their posts.

When Cyne finally stood within the walls of her castle, Aleene dropped the bar across the gate, grabbed her spear, and clattered down the stairs to stand in the dirt in front of her husband.

"What do you want?" She nearly spat the words at his feet.

"I don't want death," he said softly.

Aleene laughed harshly. "Then I suggest that you stay away from me."

"I shall take this castle, Aleene." He kept his hard gaze locked with hers. "It is rightfully mine."

Aleene gripped the spear in her hand tighter and laughed again. "Nothing is rightfully yours. If you want it, you will have to kill me first."

Aleene watched as a muscle in Cyne's cheek

danced along his jaw. "You have no way of defending this castle. If you try, your people will die." His gaze flicked away from her for a moment, then came back. "Surrender now, and no one will be killed."

Gritting her teeth, Aleene stared hatefully at the man in front of her. As she took in the considerable breadth of his chest, the long muscled legs and strong arms, she almost laughed again. She had thought this man weak. She had married him because he was one she could control. What a terrible twist of fate, to be standing here at his mercy. At the mercy of this Norman. "What is your name?"

He blinked, surprise furrowing his brow. "My name?" He shook his head slightly. "I am called Robert."

"And you fight for William of Normandy."

"Yes, I told you. I am one of his knights."

Aleene nodded, anger and guilt making her want to slap *Robert's* face. But she stilled the urge, keeping her gaze level, her hand at her side. If they fought, her people would die. If they did not, her pride would be the only casualty.

Slowly, she let go of her spear, letting it fall to the ground. "Lord Robert of Seabreeze Castle, you may bring your men within these walls."

The silence that hung over the yard beat against Aleene's body. She stood very still, her head tilted back so that she could look directly into her husband's eyes.

Emotion flickered there for an instant, regret perhaps, Aleene wasn't sure, but she did not allow herself to care. If this man she had made her husband felt anything at all, she was sure it could only be base, primal urges. He was not a man, but an animal to do this to her.

He nodded then, quickly. "It is for the best."

Aleene didn't answer. She couldn't. The hurt and betrayal that raged within her breast kept her mute. She had not cried since she was seven, and yet she knew that if she opened her mouth now, she would most probably cry. And then her pride would not even have the honorable death it now experienced, but humiliating carnage.

Cyne, no, Robert, turned and ordered one of her men to open the gate. The red-headed giant smiled hugely as the gate opened to reveal him. He thumped his chest, then led the other men through the gate, stopping next to Robert.

"Duncan, may I present my wife, Lady Aleene?" Robert kept his gaze on her as he spoke to his friend. "My lady." He bowed slightly and swept his hand toward Duncan. "Duncan."

An awkward silence hung between them for a moment and then Duncan said, "It is an honor, milady."

Aleene could only stare into the hard blue

eyes of her husband. He held her gaze, never blinking until finally Aleene had to turn away. She left them, walking through the men that stood about, and then through the doors of the hall. The women had gathered there, peering out at the spectacle taking place. They backed away as she approached, clearing a wide path for Aleene. She did not acknowledge the presence of anyone, just walked forward, her gaze never straying from before her. When she finally reached her chamber, she closed the door behind her, bolted it, and went to her father's chair.

The tears that had threatened earlier did not come, only the trembling that Aleene was used to, and a blessed numbness that seeped through her limbs and into her heart. The layers of ice were finally working.

Robert did not attempt to breach his lady's chamber. He settled his men in the castle, posting a watch and giving orders, and then he left to meet with William. They sat upon English land, a miracle in and of itself, but still the crown belonged to another. Robert could only pray that their luck would continue.

When he reached the old Roman fort, William's men had begun setting up the fortress within its walls. He watched for a moment as they pieced together the already cut wood.

"Robert!"

Turning, Robert saw William coming towards him. "William," he answered, smiling.

"You are the first Norman to win land!" William laughed, obviously in very high spirits. "This bodes well, I think, for our plans! We shall not stop until I wear the crown, and you, my boy, own lands beyond measure!"

Robert only nodded, knowing full well that with all of the land and bounty William had promised to the lords and barons who funded this project, he, Robert, would be very low on the list when it finally came time to pay back. That was the main reason he had offered to come over first as a spy. For if he lived through the battles to follow, his sons would not be landless.

"We shall ride out on the morrow, Robert." William folded his large arms across his chest and shifted his weight to the back of his heels. "I would see the surrounding area."

Robert copied William's stance, watching the men assembling the premade fort. "I have a daring suggestion, William."

William did not turn, but nodded. "Daring you say?" He laughed. "I am nothing but these days, Robert, nothing but."

"King Harold and all of his troops are still in York. They have just finished protecting that northern flank from Hardrada. March on London, William, now, and you shall find no resistance."

Robert heard his leader draw in a large breath and hold it for a second.

"No."

Robert turned. "But we shall take them by surprise. We could take London with little or no bloodshed."

"No, Robert." William continued to keep his gaze on the work going on in front of them. "I shall await Harold here, or perhaps further north at the Abbey of Fecamp. I can count on their support. Either way, I shall allow Harold to come to me and fight me honorably."

In his heart, Robert had hoped William would march on London immediately. He had known, though, that it was a thin hope. "Yes, sir." He ran his fingers through his hair and closed his eyes for a moment. There would be a battle.

"I shall see you again on the morn, Robert." William thumped Robert's back and smiled, then turned and went to help his men.

Chapter 10

❦⟳⟳❦

Aleene watched Robert leave the next morning with the duke and some of his men. They rode horses, large, powerful horses that looked nothing like the ponies King Harold and his entourage rode. It didn't matter, though, it couldn't. Harold still had more men than William. She hoped, at least, that most of them still lived after the battle with the king of Norway. With a sinking feeling in her heart, Aleene watched the men ride through the town and into the forest.

She did not leave her room that day, nor did she partake of the food that Berthilde brought to her. She stared out at the bay, the water dull and dark, the air heavy with the chill of coming rain and the sky a flat slate of gray overhead. The weather mimicked her mood as she sat, her hands placidly folded in her lap while her thoughts cast frantically about in her mind, trying to think of a plan, some way, any way, she could regain control of her castle, her life. Some way she would right this terrible wrong she had done to her people. For she had betrayed them. By thinking only of her need to rule Seabreeze, she had lost not only that, but much more to the hands of the Normans.

The only glimmer of happiness that filtered through her heart was when she saw William's company return, on foot, their horses nowhere to be seen. The mud and dirt that enshrouded each man made her smile and wish desperately she had been there to see that spectacle. With a soft laugh, Aleene wondered if they had fallen from their horses at different times or perhaps all at once. Either way, it was quite a feat.

She watched them trudge up the hill toward their fort and noticed that Cyne, no, Robert, carried William's armor as well as his own.

He was a strong man, her husband. Aleene tore her gaze from the pathetic tableau and surged up from her seat. That she hadn't realized no scrounging beggar could have such strength made her seethe. Such stupidity!

Aleene put her hand against the wall and leaned her forehead there. She had been blinded by his beauty, by the peace he had temporarily brought into her life. Oh, more the fool, she. To trust.

She must have stood that way for longer than she thought. For when she heard a knock, without thought she moved and unlocked the door, thinking it would be Berthilde with her supper.

It was not.

"Milady." Robert dipped his head as he entered, his voice low and soft.

Aleene could only blink at the intruder, her breath coming faster as she registered who it was. "How? But you . . . I thought you . . ." She cut her words short then, knowing that she sounded like a bumbling idiot and hating it. Hating him. "How dare you come to me." She straightened, squaring her shoulders and funneling all of her hatred into the look with which she speared the man before her.

He stared at her for a moment, his eyes dark.

"You cannot win, you know." She clenched her fists at her side. "You and your pathetic group of warriors think to conquer all of England? Harold has more men. He has an entire country behind him. You cannot win."

Robert showed no sign that he had heard what she said. Suddenly she remembered Cyne, her Cyne, how he would stare blankly as she spoke. Quickly she whipped around to stare out the window, giving her husband her back.

"I leave on the morrow."

She did not say anything.

"I am sorry, Aleene, for betraying you."

Aleene waited for the trick, waited for the twist that would make sense to Robert's bald lies. She stared, unbelieving, out the window at

William's standard, which flew over the Roman
fort.

She felt Robert move, felt the heat of his body
against her back and stiffened.

"You will not believe what I say now, I
know." He laughed, a small derisive sound.
"Of course, you will not."

Aleene searched her mind, trying to figure
out the game Robert now played.

"I will say it, though, for I go tomorrow into
an unknown future."

Aleene felt something near her shoulder,
whisper soft. She dropped her gaze without
moving her head and saw his hand, that beautiful work-worn hand,- reaching out, but not
touching her. Quickly, she stiffened and moved
her shoulder away.

"I would that I could take away your pain,
Aleene. That I have hurt you like this, I shall
never forgive myself."

His lies struck a hurt so deep within her,
Aleene cringed. "Do not dare, Robert!" Aleene
spun around, her anger fueled by smoldering
pride.

Robert did not move and so they stood very
close. Aleene took a deep, shaking breath into
her lungs, strengthening herself. "You come to
my bed, witless, then bring invaders into my
castle, heartless." Her words held all the vehe-
mence that pounded mightily through her
veins. "And now, dear husband, you come into

my chamber full of humility. I wonder how you shall be tomorrow?" Surging forward, Aleene brushed past Robert, knocking him aside.

"Out!" she yelled, opening the door. "Get out!"

Robert stared at the door then at her. "I *am* sorry. But know this, Aleene. If I do not return, I have William's word that you shall stay unmolested here at Seabreeze."

Aleene gripped the door with all of her might, her chest heaving with the fury that felt trapped there.

"If, on the other hand, your King Harold is victorious, you may return to your life of fighting tooth and nail for what is yours." He left then without looking at her, and Aleene shoved the door closed behind him.

With a disgusted oath she raked her gaze over the chamber she had spent two days in. Two days of wallowing in self-pity: not eating, not speaking, barely breathing. That *he* had reduced her to such a pathetic creature made her blood boil.

Aleene crossed the room quickly and stared again at the old Roman fort now teeming with another invader. *He* had made her weak, vulnerable, again. She had opened her heart and trusted. And this is what became of such stupidity.

Whirling away from the window, Aleene paced the floor, willing her thoughts away from her folly, her husband, and forcing them to formulate a plan. She would avenge the harm done her, the harm done to her people, if she died trying.

Robert stared through his mount's ears at the road before him. His back ached, his backside was numb, and his heart seemed to be crumbling away with each step. William had split up his troops, leaving some to stay with the ships and fort, ferrying the foot soldiers across the harbor mouth and leaving the knights to ride around. All of them, of course, set on the same goal of reaching the land owned by the Abbey of Fecamp. Not knowing the area at all, William felt that he could defend his position better amongst friends.

Robert sighed largely and switched his reins from one hand to the other. The wind whistled through the trees around him, biting through the seams of his chain mail and making him shiver. Cold, he could add cold to his list of grievances.

And sad. A deep, soul-taking sad. Every town they passed through the men around him went mad, ransacking homes, taking food, killing men, raping women. It made Robert want to vomit. But he didn't. He stopped the killing and raping where he could and shouted for the men to move on.

His long years as one of William's most loyal

knights suddenly seemed trivial. Never before had he questioned what he did. When he turned his back on the life his father meant for him, his great scholarly father who never believed in wars and fighting, Robert knew what he wanted was right for him.

His father felt words and knowledge to be the most important thing a person could own. Robert did not. He wanted land. He did not want to spend his life at the whim of others. He wanted land and the power to live his own life that land would give him.

But now, suddenly, he wondered if both he *and* his father were wrong. What was land, what was knowledge, what was anything, if one could not look deep inside oneself and respect what one saw?

With the thought of land and wealth guiding him, he had hurt another very deeply. From the very first night of his farce he had known that his new wife was a fragile creature. And he had begun to care for her, even as he set up the scene for her demise. If only he didn't care. If only she had been some ugly termagant with a heart of stone.

It was his mother's fault. Her caring nature had left its mark upon him. It was completely impossible for him to see a wounded creature and not feel the need to help it. Even as he shunned her way of life, and his father's, he kept within him the values they had taught him from the time he could speak.

"Robert!"

The call from behind broke into Robert's thoughts and roused him from his melancholy. With a great effort, he focused his mind on the task at hand and turned.

"Robert!"

A rider came pounding up the dirt track, red hair flying. Duncan.

"I need you to stay at Seabreeze, Duncan!" Robert said as his friend came abreast of him. "I realize you don't wish to, but I need someone who . . ."

"She's gone, Robert, gone!"

Robert knew immediately who Duncan spoke of. Fear hit him first, before the anger. "And you come after me?" he roared. "You should have followed her! She could be killed, hurt!"

"I swear I've been lookin' all night for her. She and her maid took off in a haycart. I haven't been able to find a trace of 'em."

"Damn!" Robert yanked the helmet from his head and plowed his dirty fingers through his hair. "They'll be on their way to London, I'm sure."

"Of course, she'll be off telling that king of hers all the particulars she's seen!"

Robert shrugged that off. "I'm sure many have gone running to tell their king what they have seen. I worry not about that but about her

safety." Robert turned in his saddle and surveyed the men he led.

"Damn," he said again softly. He stared
ahead of him for a moment. "Take them north,
Duncan." Robert replaced his helmet and
flipped his thumb toward the men. "I'll be there
as soon as I can." Robert wheeled his mount
around.

"What?" Duncan's fiery brows shot toward
his hairline. "You jest!"

"Never." Robert leaned over his horse and
dug his spurs in its side. They lunged forward,
leaving Duncan swearing behind them.

He looked for them for two days, his back
aching and his eyes stinging from lack of sleep.
He was nearly killed twice, coming upon bands
of men heading for London to join the forces
against William, but he quickly lost himself in
the dense forests.

It was the second night when he quite liter-
ally stumbled upon them. They had no fire, and
he was upon their cart before he realized he had
found somebody. For a heart-stopping moment
he thought it might be another band of men.
And then he made out the skirts of a woman's
tunic trailing from beneath the cart. Robert dismounted with a muffled oath, his legs nearly
giving out beneath him, and crouched down
carefully, peering through the darkness. There
was a sound, whistling air, and a dark object in

front of his face and then pain, fiery and intense, splintering through his head.

"Aaaaarrrrggghhh!" He fell backwards, his hand holding his nose. He could already feel sticky warm blood seeping through his fingers. The object came towards him once more, only this time he rolled away. It cracked heavily against the ground, sending up a light spray of dry leaves.

Robert rolled again, leaning up on his elbows and finally jumping to his feet. Whirling around, he looked straight into the dark eyes of his wife. She held a thick piece of wood over her shoulder, ready to swing another blow. Robert let go of his nose and held out his hands. "Halt, woman!"

She faltered at his words.

" 'Tis me, Aleene, Cyne."

Flinging the wood aside, Aleene spit at his feet. "Cyne? I know of no one by that name." She stomped away. "You have interrupted my sleep, Norman. Be off with you!"

Robert took a deep breath, fighting the urge to run after Aleene's weapon and beat everything within a fifty-yard radius to a pulp. His back ached, he hadn't slept in days, and now his face was a throbbing mass of pain. He reached out and wrapped his fingers around Aleene's forearm. "If you know what's good for you, ye'll not provoke me, woman."

She tried to wrench her arm away, but he only tightened his grip.

"Let go of me."

"Do you realize the danger you've put yourself in?" Robert managed to say through clenched teeth.

The murky darkness hid her intent. The first inkling Robert had that she had slapped him was the echo of flesh hitting flesh that reverberated in the silent forest. A tiny second later he felt the stinging pain in his cheek. "God's teeth!" Robert let go of Aleene and stumbled backward.

"Danger?" she fumed, advancing on him. "Danger? I put *myself* in danger? Do not patronize me so, you disgusting excuse for human flesh."

Every oath he had ever muttered poured through his mind as he turned away. He said nothing, though, just stood with his eyes tightly closed, waiting desperately for his patience to return. His head rang, his nose throbbed, and his cheek stung. He wanted to break something.

"Go back to sleep," he said finally. "Now." He did not turn around, he didn't trust himself. He didn't hear anything, though, and knew she had not gone back to the cart.

"Milady, come along." Berthilde's voice reached him, and he relaxed a bit.

"I will not sleep with this man anywhere near us!"

He turned on his heel. "You will sleep here with no protection and men clogging the roads and not see a problem with that? But you take exception when I come to protect you?"

A disgusted snort of laughter came from Aleene. "It seems I had protection enough."

"You think a plank of wood is going to stop someone with intentions far worse than mine?" Robert advanced on his wife, grabbing her arms and bringing her body flush with his. She struggled, but he held tight. She was a tall woman, and strong, and he had to exert much of his energy to keep her within his hold. "You, milady, need a lesson in your limitations."

For some reason he could not fathom, Robert bent and took her lips in a bruising kiss. He wanted to show her how easy it would be for a man to overtake her, but seconds into the kiss his senses scattered and he only wanted her close. He could feel the ripe fullness of her breasts against him, and her long legs against his thighs, and he wanted her. The memories of those nights where he had to remain pliant as she drove his blood into a roiling boil came back to him and he deepened the kiss.

All thoughts of sensual bliss left his mind immediately with the pain that sliced through his tongue when her teeth clamped down. He pushed away with a loud yell.

"Oh, yes, you are to protect us?" his hellion of a wife sniffed. "You shall bring down every person in the vicinity upon us with your screaming. And then they shall kill us all for you are a Norman."

Robert swore as he fingered his tongue and felt new blood against his fingertips. Then he whirled around and gave a tree a vicious kick.

"Let us retire, milady." He heard Berthilde say to Aleene. "This shall do us no good, and we must be rested for our long journey on the morn."

Robert swore again, his toes now throbbing in pain. William would be furious with him for leaving his post, the men were probably pillaging and raping right and left without his staying hand, and evidently Aleene truly needed him not. No man would have the patience to stick around and keep trying to do anything to such a shrew.

"When I awake, I want you gone, Norman!"

Robert kept his gaze on the tree that had probably broken his toes, but listened as Berthilde hustled his wife away. The sounds of settling down echoed around him, then silence. Robert stood there for a very long time, then slowly went to his horse, found his sword, and sat up against a tree. He kept himself awake by alternately sucking on his tongue, which stung, and pressing gently on the side of his nose, which still managed to trickle blood now and then.

He must have dozed off right after dawn, for he remembered watching the forest around him lighten from complete darkness into shades of gray. The next thing he heard was his beloved's voice.

"I am awake, but you are still here."

Robert bolted to his feet, his lids like sand against his eyes. Early morning sun filtered through the trees.

Aleene threw a wet rag at him. "Clean your face." Then she turned to the cart where Berthilde sat waiting with reins in hand. The maid did not even look at him as Aleene jumped up next to her and they started out of the small clearing.

Robert watched for a moment before it registered in his foggy brain that they were actually leaving. He bent quickly, then, to retrieve the sword that lay on the ground where he had been sitting. The world rotated in a dizzy whirl when he straightened, but he made his way to his horse and mounted.

Through the long tiring day the two women in the cart did not acknowledge his presense. At one point they pulled out some dry bread and cheese, not bothering to stop and not bothering to share their bounty, although Robert was sure they could hear his growling stomach.

Finally, just as the sun began its final descent they stopped. Robert was just in front of them, his attention intent upon the forests around them, and he did not realize they did not follow him anymore until his wife yelled.

Robert whirled his mount around, ready to fight to keep safe the woman who had made his life a living hell in the last day. She stood in the road behind him, a tied bundle in her hands. He blinked and quickly checked everywhere he could see, his sword at the ready.

"You can go no further," she said.

He frowned, taken aback when she came toward him. In reality he feared some new punishment awaited him at her hands. He could not take another whack to his head, and thanks to his mother's careful teachings he could not find it within himself to retaliate against a woman.

"Here." She shoved the bundle in her hands toward him. "Go on, take it. 'Tis only food."

He bent to take the cloth-covered offering from her.

"You cannot continue. We are within Harold's lands. Go now."

He stared at her, but she averted her gaze.

"You could take me as your prisoner. 'Twould probably make your way easier with your king."

"Go!"

He watched as she worried her lip, her eyes dark pools of uncertainty. Then she turned quickly and made her way back to Berthilde. The maid stared at him. No uncertainty lived in her gaze, just pure hatred. The old woman slapped the reins against the tired pony and the cart moved slowly forward over the rutted road. Robert pulled back so they could pass, watching Aleene intently. She kept her face forward and never turned again.

"He comes, the Bastard Duke, with the blessing of the pope." Aleene kept her head bowed as she said this.

"Oh, my poor dear Harold." Aleene felt Edith's slim hand enfold her own. "He will not take this well."

"They go north, to the Abbey of Fecamp." Aleene finally looked up into Edith's face.

Harold's hand-fasted wife smiled wanly and patted Aleene's hand again. "You have been so brave, dear, to make such a journey and bring such news."

"Courage is not what drove me," Aleene said quietly, guilt and shame making her want to turn and run forever.

"When Harold returns from the north, he shall be grateful to you, Lady Aleene, for your loyalty."

Aleene pulled her hand from the graceful one that held it and turned. "I should not be surprised if he wishes me dead."

"He has wished you many things, my dear Lady Aleene," Harold's lovely wife placed a reassuring hand on Aleene's shoulder, "but never dead."

Aleene turned and looked into Edith's smiling face, and had never felt less like smiling herself.

"And you are alive now." Edith squeezed Aleene's shoulder, then went to sit in a comfortable-looking chair. Picking up her needlework, she commented, "So you have done well."

"Ending up alive does not always mean a life led well."

Edith took a moment to smooth a silken thread. "We are women in a man's world, Aleene, survival is success." The woman nodded to a chair beside her. "Do sit."

Aleene would rather have paced and walked, in fact, she would have rather run, but she clasped her hands together and sat, keeping her back straight.

With a small sigh, Edith tilted her head and closed her eyes. "Ah, I do love the feel of sun through these lovely glass planes."

Aleene looked at the pounded glass that lined the large windows in Edith's solarium. The material did seem to intensify the heat of what outside would be a cool sun. "I have never seen glass windows," Aleene said, more to be polite than anything else.

"They are not so hard to get anymore." Edith slid her needle through the cloth in her hands and looked up. "You should order some for Seabreeze. Harold has told me that it is a striking place, your castle."

Aleene blew out a rather loud breath, unable to keep her impatience in check. "Excuse me, Lady Edith, but I am rather anxious. Perhaps there is someone here I could speak with about what I've seen? One of the king's men?"

She had been sure that Edith was the correct person to relay her news. Aleene had never met Edith in person before now, but had heard much of Harold's love for her. Edith had joined with Harold in a ceremony not sanctioned by the church. She had born the king's children and stood steadfastly by him, even as Harold sealed a more politically advantageous marriage in the church. Still, the King referred to Edith as his wife, and, it was rumored, even turned to her for counsel. But now, as they sat lazily in the warm solarium, Aleene wondered if Edith were not quite as sharp as rumor had it.

With a small smile Edith went back to her needlework. "There is nothing for you to do, Aleene. Harold will be back soon enough. And then you can tell him what you have seen."

"I truly do not think you understand!" Aleene stood quickly, moving to stand before Edith. "There are thousands of men, hundreds of horses, and they ride under the pennant of the pope. We must do something, now."

Edith rose slowly and took Aleene's hand within her own. "There is nothing we can possibly do at this very moment to help the situation. We must wait for Harold to return from

York. Until then we must be calm. For to give
Harold such news in such a state would surely
make a very bad thing many times worse."

"But—"

"No, Aleene, we must be steady." She
smiled. "It is part of our purpose. To be
steady."

Aleene shook her head, unsure of what Edith
meant, and definitely not wanting to sit back
down and wait while all around her, life
whirled with uncertainty and terror.

"We shall walk." Edith said, as if she could
read Aleene's mind. "Come, my garden is quite
lovely even though winter approaches." Still
holding Aleene's hand, she led the way out the
heavy planked door. "Steady, Aleene, be
steady. It cultivates intelligent thought, rather
than chaotic action."

As Aleene allowed Edith to take her outside
into the chilly day, a long-forgotten memory of
her mother flashed through her mind. "Your actions rule your thoughts, dear." Aleene heard
the soft voice of her gentle mother. "It should
be the other way around."

Biting her lip, Aleene steeled herself to slow
her drumming heart, to stop the dizzying speed
of her thoughts, and realized suddenly that all
of the problems she had gotten herself into
were because she had forgotten that wise counsel from her mother.

She stared at the small, fair woman beside

her and knew with all of her heart that her
mother would have said the same as Edith.

Be steady, Aleene. She heard the words this
time in the voice that populated her early childhood memories. The long-lost voice of love.

Stopping, she pulled her hand from Edith's,
covered her face, and for the first time since her
father's death, wept. She cried long and hard, a
lung-shuddering, breathtaking cry. And when
she finally felt the hand smoothing her hair, she
was too weak even to care that she had let
down her guard so.

As her breathing slowed and her hiccups lost
their strangled quality, Aleene felt the cold hard
stone beneath her and realized that she was sitting. She closed her eyes, hung her head, and
relaxed onto the bench.

Edith patted her shoulder, a comforting gesture. Not enough contact to smother, but
enough to let Aleene know that she wasn't
alone. "I do love a good cry," Edith said softly.

Without answering, Aleene used the end of
her long sleeves to dry her eyes and wipe her
nose.

"I wish you could have seen my garden this
summer. The colors were breathtaking. Although even now it is still a lovely spot, don't
you think?"

Not wanting to be rude, Aleene opened her
eyes and looked around her.

"This is my impractical flower garden." Edith

smiled. "The herbs and such I grow by the kitchens. But this place is for nothing more than aesthetic pleasure." She sighed prettily. "Oh, I do enjoy it."

Aleene dabbed at her nose again and hiccuped. "It's lovely." It was really, the ground covered with grass and moss, with stepping stones winding around and benches to sit on among the trees, bushes, and plants. But Aleene couldn't keep her mind on the garden. She had just cried harder than she ever remembered doing before. And in front of someone else. She felt dizzy and scared. Would this woman beside her use the knowledge of Aleene's weakness to do her harm?

Biting her lip, Aleene straightened, pulling away from Edith's touch.

"I will leave you here." Edith stood. She looked around, then leaned toward Aleene conspiratorially. "I know it is quite blasphemous, but I do believe this garden to be enchanted." She smiled, her entire face lighting up with the gesture. "I come here when my heart is most grieved, and usually leave feeling much better. Although, in the winter, I sometimes leave almost frozen." She laughed, touched Aleene's shoulder softly, and turned away.

Aleene watched her, tears again threatening the backs of her eyes. "Stay," she heard herself say. And then she blinked, wondering how those words had come from her mouth.

Edith turned. Her gaze seemed to go right into Aleene's heart and read it. "Of course." She sat again. Silence remained between them as a cold wind stirred through the branches of the trees overhead. Lifting her chin, Aleene watched the bare limbs dance.

"I am afraid."

"I also," Edith said slowly. And then they sat together in silence until Aleene's toes began to go numb from the cold. As if she knew of Aleene's discomfort, Edith stood, took Aleene's hand in hers, and led her back inside.

King Harold returned from York two days later. He had again marched his men straight through, never stopping. They arrived haggard, cold, and hungry. When she heard the commotion in the bailey, Aleene said a quick prayer and ran for the hall.

Edith was already there. She hugged Aleene quickly, whispering in her ear, "Be steady."

Harold entered then, his clothes caked with mud. Edith went to him and held him in her arms. It shocked Aleene that this man, the king of the English, would allow such intimacy in front of his men. But they didn't seem to notice anything amiss.

With her hands clasped in front of her, Aleene watched Edith whisper to Harold, and then swallowed against the tide of fear that rose up as he turned his gaze on her.

Releasing his wife, Harold came to Aleene. She inhaled, squaring her shoulders.

"How comes the people of Pevensey?" Worry was in his voice, not anger.

Aleene released the breath she held. "Pevensey did not see the worse of it, your highness. As I traveled, though, I came through small villages laid to waste."

He shook his head and dragged his fingers through his matted hair. "To have been at the ready for so long, and then . . ." his words trailed off and he shook his head again, his eyes closing.

"Cyne . . . I mean, the man I took to husband . . ." Aleene faltered, but then gripped her hands tighter and continued. "He was not as he seemed."

Harold opened his eyes. "I have heard."

"Messengers approach!" a page interrupted.

Harold turned. "Who is it?"

"Monks, your highness, one from the duke of Normandy, the other your own messenger returning."

Harold gestured brusquely. "Send them in when they arrive."

The page bowed and rushed away.

Aleene stepped forward nervously. "I . . . your highness, if . . ."

"Tell me what you have seen, Lady Aleene." Harold looked at her and smiled, though it did not reach his eyes. "I am happy that you have been so courageous in bringing me your news."

"I, um . . ." Aleene could not believe that he did not want to censor her. She looked around, her gaze colliding with Edith's. Her new friend smiled. Aleene took a deep breath. "The duke rides under the pennant of the pope, your highness." She bowed her head, knowing this news would hurt her king deeply.

A strangled sound came from him. She looked up just as he whirled away and went to the other side of the hall. There, on the wall, hung a crucifix. Harold stood in front of it, not moving. Silence rang through the high-ceilinged room as if not a soul stood within the sanctuary of stone.

A clatter at the door announced the arrival of the monks. They entered looking only a bit better than the king himself.

One of the men stepped forward, walking quickly toward the king. "I have a message from the duke of the Normans, your highness."

Harold did not turn. "Say it."

"He states his right to the throne of England, and offers a combat, a hand-to-hand combat that it might finally be decided."

Again silence thundered through the great hall. When Harold finally turned, his face was pale beneath the grime. "We march at once." His gaze swept the men that stood at the back of the hall. "We march to battle."

The men began speaking all at once.

"But, your highness, I implore you to think on this some more!" the monk before Harold pleaded. "It is only a combat of two the duke asks for."

Harold stayed the man's arguments with an outthrust hand. " 'Tis true that William rides under the papal banner?"

The monk swallowed noticeably, and again the men quieted, their eyes now round with shock.

" 'Tis true, your highness."

Harold clenched his hand and relaxed his arm against his side.

Aleene took a few steps forward, her heart nearly breaking at the agony she read on Harold's face. "The church has deserted me. I shall perish in hell." Aleene heard the soft sound of her king's whisper before he turned once again to face the crucifix.

"The English shall go to battle the Normans," Harold said softly. Then, thrusting back his head, he cried, "May the Lord now decide between William and me, and may he pronounce which of us has the right."

Chapter 11

The sun-dappled water danced, making it seem as if the world were full of crystals. Robert closed his eyes and watched the colors sparkle against his eyelids, blue, red, yellow. Slowly, he dragged his eyes open to see her, a dark outline against the brightness of the sea. Tall, curvaceous, sensual. She came closer and he saw that she had been swimming. Her raven hair shone with clear, sparkling droplets of water.

The beauty of the scene before him belied the feeling in his heart. Why did he hurt? How did he know her smile would turn down as soon as she realized it was him? Why did he feel so dark inside with such light surrounding him?

And then she opened her arms to him, smiling and he went to her. He felt her breasts, wet against his chest. He smelled the scent of her flesh, the sea in her hair. And his heart broke open to bring in her light and let out its darkness.

This was how it should be, he thought.

"Robert?" she asked lightly. "Robert?"

Only he couldn't answer, he couldn't speak.

"Robert!" This time her tone was more commanding. "Robert!" Harsh impatience thundered through her suddenly deep voice.

He opened his eyes and saw darkness.

"Awake, Robert de Guise!" One of Robert's men stood at the opening of his tent. "William has need of thee." He left, letting the tent flap fall behind him.

Robert swallowed once, painfully, realizing the full depth of disappointment as the happiness of his dream faded into heartbreaking reality.

With a low groan, Robert laid his forearm over his face and relaxed for a moment in his cot. In his mind's eye he saw Aleene again, at the beach. They had played like children. The woman of the wounded eyes had smiled. She had laughed. She had opened her heart, and he had smashed it beneath his heel.

He was ashamed. He had fought it at first, justifying his actions. After all, her king had stolen the crown of England from its rightful owner. But, of course, that was not his main reason for being there. He wanted wealth. He wanted the power to control his own destiny rather than be a mere underling all his life like his father before him. And so, to achieve that he had continued in his ruse.

And then he had begun to care. Still, if he had truly cared, he should have left. He should have lost himself to her so she would never know his true identity, never know even more heartbreak than she had already.

Robert huffed a dark laugh as he hauled himself from bed and pulled on his leather shoes. He had been torn. Caring for the woman, he began to see through the layers of armor, and caring also for the wealth she could bring him. Robert shook his head. He needed to forget for now, put her from his mind. He had a war to help win.

Into the dark, crisp night, Robert trudged, his breath making a soft white mist in front of his face. He pulled his cape up around his ears and hunched his shoulders. It was getting colder, and they had no supplies.

They would have to do something soon, or die out here. As Robert nodded to the sentries on duty outside William's tent, he chuckled. It sounded hollow and foreboding in the chill night. Wouldn't it just be perfect irony if William accomplished the imposing feat of bringing an entire army across the English channel, just to have them all die of starvation?

"You laugh, Robert de Guise?" William's voice broke through his thoughts, and Robert focused on his leader's candle-lit face in the dark tent. "You are happy, then, about our surprise visitor?"

"De Guise?" Another, familiar voice came from the shadows. "How fitting."

Robert turned, straining to see her in the flickering light. "Aleene, what do you here?" He looked sharply at William. "Have you kidnapped her?" Robert moved quickly toward the duke, stopping just in front of him. "You cannot, my lord. She is my wife, before God." He could barely speak through his labored breath. "She is my wife."

William looked as if he might speak, but then Aleene said, "I come of my own accord, dear husband. Although it is quite heartening to see that you care so very much for my welfare. I am glad, also, that your nose is looking so much better than the last I saw."

The bitterness made Robert wince. He took a deep breath, his hand going unconciously to his still-tender nose.

"Your wife accompanied Hugh Margot, who took the message to Harold. We are to have a battle."

The duke kept his voice light, but Robert knew that his leader's heart was anything but. Robert knew that William spoke flippantly for Aleene's benefit. He wanted no one to know the pain this confrontation caused him.

"And your wife has come to be with you in what may be your last days upon this earth."

William smiled toward Aleene. "A most heart-warming gesture."

Aleene smiled back. Her ice-smile. Robert recognized it. He had melted the smile before, but he had many doubts of his ability to do so again. He looked from his wife to his liege, his loyalties to them at odds with each other, but still present within his one heart. And one always the more important. Robert's gaze came to rest upon William.

"Take your wife, then, Robert. Take her to your tent and thank her rightly for coming to you on this bone-chilling morning." William turned his gaze back to Aleene. "Keep her close to you."

Robert read his warning and nearly laughed, but bit back the bitter sound. Aleene lifted one side of her mouth in an ugly smirk. Obviously she also realized William's warning. Another irony, that she should now be the spy among his people as he had been among hers.

As he took her elbow and led her out into the cold dawn, he wished them all to hell. His people and hers. It seemed absurd, suddenly, that they should both fight so hard for their separate causes. Did those causes care one whit for the people they were? He and Aleene? But then he stopped those traitorous thoughts, his mind confused at the way his heart had taken over.

Aleene jerked her arm from his grasp, and he sighed. "Why did you come, Aleene? You would be safer elsewhere. Truly you should be safe at Seabreeze. Duncan would see to that."

"I don't wish for safety!" She turned on him, her shoes squishing in the mud. "Especially in the hands of a Norman!" she spat the word as if it tasted vile.

Robert again took her elbow and urged her forward. She went, fortunately, although she shook free of his hand. "Duncan is not a Norman. He is Scots."

"You think that makes subjection easier?"

"It is not subjection. You are still the lady of Seabreeze Castle. In fact—" Robert held his tent flap open for her, only she did not bend to enter. Instead she stood, pinning him with an icy glare. "In fact," he said on a sigh, "I am probably the only person in the world who will actually fight to keep you as such."

With a disgusted grunt, Aleene broke eye contact and went inside the tent. Rolling his eyes, Robert followed. This promised to be a wearing morning.

"You dare to say such a thing?" Aleene said as he entered, her back still to him. "You dare?"

" 'Tis but the truth."

"Ahhh, and so now you are a bringer of truth?" Aleene whirled around. "Forgive me if I find that hard to believe, my lord."

Robert took a deep breath and scratched at the beard that had grown in the last couple weeks. He had thought to purge her from his thoughts and now she stood before him in the flesh. He was doomed to have to deal with this now. He decided suddenly to use a stratagem taught to him by his mother, one he hadn't often used. He told the truth. "I have come to care for you, Aleene."

"No!" She came forward and slapped him hard across his face.

He winced at the sting, but did nothing else. So much for the truth.

"Do not take me for a fool twice, Robert *de Guise.*" Her chest rose and fell. He could hear her harsh breathing, taste the hate that vibrated from her. "I will not allow it. You do not care. You take. You have come to take a land not yours. You have taken my pride. You have taken the trust of the people of Pevensey. You will take no more."

He could say nothing, for what she said was true.

"King Harold is the king of our people. He will not allow you and your Bastard Duke to take what is ours. And I will do anything possible to make sure that you don't. I was stupid before, seeing only what I wanted. I must thank you for that one thing. You opened my eyes. With a Norman ruling Seabreeze, I now realize that I had more to fear than Aethregard in that position."

"Aleene, I . . ."

"No! I will listen to no more. You made me

a traitor to my people, and I will listen no more
to your lies."

"A traitor?" Robert shook with fear. "They
have branded you a traitor?"

"No, *you* have branded me a traitor."

"Do they pursue you? Is that why you are
here? Do you run for your life?"

"King Harold is a man of God, you piece of
filth." The venom in her eyes was pure hatred.
"He has forgiven me my stupidity. But I have
not. Nor will I ever. I will fight to my death to
right the wrong I did when I married you to
preserve my own holding."

Robert sank to the edge of his cot, running
his fingers through his hair. "Ahhh, Aleene, I
am sorry for this. What I did was wrong. But
at first I saw only the opportunity. And then I
felt such pity for you."

"Pity?"

Robert clenched his hand in his hair. Wrong
word, Robert, he thought.

"You dare to pity me?" She moved away
stiffly. "There is nothing to pity, Norman. I am
the wealthiest woman in all of England. An England that shall never be under the rule of any
Bastard Duke. There is nothing to pity." She
turned and left quickly.

He knew he should go after her. William
would not want her alone within his camp. But
Robert let her go. For in that moment he wished
William to hell. And it scared him.

*   *   *

She didn't look around her as she stalked outside. She did not count men, or inspect their arms, or investigate the number of horses. She went through the camp, looking neither left nor right, and made for the trees. Once there she sank down on a rotted log and wished for oblivion. She wished it for a long time, in fact, but it never came. The cold sun kept filtering through the trees and the leaves kept swirling around her ankles as a bitter wind kept slithering through her clothes to trail icy fingers along her skin.

Nothing stopped.

It seemed it should. How could everything continue as if nothing had happened? As if she were still the undisputed heir to Seabreeze, fighting to keep control? As if an army did not sit beyond these trees, waiting to tear apart her people's world? As if some beautiful, hateful man had not torn apart her defenses and stormed her keep . . . her heart.

"I have brought you dinner."

She had heard someone approach, and so she didn't jump. She had been half-hoping that oblivion finally did come to her on stealthy feet, through crackling leaves. But, alas, it was only Robert. The very antithesis of oblivion. Aleene sighed and kept her gaze on the small woodland creature that pushed its nose from its burrow. Would it brave the outside after hearing them? She watched.

" 'Tis not much." He sat beside her and opened a folded cloth. "Hard bread and harder cheese."

The nose peeking from the ground twitched. Ah, the terrible agony the poor creature faced. She knew his fear, yet he hungered. And now what must to him be a tantalizing aroma drifted toward his small, hidden home.

She felt something being pressed into her hands, and she wrapped her fingers around it.

"I did not pity you."

She listened, barely.

"I admired you, your strength. I hurt for you, your pain."

Before she might have struck out at that. Her pain. She had not acknowledged such a thing. Now she realized she lived with it constantly. The pain of betrayal. The pain of a loveless life. It would not have been so painful, truthfully, if it had not been preceded, so closely, by the life she had shared with her father, a life full of love, a life full of contentment.

And yet the pain had forced her strength. The pain had been necessary for her to realize the fleeting character of those things she had believed so strong before, love, loyalty, security.

"I would rather you be angry with me than enforce this silence."

The creature on the forest floor had stopped

moving, but she could feel his anxiety still. He wanted the dinner in her lap, but he feared her.

"How is it," she finally asked, "that William rides under the banner of the pope?" She did not ask to fulfill her wish to spy on William and his men. She asked because it was one thing she truly didn't understand.

"Lanfranc secured that."

Aleene finally turned, the stunning beauty of the man beside her still causing a breath to catch in her throat. But she squinted against the sight of his bright hair and strong chin and asked again, "How?"

It was Robert's turn to look away. "William put his plans to invade England in front of the pope as a crusade."

"A crusade?"

Robert cleared his throat. "Yes, a crusade to reform the English church." He crumbled the bread in his hand and threw the crumbs on the ground.

"Explain." She could say no more.

Robert threw some of his cheese on the ground. "It is hard, Aleene, to explain. Edward the Confessor promised the throne to William years ago when Harold and his father, Godwin, were in exile. William even obtained Harold's support. The man promised that support by swearing an oath over sacred relics. I know, I saw it happen. And then Edward died, and Harold used trickery to seize the crown . . ."

"Seize the crown?" Aleene surged up from the log, scattering her supper upon the ground. She heard something flutter about in the leaves and realized that the creature had come out of his burrow to eat the food Robert had thrown for it. She stopped a moment, watching the animal's backside disappear again into its hole. She shook her head and turned back to Robert. "How do you say Harold seized the crown? No such thing happened."

"He is not in line for the crown. If not from force, how did he obtain it?"

Aleene closed her eyes for a moment, amazed at Robert's accusation. "The witan."

Robert looked blank.

"The witan, the council of wise men, met and agreed that Harold should wear the crown." Aleene could not believe what Robert had said. "In fact, from what I have heard, Harold was reluctant to become king. How do you come to think otherwise?"

"It is what William told us." Robert looked away from her and gently threw out some more bread. "He said Harold had seized the crown that rightfully belonged to William."

"And the pope believed this?" Aleene turned away, her skirts stirring up the dry leaves on the ground. "But that does not explain why the pope would hand over his banner to William."

Robert hesitated, and Aleene turned again to stare at him.

"Lanfranc and William decided that the only way to truly encourage the invasion of England was to make a crusade of the project. They knew then that the men would not only be fighting for land and riches, but for"—Robert took a deep breath—"for salvation."

"I think I shall be sick." Aleene sat again, this time on the ground. She pulled her knees into her chest and stared at the ground.

"William sent an emissary to the pope, persuading him that the church here in England had begun to go its own way, that it needed reform."

"And through such lies, William rides with the pope's blessing, while Harold, the true king of this isle, shall be excommunicated if he fights." Aleene turned again to stare at the man beside her. "Your men will obtain salvation, and my king will burn in hell?"

Robert said nothing.

Aleene shook her head. "This world is not one I wish to be a part of any longer." She stood. "You men and your lies make me ill." She turned away.

"Aleene!" He grabbed her arm, stopping her. "What do you mean? What do you think to do?"

"I am going to Harold and tell him of this treachery. He must know that he risks not his soul if he fights against William."

"But he does, Aleene, he does." Robert continued to hold her arm, but it was a gentle touch, not harsh or hurtful as so many men had dared before. "The pope has ruled on this subject. William has his blessing. Any that go against it risk excommunication."

Aleene pulled away from his grasp. That the man before her had once again betrayed her loomed in her mind. She had thought him innocent. He was not. Still, even when Aleene had been confronted with the knowledge that Robert had pretended his simpleness, she had believed him to be a good man. He was not. He had been a part of this treachery. He still was.

"How could you?"

He read her mind, it seemed. For he lowered his gaze. "I thought William had the right to wear the crown of England. I supported anything he needed to do to obtain it."

"You thought William had the right to wear the crown?" Aleene made a huffing sound of disbelief. "More likely you saw the chance to become rich, Norman."

Robert nodded, staring now at the hedgehog who had come back out of his hole to snack on the crumbs that surrounded his burrow. " 'Tis truth you speak." He lifted his sky-blue gaze to her. "I wished for land. I wished to give my sons and daughters a name."

"And you shall, Robert *de Guise*. If you live to have them." She walked away, her heart no longer numb, no longer encased in ice. It hurt. Oh, it hurt.

"Do we not all do things we are ashamed of in the guise of our heart's desire?"

She heard him, but kept walking.

"Do we not all make mistakes because we cannot see clearly what our future should hold?"

"And so you think you have made a mistake?" she yelled, turning back to him. "Have you?"

"Yes." He rested his hands on his hips, his eyes piercing through to her unguarded heart.

She chewed on her inner lip, unsure. She had been so sure before. She had one goal: to be the Lady of Seabreeze. Nothing else mattered. And now, since this man had walked into her life, she always felt so uncertain. She felt so strange now, right now, at this very second. This man had betrayed her completely. He was an enemy with incredible potential to hurt her. To hurt the entire world she knew.

And what of her world did she want to protect? What of her world was so dear to her? What of her world gave her any peace, any happiness?

"Damn you," she said, clenching her fists against her side. She went to him. "You have changed everything. I can no longer be what I was, and yet you have given me nothing to look forward to. There is no world beyond this day. All that I have known is no more."

He reached for her. "Understand this, Aleene. I feel the same. I am bewildered and unsure. I came here wanting one thing, land. Now it is mine, and it means nothing. Everything I have believed until now seems to mean nothing."

She wanted this to be true so badly it made her entire body tremble. Please, she wanted to plead, tell me that what you say is the truth! And then she heard herself ask in a shaking, intense voice, "Are you true to me, Cyne? Do you speak your heart?"

And he kissed her, hard, his mouth taking hers, covering hers heatedly.

"With God as my witness, I am true to thee, Aleene," he said against her mouth, and then kissed her again, softly this time. He threaded his fingers in her hair, knocking her veil askew, and gently tongued her lips, kissed her neck, and took her mouth again.

Her body shook and her knees went weak. She held tight to her husband so that she would not fall. She felt one of Robert's hands trail down her back, pressing her into him. And she fit perfectly. He was tall, but so was she, and her body molded to his with perfect symmetry.

He surprised her by pulling away, and she realized with a start that she had surrendered to him. She stiffened and released her hold on him.

"Do not retreat from me," he said taking her hand in his. "I just think we should go somewhere more private."

"No." She yanked her hand away and twined it in her gown.

Robert stepped closer and put his arms around her. "Don't, Aleene. There is enough pain these days without adding to it. Let us at least be one in heart, if not in mind."

Aleene shook her head and broke from his hold. "How can you say that? We cannot be one in anything."

"I believe the kiss we just shared makes that untrue."

"A kiss? A kiss is nothing but lust. You betrayed me, you lied to me." She looked into his eyes and had to swallow before she said, "You are my enemy."

Robert feathered his fingers through his hair and closed his eyes for a moment. Aleene looked away in relief. She must remember not to look straight into those sky-blue eyes of his. They made it impossible to think.

She felt his hands against her chin, turning her face toward him. She resisted for a moment, then gave in, but kept her gaze at the collar of his rough tunic.

"Something happened to you." He stopped and Aleene watched as his Adam's apple bobbed in his throat. "Before. I know not who, or how, but you were hurt."

Aleene began to tremble. She clenched her fists.

"I would that I could kill the man, Aleene."

A black hole opened inside of her heart, sucking at the rest of her. The memories whirled through her, resisting the pull of the black hole.

Robert brushed her cheek with his thumb. "Tell me, Aleene, for you must realize what we have is very different from lust or anything dirty or bad."

Aleene jerked away from Robert's soothing hands. "Tell you?" she screamed, trying to make herself heard over the rush of noise inside of her. A cacophony of sound, the memories, the feelings running through her and the black hole pulling at them. "I can never tell you anything. I told you too much already when I believed you simple. When I thought you could never hurt me."

"I won't hurt you."

"You did hurt me!"

He grabbed her shoulders, but still did not hurt her. "I swear on my honor, Aleene, I shall never lie to you again! I shall never intentionally hurt you again."

Steeling herself, Aleene looked back into his eyes. "Honor? What do I know of honor?"

He blinked, his hands tightening on her shoulders. "Who did it, Aleene?"

She stared at him as the roiling emotions within her began to settle. She forced them down, made herself numb. "My stepfather." She shook free from Robert's suddenly limp hold. "If you take me to your bed now, Robert, you will not be the first." She turned on her heel and walked away. She knew he would not follow. He would think on her with disgust now. Which was for the better. No matter the strange physical pull between them, he was her enemy.

Chapter 12

⟨◦◦⟩

He stood frozen for a only a moment, his mind numb with shock. He had heard of such things, of course, but never had he been confronted with them. He had known only love his entire life. His parents doted on both him and his brother, though some thought his brother should be shunned because of his simple mind.

Now, his heart hurt for the woman striding away from him, her shoulders squared, her back straight. Tears blurred his vision, but he hurried after her, grabbing her hand and pulling her into his arms.

Yanking her veil away, he buried his face in her hair and held her. "I wish that I could kill him." He squeezed his eyes shut. "Savagely."

She resisted, standing like a board in his embrace, but he did not let her go. "You are so strong, Aleene, so strong and beautiful. You have endured terrible things alone, and I know you can endure more. But I don't wish you to. I want to be with you. I wish I could take all the pain from your life, but since I can't, at least allow me to stand with you in the pain."

She pushed away then. "What nonsense you speak, Robert de Guise. You are my pain."

Where Aleene's body had warmed his, now he felt the bite of the frosty wind. Robert noticed her fists at her sides, clenched as if awaiting a fight, and he knew a moment of complete frustration.

He wanted to grab her, force her to accept his arms around her, his comfort. But the thought of another man forcing himself upon Aleene stayed Robert's hand. "Come with me," he said finally, and turned toward his tent. He walked slowly, hoping she followed, but not turning to make sure.

When he reached the tent, Robert pulled aside the flap and turned. Aleene stood behind him, waiting. She had followed. "Come, I want to show you something."

She blinked at him, hesitating.

"I will not hurt you."

They stared at each other, the tent shuddering in the wind. Aleene broke their gaze, bending and entering the tent suddenly. Robert followed. His cot was small, so he grabbed the thick blanket his mother had sent with him and threw it on the ground. Then he carefully took his wife's hand. Although her fingers did not curl to grasp his, she did not pull away. Robert lowered himself to the blanket, pulling gently at Aleene's hand. She resisted for a moment, then followed.

"It is cold outside." He took Aleene's frigid hands and warmed them between his own. "Can you hear the wind?"

"Of course," she snapped. Still she did not pull away, so Robert knew she was intrigued.

"All around us is cold and war. The muddy ground has frozen into the ruts, the wind pierces clothes and touches skin with its icy fingers." Robert inched forward, erasing the space between them. "An army prepares for battle." Slowly, Robert reclined, pulling Aleene down with him.

She yanked her hands from his and stayed upright. "What are you doing?"

"I will not hurt you, Aleene. I promise."

She furrowed her brow and watched him with narrowed eyes as he took her hand again.

"Come." He tugged, and she stiffened. He sighed, then thought of something. "Here," he said, pulling a small knife from his boot. "Take this."

She stared at the blade in his hand, then looked back at him with trepidation.

"Take it, and keep it. If I hurt you, kill me."

Her eyes widened in shock.

He smiled at her and put the hilt of the knife in her hand. "Do you think I wish to die?" He reclined again on the blanket. "Come." He patted the ground beside him.

"I do not understand you, Norman," Aleene said as she came down beside him. Robert moved so that he pillowed Aleene's head on his arm. He tucked the blanket around them and got as close to Aleene as he dared since she still held his blade.

Aleene did not move.

"All of those things are still there, Aleene. The cold, the wind, the army. And yet here we lie together, warm."

He felt her body relax a bit. Robert stroked her back, hoping that the love he felt for her would transfer from his fingertips into her very soul. Maybe then that soul would have the strength to unearth itself.

"I love you," he said softly, looking into her dark eyes.

She blinked, breaking their gaze and staring at his chest. "Don't, Cyne. Robert."

He tried to lift her chin with his finger. "But . . ."

"Don't." She jerked her head away from his hand and reached around him.

For a startled moment he thought he was about to feel the blade of his knife in his back. Her lips against his made reason flee. She kissed him hard, and he lost himself in her until he knew that he would not be able to control himself if he went any further.

She tightened her arms around him as he pulled away.

"Do not leave me."

The sound of her voice near his ear sent shivers racing down his arms. He wanted her so badly it hurt, but he didn't want to frighten her. And he didn't want to hurt her.

"Ah, Aleene, I wish to never leave you."

"Then don't." She pressed against him, and kissed his lips, and then his chin and then his throat.

She dropped the knife then, because it truly did not matter. It really never had. She would never have been able to hurt Robert. And she knew deep within her heart that he would not hurt her.

All she cared about now was the force that seemed to pull them together. Her anger, hurt, everything had dissipated with the heightened sensitivity of her body. All she could think of was the storm that had begun to wage within her body, her heart hammering at her chest, her nerve endings hot as lightning bolts of sensation shot from her husband's fingers across her skin.

She heard the knife thud against the hard, dirt floor and plunged her fingers into the hair at Robert's nape.

They kissed, and Aleene felt dizzy. Wrapped in each other's arms beneath the blanket, the warmth sent beads of sweat slipping down

Aleene's temples. Robert groaned against her mouth, cupping her breast in his hand. The storm within Aleene strengthened.

With a deep shudder, she arched her neck, breaking their kiss. She could feel her husband's fingers at her throat, tugging at the string that gathered her gown there. Slowly and gently, he smoothed her gown down her shoulders. And then he dipped his head and nuzzled, just beneath her collarbone. Aleene swallowed and tried to breathe as Robert trailed light kisses down her neck and between her breasts.

She clenched her fingers in his hair.

He breathed hotly against her and continued his exploration, nibbling lightly at the underside of one breast. His hand wandered down her side, cupping her hip and pulling her more firmly against him.

Aleene closed her eyes feeling him against her body, his lips, his fingers. Fear had no place in her mind. It was as if they had been thus long before, only they had forgotten. And now they were together again.

"Is it good, Aleene? Do you feel the rightness of it?"

She trembled, for he had not moved away when he spoke and his breath heated her already hot skin until it seemed to burn. She opened her eyes and looked down at her husband. It was a moment of stillness; his eyes, dark in the blackness of the tent, stared up at her from under his brows.

"Don't stop, Cyne."

His entire body slid against hers as he pulled himself up to be level with her. Her womanly place seemed to clench, and she made a small sound of pure pleasure.

He kissed her mouth again, and she opened for him. The moment of peace passed, and her body took on the rhythm of the storm once more. Cyne trailed a line of kisses down her breast bone and slid his arm around to cup her bottom in his hand.

He nipped at the side of her breast, and she bucked toward him. Aleene bit at her bottom lip as he trailed kisses toward the tip of her breast. The loud rushing sound in her mind lessened as she waited, all feeling centering upon her husband's tongue on her body. Finally, Robert laved her nipple and sucked gently. As if a hard wind had gone through her, Aleene's entire body trembled as she dug her fingers into Robert's scalp.

Her legs came up, her heels pushing at the ground, lifting them both. She needed fullfilment. Robert rose above her, kissing her mouth as she pulled at the ties of his hose. He pushed them down and lifted her gown, still tangling his tongue with hers.

His hardness met her softness, and she stiffened. Her frenzy and need slipped slowly away as the same awful memories began to slither into her mind.

"Shh, darling," he whispered against her mouth. " 'Tis nothing to be afraid of. It will be even better than what we have been doing."

She breathed irregularly, and Robert kissed her again, lightly. The urgency that had led them to this point calmed. Aleene could feel her husband, still hard against her, but she could also feel his control as he said calmly, "I will never hurt you, Aleene."

He moved, sliding off of her. She made a whimpering sound, her hands folding in his tunic and stopping him. "Please, I'm afraid, but do not leave."

"I'm not going to." He smiled, then settled himself next to her on the floor and lifted her over him. "We shall do this with you in control, will that not make it better?"

She gasped, her legs automatically straddling Robert's.

He laughed. "Come, come, Aleene, you did very well this way the first time." Robert ran his hands up her thighs. "This time we will finish."

"Oh." Goose flesh covered her legs, and she shivered when he reached her hips and squeezed.

"Bring me into you, Aleene." He moved beneath her.

She sat up on her knees slowly. When she

moved, she saw the blade of Robert's knife on the floor beside them. She stared at it for a long moment, then turned her gaze upon her husband, at her mercy beneath her. She closed her eyes for a tiny second, then reached down and shoved the hilt of the knife so that the weapon skittered away from them.

Robert never moved.

"I wouldn't want us to hurt ourselves." She smiled and reached between them, taking him in her hand.

Robert held his breath, clenching his teeth together.

She moved forward slightly, her exposed breasts bouncing against her ribcage, her gown dropping even lower on her arms. He felt her wet against him and hitched in a small breath of air.

Aleene supported herself for a moment on her knees, her eyes dark, sensual, and, finally, trusting. He held himself still, waiting for her to move. All the while everything within him wanted to thrust forward and feel himself deep inside of her. Another breath, this one a bit deeper. Would he live through this? Surely he would die of agony.

She did not move down on him, but she took one of her hands and cupped his cheek. "I am so afraid, Cyne."

"Do you wish to stop?" Could he?

"No." He felt her quiver against his manhood. "The dark memories do not come. But I am still afraid that they might."

"If they come, I will stop."

She only nodded.

"Move against me, Aleene, feel me."

She rocked forward and then back, slowly, so slowly. Her eyes drifted shut, her head bent backward. He could feel her hair against his legs, trailing forward, then back. He would die soon, he knew he would.

He needed her down on him. Her breasts moved with her body, her throat exposed for his lips, but he could reach neither. He tightened his grip on her hips, willing her down.

And finally, she lowered herself. An inch at a time, she came upon him, the breath leaving her lungs in an audible woosh when finally she straddled him completely.

His member moved inside of her, and he held his breath, afraid he might spill his seed at any moment. He closed his eyes and tried to think of anything else. The hungry men outside, the battle soon to be fought, his wife above him, moving.

His eyes snapped open as he felt her bend toward him. Her breasts flirted with his chest. "Ah, Aleene."

"Oh, Cyne," she murmured back, her lips meeting his, her hands coming to rest on either side of his head.

They kissed lightly as Aleene moved her

body slowly over him. "That's right, darling. Do what feels good," Robert said against her full lips.

She moved faster and their kiss deepened. Robert felt as if he might drown in her. The dark, swirling kiss took on the rhythm of their mating, and Robert knew he had never felt so aroused. Every part of him moved with his wife, his tongue, his manhood, his heart. He groaned, taking her tongue deeper into his mouth and clutching her hips.

He was lost, completely. That she could do this to him seemed miraculous for she was truly a virgin no matter that she had no maidenhead to breach. He opened his eyes, saw her beautiful face above him, her dark hair enclosing them in their own world, and bucked forward, needing to be completely within her.

She gasped, and he came. Hard and fast, he felt himself convulse and pulse inside of his wife. She continued to sway above him, as she broke their long kiss and flung her hair aside, breathing erratically. He came so long he thought he might die, but then he realized that it was no longer him. He had spent himself, but his wife's body clenched his spasmodically. Robert watched her, running his hands up her sides to cup her heaving breasts.

"Ah," she moaned and shivered when he thumbed their peaks. And then she came down upon him and buried her face in his neck.

"Ah," he agreed, smiling and stroking her hair.

The silence in the tent seemed deafening, and he wondered if they had been loud. He tightened his arms around Aleene, not caring. Let everyone hear them, and envy them their closeness at this time of heartache. He turned on his side, feeling himself slide from Aleene's warm body, and held her tightly against him.

After a few moments her breathing lengthened and he felt all the tension leave her limbs. She slept.

But such a reprieve did not come to Robert. For his heart now loved as it had never done before. And it hurt. For his love was on the other side of the battle he must fight. He had promised never to hurt her again. And he wouldn't. But he would fight. His heart would no longer be in it, though, for William had lied.

Robert knew that William had been promised the crown, he had witnessed it himself. And for that Robert's loyalty still lay with his liege. But William had lied about Harold taking the crown of England by force. He had lied to secure backing from his people. And then he had lied again to secure backing from the pope. No, his heart would no longer be in it.

Robert looked at the shadowy figure of his wife beside him. He reached out and smoothed dark strands of hair from her face. His heart would be here, with Aleene. All he could hope is that she would understand. And that she would leave, so that she would be safe.

"I will not leave!"

"Shh, Aleene, you will wake the men."

"I do not care, Robert, I will not leave."

Robert sighed and ran his fingers through his hair. "You are truly the most stubborn woman."

"Do not call me names." She sat up. "You are being just as stubborn as I."

He pushed himself up and pulled her into his embrace. She went willingly, for even in anger she coveted his closeness. "I want you safe."

"And I want you safe, Robert. Come home with me."

He pulled away from her, his face in dark shadows. "You know that I cannot."

Aleene breathed in deeply and held it. On a sigh she said, "I know."

"We fight tomorrow. I want you to go to King Harold tomorrow morning at dawn before the fighting begins."

"No!" Aleene dropped her head into her hands. "Do not speak of the battle. I cannot bear this, Robert, I feel as if I am torn into a dozen pieces."

"I know, Aleene. I think I feel the same."

She looked up at him, grabbing his arms. "Then let us run. Now, Robert, let us run. Let us go somewhere far from here. Somewhere we can live without English or Norman. Somewhere we will not be enemies."

"Are we enemies, Aleene?"

"Do not speak word games, Robert. I swear I cannot ever believe I thought you simple!" She threw off the blanket that had twined around her waist and stood. Her dress hung in a rumpled circle at her waist. She tried to pull it up, but couldn't find the arm holes in the dark.

Her husband's hands stopped her. "We cannot run, Aleene." He pushed the gown down over her hips. "I will fight for my lord, you will fight for yours."

"I do not know what to fight for anymore, Robert, you have taken all the certainty out of my life."

Robert came against her, their naked bodies touching and warming each other. She shuddered. "Have I, Aleene? Have you no certainty in your life?" His large, beautiful hands rubbed her back, then slipped down to cup her bottom.

She clenched her fingers around his shoulders, holding him to her, yet keeping him away. "Yes!"

"Stubborn wench." He nipped at her lips.

"Don't call me names."

He chuckled and kissed her this time, deeply. Thought spiraled through her head and left, like the leaves on the wind. The blood thrumming through her veins, and the need of her body for her husband's took over all else. She melted against him, and he lowered her to the ground gently.

He came over her, a shadow in the dark, yet ever so comforting. And she surrendered to his touch, the callused fingers on her breasts, the warm lips against her throat. "Oh, Cyne."

He thrust inside of her, moving against her slowly, then coming faster and faster. Aleene came up to meet him, her hips moving against his. And the feeling came again, only this time faster. Her insides centered wholly on the point where their bodies met, a whirlpool of all her emotions, moving around and around until she was sucked down inside and came out the other side, convulsing with the most intense beauty and release she had ever felt. Her whole body shook with the force, and she shuddered with the effort to breathe.

He kissed her lightly, then pushed the tangled, wet hair from her forehead.

"I shall never be cold again," she said.

"I pray so, Aleene."

The next morning as the men prepared for war, Aleene left. With her back straight, and her eyes forward, she swore she would not turn around. But her newly melted heart would not allow such icy tendencies. She turned at the edge of the forest, and caught the gaze of her husband. He brought his fingers to his lips then blew a kiss to her. She forced her mouth to curve in a smile and pretended to catch his kiss.

Only she didn't put it to her mouth, she placed
it above her heart. And then she turned her
mount, made sure that her banner flew high,
and pushed the beast into the trees.

On the other side and up a hill, she met with
her king's men. They welcomed her, pointing
to Harold's tent. Aleene wanted nothing more
than to turn around and stay behind the lines
of her enemies, to stay with her love, but she
forced herself forward.

Harold sat with his brother and many other
earls, counseling before they went to war, but
he stood when he saw her and helped her from
her horse. "Aleene, I am happy to see you
safe," he said, his eyes weary and his voice as
unhappy as she had ever heard it.

"I have seen their troops, your highness,
would you like me to report?" she asked reluctantly.

He smiled a sad smile and shook his head.
"No, my dear, that will not be necessary. We
already know what we must, and you should
not be put in such a position to be disloyal to
your husband."

She fell to her knees and took her king's
hand. "I wish to be loyal to you, your highness." She felt as if she might crack in two.

"I know, Aleene, I know." He pulled his
hand from hers and patted it. "Arise and go to
Edith. She has professed her hope that you
would be with her this day."

Aleene swallowed hard and stood. "Of course!" She curtsied.

"She is beyond our camp, well away from harm. Go be with her, Aleene." He stepped away, but then turned back. "Always remember, Lady Aleene of Seabreeze Castle, you have been a woman worthy of my esteem, and I count myself grateful that you are with me." He smiled again and turned back to his circle of confidants.

Aleene stood very still for a moment. Her thoughts returned to the time she had just spent with her husband, and she closed her eyes. Was she worthy, truly, of her king's respect? Or had she again commited an act very close to treason? The agony of split loyalties churned within her breast as Aleene hitched up her skirts and walked through the cluster of lingering men.

She left the horse where it stood, knowing that another would use it. The heavy dew soon drenched her skirts as she strode toward the small tent she saw in the distance, but she did not feel chilled. She was not sure she would ever feel anything again. With that thought she remembered her husband's warm hands against her bare skin, and knew that she would definitely feel again, but only if she had Robert back. "Please, God," she prayed softly, "let him live."

With that prayer on her lips, she came to the tent. Edith sat next to a small fire on the ground, her slender hands cupping a bowl of warm broth. A servant busied herself at Edith's side.

With a sudden intake of breath, Aleene realized that if she had her wish, Edith would most probably not have hers. The agony hit her like a physical blow. They would sit here, in their new friendship, hoping for opposite outcomes of the same battle. Aleene froze, suddenly unsure if Edith would truly want her there.

Her friend looked up then, her eyes sending only a message of love. "Aleene!" Edith stood. "You are here!" She put her bowl down and rushed forward, engulfing Aleene in a warm embrace. "I prayed that you would come, I do not wish to be alone today."

Aleene stood still. "But are you sure?"

Edith hugged her tighter, forcing Aleene to return the gesture. "It is the only thing I am sure of this sad morning, Aleene."

They broke apart, and Edith took Aleene's hands in her own. "My goodness, you are like ice, Aleene!"

Aleene smiled then. "No, Edith, I am not. Finally, I am not."

Chapter 13

❦

They watched from afar. Aleene felt as if she might die at every clang of iron against iron that echoed up from the battlefield. She saw blood. She watched men die. But she was too far to see who they were. With every fallen man, she knew that Robert could be dead.

And then it seemed the English had won, for they had beaten away at the Normans, and the men from across the channel turned and ran. The English followed, yelling their success, and Aleene bowed her head. She felt a shallow relief, but could only pray that Robert still lived. As she prayed she heard Edith gasp beside her. Aleene glanced up, then clutched at the neck of her gown in disbelief. A large group of English had rushed after the seemingly retreating Normans only to be engulfed in another siege of fighting.

Aleene looked sharply up the hill to where King Harold stood. From where she sat, Aleene could not tell what was happening, but it didn't seem that the king was taking control.

"He is torn," Edith said from beside her. She shook her head. "My poor Harold cannot fight with all of his heart for he knows he fights not under the church's pennant."

"But the men!" Aleene again looked toward the English being slaughtered on the field. She could only watch in horror, until finally she closed her eyes against the ugliness of it all.

There were lulls in the fighting in which Aleene could see Edith's gaze frantically searching for her husband. Aleene herself no longer watched. At another gasp from Edith, Aleene knew that again a flank of Englishmen had been surrounded and subsequently slaughtered. She could only sit with her hands clasped, her mind trying valiantly to focus on prayer. And yet, she knew not what to pray for. Suddenly, she felt that all of her ambitions had been wrong. They had been bad. She was the reason that men were dying this day.

She knew that to be a foolish, even arrogant thought. Even if she had not been so prideful and allowed another to rule Seabreeze, William would still have come. She did not amount to anything more than a slight convenience in William's campaign that seemed filled with luck and conveniences.

Yet now, there was no convenience, only death.

She knew when she heard her friend sob, the end had come. Finally, Aleene looked up from her scattered prayers and thoughts. Edith stifled another sob, then stared back at her.

She wanted to reach for her friend, hold her, give back to her the comfort Edith had given. And yet, still, Aleene held back. Truly, she still knew not how to give of herself.

Edith finally came forward, putting her arms around Aleene. Neither woman cried. They only stood in the growing darkness, willing strength into each other.

Aleene spent the night not knowing whether Robert lived. She knew that he could not come to her, for their small camp was in the forest. The Norman men would not venture past the trees, for fear of traps. Aleene and Edith had watched all of the Englishmen flee, though. None remained behind trees to spring out at an unsuspecting Norman. None but the two women. Edith said that she had seen Harold fall, but she gave no further information. And Aleene did not wish to hear it. She still blamed herself.

When the sun finally showed itself once again, a messenger came from William. He wished Edith to pick Harold's remains from the dead. Aleene could only stare in shock at the messenger. "He cannot do such a thing himself?" she asked, her voice a high unnatural sound in the quiet morning.

"The bodies on the field are quite mutilated, my lady," the man said matter of factly.

"Shh, Aleene." Edith placed her steady hand over Aleene's trembling one. Then she turned toward the messenger. "Tell William, duke of the Normans, that I shall come to him after I have broken my fast."

The man nodded, bowed and left them.

Aleene shook with anger for her friend, for the island of the Englishmen. Her heart trembled with fear for her husband, her enemy. Would not the messenger have said something if Robert were alive? Was he also on the field, a mangled body?

"Will you come?"

Aleene looked toward her new friend.

"It is selfish of me to ask, I know."

" 'Tis not selfish, Edith. It would be my honor to come with you." She looked away. "I only wish I could be a better support to you in your need."

"You have helped me more than you know." Edith smoothed a hand over Aleene's veil.

Aleene could only nod. Her own need to go with Edith was more selfish than Edith would ever understand. She needed to know if Robert lived.

"Be not torn, Aleene."

Aleene jerked her gaze up. Edith's own eyes

were filled with such understanding it made Aleene shudder. It was a sad shudder of remembrance. Her mother had looked at her in such a way, many years ago, in the years before Tosig.

"Be steady."

Aleene swallowed hard and nodded.

Messengers were again sent to escort Edith and Aleene to the edge of the bloody battlefield. As they came upon the men who stood there, Aleene immediately recognized Robert. He watched her, his eyes keeping her upright. Inside she quaked with the realization that her husband lived. She could only stare at him across the muddy cold grass.

"We need you to identify the body of Harold, my lady Edith," William said in his booming voice. Aleene jumped, her thoughts focusing suddenly on her friend.

Edith only nodded. She looked out over the destruction before her, then took a few steps forward. She halted. A noticeable shiver ran the length of her spine, and Aleene watched as the woman clenched her fists at her side and took a deep breath, then waded, alone, into the sea of shorn limbs and bloody corpses. Biting her lip, Aleene clasped her hands tightly together and watched as Edith walked, her shoulders back, head high. The woman stopped beside a dead soldier and bent down next to him. Holding her breath, Aleene waited, hoping desperately Harold's lover had not found her king.

Edith touched her fingers to the eyelids of the dead man, closing them, and then stood again and proceeded into the horrific aftermath of death. Aleene let her breath out slowly, closing her eyes and giving a quick prayer of thanks. She still hoped deep within her heart that Harold had somehow gotten away and was at this very moment hiding, waiting to gather his people again and defend their country against invasion.

Opening her eyes, she looked over to where William stood, chest puffed up, hands behind his back, feet braced apart. She hated him. Glancing sideways, Aleene watched Robert bring his hand over his eyes for a moment.

As if sensing her gaze, Robert dropped his hand and looked at her, his eyes mirroring the clear blue sky. And she wanted to cry. For as much as she hated William, Aleene loved Robert with just as much intensity. But, for what it was worth, they were one man, for they had the same goal. To take England away from her people.

Aleene swallowed hard and clenched her fists. That she had wanted to stay with her husband the day before the battle suddenly made her feel sick. She had betrayed her king, her people. Not once, but twice, she had let her own feelings and needs lead her. She had done wrong. With a disgusted sigh, Aleene closed her eyes for a moment and berated herself for her weakness.

She had *not* deserved Harold's respect the day before. She had prayed for Robert's life, but not the life of her people. She fought the memories of warmth and security, and tried to fill her heart with strength. She would not be traitor to her people, she would not. Opening her eyes, she stared hard at Robert. His being was one of beauty, and she suddenly felt as if she could never look away.

Aleene forced her attention from him, forced herself to watch Edith's pathetic trek through a maze of broken bodies. With her heart, Aleene willed Edith to feel the strength of her gaze, feel the need in Aleene's soul to be there with her, help her through this.

What if it had been Aleene out there, searching through the remains for her lover's body? One sure to be found missing a head, an arm, a leg. Marked with blood, cuts, death. A tear streaked down her cheek, and she let it fall. Another followed, and then another, blurring Edith's image. She did not wipe them away or hide her face. What did she care if William saw her cry? What did she care if the whole world saw her cry? So they knew that she had vulnerabilities, so what? Let her enemies strike at them, for she knew herself to be strong enough to shield her weaknesses from attack. But she was no longer strong enough to hide them.

A great tearing cry startled Aleene from her inner thoughts and brought them back to the scene she witnessed. Swiping the tears from her eyes, Aleene saw that Edith kneeled on the muddy field, her head bowed over something that Aleene could not see, but could only guess to be the body of King Harold.

Aleene took up her skirts and ran toward Edith's hunched form. Her steps faltered as she neared her friend and saw the carnage that lay before her.

With another bitter cry, Edith stood and swung away from the body that no longer resembled anything human. Aleene opened her arms to her friend and pulled the weeping woman against her, holding her, rocking her, but saying nothing.

Aleene squeezed her eyes shut against the nauseating sights around her and listened with agony to the sobs that ripped through Edith's body.

"Are you sure?" she finally asked softly when Edith had stopped crying. Edith nodded against Aleene's shoulder, not letting go to look into her face. Aleene squeezed her friend tightly and they stood silently for a long moment. One woman saying goodbye to a lover, the other saying goodbye to her king and country.

A movement behind her made Aleene start,

and she saw that some of William's men had come to take Harold's body.

"No!" Edith separated herself from Aleene and held her hand in front of her. "Touch him not!" Her gaze angry and hostile, Edith took from a voluminous pocket of her gown a folded purple cloth which she laid out on the ground next to the broken and dismembered body of her love.

Aleene watched with growing horror as Edith moved to pick up Harold's head. "No, Edith do not do this to yourself!" she cried. "Come away with me. William would not dare but to give Harold a Christian burial."

Edith looked up into Aleene's eyes, her own shimmering with tears. "I know, Aleene." She paused, biting her lip. "William shall bury the king of the English in the church, but I need to bury the husband of my heart." She turned to her macabre task once again.

Aleene watched, her stomach churning with sick fury at what her friend must do. With a quick backward glance at the duke who stood silently watching, and her own husband, Aleene knelt beside Edith and carefully helped the woman move Harold's remains to the cloth.

Her hand's shook as she bit back the bile that collected in her throat. A cold, screaming wind rattled through the leafless trees around them, and an uncontrollable shiver racked Aleene's body. And then she felt warmth, a comfortable, loving warmth that could come from only one person. His large hand came over hers, stilling it for a moment, and his arm encircled her waist from behind. For just a small second in time, they stayed that way, Robert's warmth chasing the chill from her heart. She knew she would hate herself later for allowing the closeness, but at that moment she needed anything human to help her through such an inhuman task.

And then he moved, helping the women as they brought Harold's scattered remains to the purple cloth and wrapped them. As Edith went to hoist the heavy, bulky package, Robert stopped her. Without a word, Aleene's husband reverently took the cloth and its sacred contents from the woman.

Aleene held her breath, waiting to see what Edith would do. But the mother of Harold's children only stared into Robert's face, and then turned. With long, strong strides Edith walked east, toward the ocean, away from them.

Robert followed a few feet behind the straight form of the proud and devoted widow.

Sure that at any moment, William's outraged bellow would echo through the small, shallow valley, Aleene waited for a moment, her gaze never leaving her husband.

Out of the corner of her eye, Aleene saw the bulky form of the Bastard Duke as he also followed Edith. Turning her gaze full on him, Aleene realized that he was neither angry nor about to bring Edith back. He just followed, his head bent against the wind, his battered helmet held at his side.

A tear escaped and splashed down Aleene's cheek as she too went after the somber entourage. *Oh, if only!* Her thoughts screamed through her as she trudged along the muddy ground and through the remains of death that surrounded her. *If only!*

But if only *what* came back to her. If only William had stayed on his side of the channel? Then Robert would never have found her. If only Harold had been victorious? Then she would now be taking her husband's battered body away to be buried.

That she couldn't stand to think of Robert dead made Aleene quake. She shouldn't care. She hated the part of herself that was so very glad that she could look ahead of her and see the wide, strong back of her husband before her. She rebelled against that part of her. Her people now faced death, poverty, and subjugation. And her husband had helped to establish that.

Oh, if only there were no such thing as war, hatred, hurt, her heart cried out. *Oh, if only!*

As they came nearer the cliffs that looked out over the gray, churning sea, the wind strengthened, tugging at Aleene's gown and swirling her hair about her in a tangled mass. Pulling her hair back with one hand, Aleene looked before her and realized that Edith had stopped.

When she reached the others, Aleene saw that some of William's men were bent over, digging. Using rocks and helmets as tools, they dug a hole in the cliff overlooking the sea.

Alarm raced through Aleene. Did Edith wish to bury Harold here, on unconsecrated ground? Surely not! It was paganistic! "Edith!" Aleene cried, coming to stand next to her friend. "You cannot bury him here!"

Edith turned, her eyes sedate and now tearless. "I was never married to Harold by the church, Aleene. When the people of England bury Harold in their church, they will bury another man, another's husband." She stared down at the growing hole, then looked back at Aleene. "This day, here, I shall bury *my* husband, my love."

Aleene backed away a few steps, her mind trying to grasp what happened here. Robert still held Harold's body wrapped in the purple cloth, but his gaze found hers. He held her there, communicating his strength through his eyes. With a questioning expression, he nodded. Lowering her lashes, Aleene answered his question with her own nod. Yes, she was all right. If Edith could do this, so could she.

As they stood on the wind-whipped cliff, no one spoke. The only noise was that of stone pounding against earth. And, also, stone hitting stone as William Malet, one of Harold's companions, one of his monks, chiseled out an epitaph.

Aleene watched the man work, slowly reading the words that he painstakingly brought out of the stone. *By command of your wife, you rest here a King, O Harold, That you may be guardian still of the shore and sea.*

Numbed by the cold wind and even colder emotions that seemed to freeze her very heart, Aleene could only watch as, finally, Edith buried her husband in the earth, covering him with dark soil and the stone that said what she wished it to say.

Through it all William stood silently watching, allowing Edith to do as she wished. When it was over, Edith bent and kissed the grave, then turned and walked back from where they had come.

William threw his head back then and proclaimed with a large booming voice, "I now take the title of king of the English!"

His men hurrahed mightily, all except for Robert, who only watched Aleene. At the yell, her heart seemed to drop like a stone to her toes, and she wobbled, her knees suddenly buckling beneath her.

Robert reached her in two strides, his arms coming around her, his warmth seeping through her clothes to war with the numbness that pervaded her soul. "Let yourself hurt, Aleene. I shall hold you up."

Closing her eyes to the great rushing tide of relief that swamped her with his words, Aleene straightened away from her husband. Stiffening her shoulders and tilting her chin in the air with a bravado that came from someplace hitherto untapped, Aleene moved away from Robert and from William and followed Edith.

Edith walked alone and so would she.

Part III

Chapter 14

"Men are stubborn, weary creatures."
Aleene dragged the veil from her
hair and plopped down upon a chair. She
sighed, then looked at Berthilde. "The archbishops are on the verge of giving up. I know. I can
see it in their eyes."

"Perhaps we should be gettin' home then,
milady." Berthilde bustled about the small
room they had lived in for over a month. The
noise from the London street outside filtered
through the small window, and Aleene had a
sudden yearning to hear the crash of waves
against rocks rather than the cacophony of
voices that never seemed to cease.

"No." Aleene pushed the homesickness
away. "I will not give up. We cannot just lie
down and allow a foreign man to be king."

" 'Tis not your fault, milady, that the Bastard
Duke prowls about upon English land." Berthilde went to the window and dumped a pot

267

of wash water down to the street. "You have spoken to the archbishops." She turned, the old ceramic pot in her arms. "You have spoken with the witan. You've done what you could. 'Tis home we should be gettin' to now, and leavin' the guilt behind." She nodded as if that ended the discussion and went back to her chores.

Aleene huffed a small laugh. "You do not approve of my exploits, Berthilde?"

"I approved. You wished to help bring Edgar to the throne. You've done all you can. You can do no more here."

Aleene heard the serious harshness in Berthilde's voice and the amused smile left her face. "You have heard something."

"Only that William's army has reached Wallingford. There is sure to be another battle soon."

Aleene sighed and dragged her fingers through her tangled hair. "I have heard the same." She sat silently for a moment, her thoughts on her husband. He was close. Oh, so close. She had not seen him in over a month, and truthfully, she missed him desperately. But she would not say it, not out loud. For she wished that she didn't. She wished that she had never met him. Her own involvement in the landing of William's troops haunted her, as did her torn loyalties as she had watched King Harold brought down before her eyes. She would not, could not, stray from her course now. She would fight William and her husband with everything she had, for to do anything less would be to kill her soul.

She jumped from her sprawled position and yanked her veil back on her head. "I go back to the great *men* of England." She secured the veil haphazardly. "I cannot sit about when I could be persuading these good-for-nothing men to get off their duffs and do something."

"Get off your arse, you son of a bastard pig."

Robert looked up startled, the hard bread slipping from his grasp and landing on the frozen ground.

Duncan laughed and squatted beside him. "Scared ye, didn't I?" He laughed again, the great belly laugh that always made Robert smile. "I do like to scare ye, Robert de Guise, I do like to scare ye."

Robert snorted and grabbed the bread at his feet. "I thought I told you to stay at Seabreeze." He tried to tear off a piece of bread with his teeth, but couldn't. He pulled harder.

"And let you have all the fun?" Duncan took a folded cloth from one of his pockets and slowly uncovered a beautiful loaf of bread.

"Holy Jesus and Mary." Robert stared at the food in Duncan's hands.

"Not quite." Duncan laughed again and handed over his prize.

Robert had to take a deep breath and steady his hands. It had been a long time since he had partaken of fresh food. He no longer cared if Duncan had left Seabreeze in the hands of a nanny goat, all he could think of was putting his mouth around that loaf of bread. But he controlled himself and tore off only a small piece. Then he tried desperately to savor every crumb as he chewed.

"From the looks of it, I'd say I was wrong about you having all the fun," Duncan said, then refused the bread Robert offered. "No. 'Tis for you, Robert."

Robert stared at it for a moment, then stood and took it to some of his men sitting around a small fire a few feet away. He broke the bread and handed it out, then returned to Duncan. "And so, Duncan, tell me now what you do here."

"Aw, Robert, 'tis boring at Seabreeze. Your lady wife is not there, the people stare at me with hatred. Your property is in good enough hands. I needed to be here, where things are happening."

At the mention of his wife, Robert stared off in the general direction of London. He knew she was there. Duncan had informed him that she had never returned to Seabreeze. And spies had reported of an outspoken woman trying to persuade the people of London to fight against William. He sighed. He knew why she was there. It was as if she were doing penance for her sins. But they were not her sins.

A movement near William's tent caught Robert's eye, and he turned to look. A man shook William's hand, then strode to one of the small ponies the English rode and took off down the muddy track. Robert squinted after the man's retreating form. Something about the man struck Robert as familiar. But the strange thing was that the man who had just clasped William's hand in a conspiratorial grip was English.

Aleene stood again before a meeting of the archbishops and the other great men of England. She rubbed at her forehead and nearly laughed. The great men of England were now mostly boys. Edgar, the one she was fighting to be made king, was not yet grown. He spoke still in a high childish voice, looking more like he should be out playing with his peers than sitting upon a throne.

And yet, she would rather he were to rule than a foreigner. Aleene dug her fingernails into her palms and cleared her throat. "Gentlemen, we cannot allow fear to guide us."

"You ask us, then, not to fear God?" Stigand, archbishop of Canterbury demanded, his brows furrowed.

"She asks you to be killed, that is what this woman asks."

The booming voice from behind her made Aleene jump. She turned to see Aethregard stride into the room, his soulless gray eyes hard on her.

She had heard nothing about him for so long, that truly she had hoped he was dead. Now, to see him before her very much alive and obviously strong and healthy made her legs go weak.

"Harold banished you from court, Aethregard." Aleene gritted out between her teeth. "You tried to kill me."

"I did no such thing, sister mine. And, may I remind you, Harold is dead." He flicked a cold glance over her, then turned to the men who stood about the long wooden table. "Why do you let this woman speak as a man should?"

Aleene felt a burning spark of fury ignite within her at his words. "How dare you!"

"She is a woman of wealth, Aethregard, a woman of property." One of the men interrupted her.

"A woman who handed over her property to a Norman. A traitor."

She wanted to slap him, wanted to see the red outline of her own fingers on his cheek, but she took a deep breath and waited a small moment to calm herself. "Why do we speak like this of each other? We are on the same side in this fight, Aethregard. Let us work together to keep England out of the hands of a foreigner."

"A foreigner?" Aethregard lifted his chin and let out a belly laugh. "You surely are one to speak, Aleene of the black Spanish eyes."

The silence that surrounded them at that taunt seemed to slice right through to Aleene's heart. She had spent her life as the outsider. But still she was English, no matter what she looked like. She had made a mistake in taking Cyne into her home, and now she wanted nothing more than to right that wrong and fight for an English king. "Aye, the eyes are from Spanish blood, my brother," she finally said, pinning him with an icy stare. "But the heart is English. Now," she turned to survey the men before her, "let us not allow a foreign bastard the right to reign over English men."

" 'Tis not so easy as that, Aleene of Seabreeze." Stigand said slowly. "William rides under the pennant of the pope. Our defeat at the hands of the duke shows the will of God."

"I have already told you, sir, while I was within the enemy camp, I learned that William used trickery to secure the pope's backing. How could he not? Harold was never even brought before the pope to state his own side."

Aethregard cleared his throat. "If I may," he smiled at Aleene, then turned toward the assembled men. "Of this trickery she speaks, I know nothing. But I do know the pope speaks the word of God and the pope has spoken in favor of William. That means God has chosen

William as our king. God has spoken, but we still stand about listening to a woman." He spat out the last word with disgust.

Aleene turned on Aethregard. "And you call me a traitor?" She took a step toward him. "What you say here today is the ultimate in cowardliness."

"You are most definitely a traitor if you call me, a warrior at Harold's side, a coward."

"A warrior? Ha!" Aleene stepped closer to her stepbrother, her hands clenched at her side. "I did not see you there, Aethregard. You did not fight at Harold's side." She turned to the men seated at the table. "This man should have no say here. Harold banned him from court."

"No, Aleene." Stigand stopped her, his hand raised in front of him. "Wait." He stepped away from the table and walked toward Aleene and Aethregard. "Do not bring your sibling squabbles here. We do not have time for them." Then he turned toward the men. "It is hard for me to do this. I want an English king with all of my heart, but I fear on this point Aethregard is right. God has spoken. Since he rides beneath the banner of the pope, I must, as an archbishop, support William of Normandy. Tomorrow morning, I shall ride out with the other archbishops to where William camps and tell him of our decision."

"No!" Aleene cried, rushing forward.

Stigand held up his hand once again, stopping Aleene. "It is the will of God."

Aleene shook with the anger that roiled through her, but all she could do was watch as the men nodded and bowed their heads in prayer.

Aethregard also bowed his head, but his gaze caught hers before his eyes closed. Triumph gleamed there, and pure hatred. Aleene heaved a sigh of deep frustration and stalked from the room. She stopped only long enough to whisper to her stepbrother, "If I see you again, ever, I shall kill you."

"As you did Tosig?" The hatred from his gaze now coated his words.

Aleene blinked. "Tosig?" She shook her head, then, sure that Aethregard was touched in the head. "I only wish I could count his death as one of my deeds!" She turned her back on her stepbrother, hoping never to see those soulless gray eyes again.

The weak sun had dipped below the horizon, leaving a gray, cold, darkening dusk. Robert hunched his shoulders against the sharp wind that scattered leaves about them with a lonely whining sound. Duncan had gone to bed already, but Robert could only sit staring into the fire, watching the flames form into faces and ghosts. His father was there, a book in front of him. His brother and mother danced before him, their smiles turning garish as the flames licked at the blackening night. He thought of the warm hearth in his mother's home, where he had sat and learned his studies from his father, and where his mother had told stories on cold nights. Until Robert had been ten, she had told stories to him and John, and then she had kissed them both and tucked them into bed.

Finally, Robert had ducked away from the kiss, and told her he was too old. Now Robert stared into the fire and wished he had let her kiss him until he was thirty. She had wanted him to follow in his father's footsteps, be a learned man, stand behind the dukes of Normandy. But Robert had more ambitious plans. He wanted wealth. He wanted property. He didn't want to be at the whim of some over-haughty simpleton.

Robert laughed, a hollow sound in the night, and threw a small stick into the fire. Wealth. He had it now. He was the lord of his own castle. He had everything he had once only wished for. His dreams were his, they were in his hands. He looked down at his dirt-stained fingernails. But now that he had them, he realized they were not what he wanted.

He wanted Aleene. He wanted what his mother had always taught him to want. Love, hope, caring. His home had been full of those things, and now, more than anything in the world he wanted to give them to Aleene. He wanted to fill her life with laughter and light.

He wanted to see her smile, watch her dance, and feel her happiness. He wanted to make love to her body, and hold her heart in his hands. Robert turned his palms up in his lap and stared at the calluses that hardened them. Instead his hands were empty, and his own heart was being eaten away by despair.

A noise from the track that ran along their camp caused Robert to lift his eyes. A man on horseback clattered down the road, his outline dim, but still noticeable. Robert watched as the man headed for William's tent.

The man swung off his small horse, slicked his fingers through his hair, and went to the tent door. And in that instant Robert knew him. The feelings that had pushed him to kill in battle were nothing to the hatred that seethed inside of him now. He stood, throwing the blanket away from his shoulders, and marched toward William's tent. He brushed past the sentries and threw open the flap. "How dare you come here, you cowardly son of a dog!" he yelled.

Aethregard turned quickly, his face blanching to a grayish hue.

"Robert!" William interrupted his next outburst. "We have good news!"

"I have no care for good news, I wish only to kill this man." Robert took a step toward Aethregard, who retreated until his back was against the side of the tent.

"I do not have to take abuse from you!" It was a whine more than a statement and Robert scowled at his wife's stepbrother.

"You are horse dung beneath my feet."

"I would say the two of you are acquainted?" William asked, walking to stand in front of Aethregard. "Robert, do listen, Aethregard has brought good news. Our quest shall be one step closer to the end tomorrow."

Aethregard nodded. "Yes, Stigand, the archbishop of Canterbury comes over to our side tomorrow. It is only a matter of time now."

The news should have made him beyond elated. Instead, Robert could think of nothing but Aleene's sickening cries as he thought she lay dying after ingesting the poison given to her by the man now hiding behind his liege. "So, you are a traitor now, Aethregard? How fitting."

"I am not. I fight for what is right."

"You fight for who is winning, you swine."

"Come now, Robert." William laid his hand on Robert's arm. "There is no need for this. We celebrate, for tomorrow we come closer to victory."

"You celebrate." Robert shook off William's hand. "I shall leave Duncan here in my place. I have business that must be attended to." William raised his brows, his eyes narrowing. Robert knew he had probably lost any more land or booty that William might have given him, but he didn't care. He didn't care in the least.

Aethregard stepped out from behind William, his demeanor triumphant. "Robert, your diplomacy is a trifle lacking, is it not?" He smiled showing graying teeth and blackened gums.

"You have seen nothing, yet." Robert smiled hugely, pulled back his fist and hit Aethregard as hard as he could in the face. Blood spurted from Aethregard's nose as he bent forward screaming. "That was for Aleene. Don't you ever touch her again." Robert swiveled on his heel and left the tent. The despair he had felt only moments ago was completely gone. Hope reigned in his heart once again.

She was asleep, she knew, but it seemed that some frantic activity happened around her. Finally, Aleene opened her eyes to see Berthilde throwing clothes into a trunk. Aleene leaned up on her elbow, squinting in the dim light of a single candle. "What do you do, Berthilde? Why are you up?"

Berthilde turned to her just as another figure entered the room. "Ah, you awake my sleeping beauty."

Her heart fluttered and then beat heavily against her chest as Aleene stared at the large outline of Robert in the shadows. "You!"

"We wanted to let you sleep as long as possible." He came forward, the candlelight illuminating the planes of his face. "Now, though, you must be quick."

"Quick?" She sat up and rubbed her eyes. "Why are you here?" Aleene opened her eyes and stared at her husband. "What in the name of heaven is going on?"

"I am taking you home." Robert went down on his knees at the side of the bed, taking her hands in his. "We both fight for a cause that is beyond our governing. We can do no more."

Aleene yanked her hands out of Robert's. "What do you say? I will not leave here!"

"Aleene, Stigand is going over to William's side tomorrow morning. It is only the beginning of the end for the English resistance. Surely you know that you can do no more."

"How is it that you know such a thing, Robert de Guise?" Aleene narrowed her gaze on Robert's haggard face. "Have you been spying again?"

"No, 'tis another that spies now, Aleene." He sighed heavily and pushed himself up to stand next to the bed. "You can do no more here, Aleene. And I wish only to take you home and begin the healing. I am tired of fighting."

Aleene threw back her covers and jumped out of bed. "You should have thought of that before, Robert." She turned to face him. "Perhaps before you journeyed across the channel to kill."

Robert sighed. "Please, Aleene, let us go home."

"I shall not go with you!"

"You shall."

"What do you propose to do? Tie me to a cart and haul me away?"

"If I must."

"Oh!" Aleene whirled away but had nowhere else to go in the tiny room. "Oh!"

"I don't want to do such a thing, but I will do what I must. And right now we should be home."

"Home?" She clenched her fists at her sides. "Home? So you will go back to Normandy?"

"You know what I mean, Aleene. We must begin the . . ."

"Healing?" Aleene turned on Robert. "Yes, you said that already. You wish to heal the wound that you ripped open? I fear 'tis not possible, Robert. I fear 'tis a fatal wound you have inflicted upon *my* home."

With a thump Berthilde closed the chest she had shoved full of clothes. "This is ready to go, my lord," she said to Robert, then turned to her mistress. "I have laid out a kirtle for you, Lady Aleene. It will do ye well for the cold journey ahead."

Aleene could only stare. "You would follow this man? Our enemy, Berthilde?"

Robert sighed as he shouldered the heavy

trunk and left the room, but Aleene continued to watch her old servant.

"Choose your enemies well, milady. 'Twould do no good to put a friend in that role." She arched her brows and nodded, then left quietly.

With a low, frustrated groan, Aleene dropped onto her bed. "I cannot leave now. I cannot," she wailed into the scratchy wool coverlet. She had to stay. She had to try and right the wrong she had started with her marriage to a Norman spy. Oh, but she did *want* to go. She did. She longed for home, longed to hear the waves as she slept and feel the salt air on her skin.

"We are leaving, Aleene."

Aleene looked up to see Robert standing in the doorway. She stood and slowly pulled the rough kirtle over her head. Turning away from him, she fingered her heavy hair. Berthilde had left a veil for her on the table by the window. Aleene felt a bitter smile curl her lips as she lifted the material, then anchored it to her hair. Just a few short weeks ago she would have never dressed so, not caring that her shift was wrinkled, that her veil was askew, her hair unbrushed. And to do it all in front of a man. Aleene turned again, her eyes searching out Robert's in the wavering shadows.

"You have taken everything I value." She hadn't meant to say it aloud, but it didn't matter.

"Perhaps it shouldn't have been."

"But it was, nonetheless."

Robert advanced on her, and Aleene stiffened. He stopped just short of touching her. "I wish to give you all that I have ever valued."

"And that is what I should hold dear? Such a high-handed attitude, my lord."

Robert cocked his head to the side, his eyes never leaving hers. "I would hope that we would not fight over every small word, Aleene. I love you, and I want only to give you everything you always deserved to have."

Aleene blinked, then brushed past him rudely. She did not turn around as she said, "I shall fight you, Norman, be sure of that."

Chapter 15

The icy wind had hardened the muddy ruts beneath the wheels of the cart, making their journey difficult in the extreme. The frozen demeanor of the woman at his side did nothing to help. Robert grunted as the cart slammed over another stone, then nearly bit his tongue clear off when they bounced over a large hole in the road.

"My backside shall never be the same," Berthilde grumbled from her place in the back of the cart.

Aleene did not make a sound. She steadied herself by holding to the plank upon which they sat, her knuckles white with the strain. Her face, though, showed nothing but an icy indifference.

He had tried over the last couple of days to speak to her as they made their slow way through the countryside. Aleene would not acknowledge him with even a nod. As they passed through several burned-out villages, she paid more attention to the few remaining people, all sick and hungry. Aleene gave away their own meager provisions, then turned back to him, her face devoid of emotion. He thought he detected a hint of defiance glinting in her black eyes the first time she gave a poor woman some of their bread. But instead of trying to stop her, as he was sure she wished, Robert helped her disperse of their small hoard.

The first night they stopped, he had been able to kill a couple of rabbits. They had eaten one and saved the other to give to the hungry they knew they would encounter. Fortunately, Robert's luck with his bow had held out, or they would have been weak with hunger now.

The first salty smell of ocean Robert caught was on the third day of their journey. He sat straighter, hoping it hadn't been an illusion.

"Be home right soon now, my lord." Berthilde nearly laughed from the back of the cart. "I can see that snout of yers pulling at the air like a dog after a bone." She chuckled at her own words.

Robert couldn't help the smile that spread over his face. "Ah," he sniffed mightily. "'Tis the best thing I've smelled in a long while."

Beside him Aleene showed no reaction to their banter. He turned to her. "Aleene, do you smell your home?"

She blinked down her nose at him. "I smell

the rotting stench of a Norman swine," she said, then pinned her gaze on the track in front of them.

Robert let out a large sigh and flicked the reins over the ponies' backs. He had hoped she might be ready to speak with him by the time they reached Seabreeze. Obviously, that was not to be the case. They journeyed on in silence except for the grunts Berthilde emitted when the wagon hit a particularly large rut.

The trees around them thinned finally, and they saw Pevensey before them. One of William's ships sat anchored in the harbor, looming dark behind the small, quiet town. And the temporary fort William had built in the Roman ruins still sat upon the hill. No children rushed about them as they went through Pevensey. The quiet grated on Robert's nerves as he snatched quick looks at Aleene out of the corner of his eye. He couldn't help but remember the day they had walked through the village, everyone boisterously happy and excited about the new lord of Seabreeze Castle. They were no longer thrilled with him Robert realized as he noticed accusing eyes watching him from out of darkened huts.

Clenching his teeth and facing forward, Robert took a deep breath and resolved again to make everything right. A daunting task, and probably completely unobtainable, but he would try. His loyalty still lay with William,

and always would, for he had grown up with
William. He understood William. But he had
seen enough bloodshed. William had gotten
what he wanted; now Robert needed to set his
sights on his heart's ambition. A home. Not because with it lay wealth and power, but because
with it came love and happiness. Robert
glanced over at the beauty at his side and tightened his grip on the reins. At least he hoped
that love was still there. He hoped with all his
heart he had not killed the only thing worth-
while in his life.

The men at the guard tower were his men.
Anger clawed at her breath, forcing her to gulp
air into her lungs. He looked over at her, and
she sat very still, keeping all of the turmoil that
roiled about inside of her from showing on her
face. The gate opened slowly, and they rode in.

"We shall need supper, Berthilde." Robert's
commanding voice sounded beside her, startling Aleene.

"Yes, milord." Berthilde bounded from the
wagon as if she were twenty years younger and
immediately began yelling orders at people.

"Take care of the ponies, Wat." Robert
handed the reins to one of her servants. "Nan,
see Aleene to her chamber. Order hot water for
her to bathe."

Robert turned toward her. "Supper should be
ready soon so that we might get rid of the hun-

ger that has plagued me for days." He smiled.

Without a word to him, Aleene slapped away the hand Nan offered to her and descended from the cart on her own, praying that her lungs would continue to draw air. She gazed quickly at the people gathered about. They looked back at her, hatred and pure animosity in every eye.

The little progress she had made after Tosig's death was gone. Now, not only did her people think her unworthy of being the lady of Seabreeze, but clearly they thought her a traitor. With a deep breath, Aleene drew to her full height and began to make her way toward the great hall.

Like so many times before, Aleene had to cover her weakness with a show of strength. Only now she had to use so much more energy to find that strength.

She actually felt tears threaten the back of her eyes and burn her throat. Tears had never been a problem before. They had never been an option before. Aleene took a deep breath and cursed Robert. He had given her security and then taken it away, and that was harder by far than never having experienced such a feeling in the first place.

The people standing about parted before her like the Red Sea at Moses' bidding and it reminded her of the day William had landed. That fateful, humiliating day when she had watched Cyne turn into Robert, then had been forced to hand over Seabreeze to the monster. How dare he do this to her again?

Twice he had ground her authority beneath his boot heel. Aleene squared her shoulders as she made her way quietly to her chamber. Passing his men at the entrance to the great hall, Aleene had to use all of her control not to spit on them. She looked at them, hoping that all of her hatred was clearly readable in her eyes, then went to her room and closed the door gently behind her. He would not win. For him to win meant death to her. She would not submit again to a man whose only history with her was hurt and deceit.

She waited for morning to mount her defense. At dawn, though, she went forth to stake her claim as lady of the castle. She found Berthilde in the kitchens. "Tell Cuthebert I wish to speak with him," she said, then turned to the women working with Berthilde. "I shall supervise the women."

Nan glanced up from her work near a steaming kettle. Her brows lifted in defiance, but she said nothing and went back to stirring with a long wooden stick.

Berthilde glanced from the women back to Aleene and shook her head.

"Now, Berthilde, go."

Her old maid stared at her for a long moment then left.

Aleene took a deep breath, feeling with every nerve of her body the anger that emanated from the women around her. Again, she felt the fear that had controlled her every action the months after Tosig's death. She hated to fear her people.

Just as she determined to say something, anything, something hit her from behind and she fell.

" 'scuse me." Perry from the stables held a hand out to her. "Was carrin' them rags in and didn't see you there."

Aleene blinked at Perry's outstretched hand, then back at the small mound of cloth at his feet. Not exactly a mountain of rags, definitely not enough to make it hard for the man to see where he was going. Aleene laid her own hand carefully in her servant's. He pulled her roughly to her feet, then gathered the rags and continued through the large room. Aleene bit at the inside of her lip as she realized that Perry had forgotten to address her properly.

She stood a bit straighter and tried to dredge up her facade of courage. She pursed her lips and squinted about at the women who stood watching her.

Nan stood with a fist at her hip, a slight tilt to her lips. Hedwig's brows were raised comically as she nudged the young girl next to her. Aleene heard a muffled snicker from behind her mingle with the soft roll of boiling water.

"Cuthebert awaits you in the hall, milady."

Berthilde interrupted the tense moment, bustling into the kitchen and wiping her hands on her apron. "I'll see to the cooking now."

Aleene let her hard gaze fall upon each woman in the room before she nodded at Berthilde and left. She kept her head high as she made her way through the bailey. Cold, angry eyes turned in her direction as she walked; nudges, nods, and hissed words followed in her wake.

"Norman whore."

She heard the softly heated words and stopped. When she turned, though, every head was bowed to a job, all hands were busy. Aleene searched the bailey with her gaze. "I am the lady of Seabreeze Castle. If any of you wish to forget that, you may leave this place!" She continued to look about her for a long moment, then turned on her heel and entered the hall.

"Cuthebert!"

Her steward looked up quickly from the ledgers spread before him. " 'Tis busy I am, Lady Aleene, what do you wish to speak to me about?"

Aleene's frustration grew stronger. "Cuthebert," she said as she went to sit across from him. "I am the lady of this castle and if I wish for you to go catch frogs at the stream you will do it with pleasure!" The minute she said it, she knew that she shouldn't have. Aleene sighed, but kept her back straight and her gaze upon the angry little man before her.

"Really, *Lady* Aleene, you would have me catch frogs rather than keep *your* castle running smoothly?"

Aleene leaned over the table. "I shall not tolerate another word of impertinence. Do you understand, Cuthebert?"

"*Impertinence*? And which word was *impertinent*?"

Aleene stood quickly. "You try my patience."

Cuthebert did not even bother to look at her as he slowly gathered the ledgers from the table. Finally, he stood.

"From the strange death of Tosig to the way you broke your betrothal with our lord, Aethregard, you have brought nothing but tragedy to this place."

Aleene swallowed against the bile that rose in her throat, for she did feel responsible for her people's plight, for the downfall of England itself.

One of the women who had been sweeping up rushes paused in her work and looked over at them. Aleene realized that she had to show her dominance, quickly.

Cuthebert continued before she could say anything, though. " 'Twas not enough that you rid this keep of its beloved lord, but you had to fight his living wish that you marry his son, also."

Aleene forgot all else but what Cuthebert had just implied. "What do you say, Cuthebert? Do you accuse me of murder, perhaps?"

His wiry, gray brows rose tauntingly. "I do not accuse. I know. You killed and you broke promises to wrest control of this holding."

"Wrest control?" Aleene could barely contain her temper. "This castle has been mine since the day my mother died, you impertinent little twit. Seabreeze was never under the control of Tosig or his sniveling swine of a son."

"But it should have been!" Cuthebert spit at her feet. "Look what has happened since you have controlled it!"

"What is this?"

Aleene was surprised the hall did not collapse about them at the force that the deep resonance of those words had as they rang through the room. She stiffened.

Cuthebert dropped his ledgers and blinked, startled.

"A bad taste in your mouth, Cuthebert?" Robert stalked around Aleene and grabbed the front of her steward's tunic. "Did I not see you spit at your lady's feet?"

Cuthebert finally showed signs of fear, which only made Aleene just that much angrier. That she needed a man to control her servants made her want to throw things.

"I . . . er," Cuthebert glanced furtively at Aleene.

"He choked on a bone, Norman." She gave Cuthebert a pointed glare before Robert turned toward her.

Her husband stared at her a moment. "Really?" He dropped Cuthebert, who had been standing on his tiptoes to avoid strangulation. As the man staggered backward, Robert turned his full attention on Aleene. "And he got it out with one spit?"

"Aye, he did." Aleene watched Cuthebert gather his ledgers from the rushes and scurry away. She had once been able to control the man. Even though he had shown his defiance in many of his actions, he had still never been as outspoken in his hatred as he had this day. Feeling wretched and defeated, Aleene closed her eyes and sighed.

"Aleene . . ."

"Leave me be, Norman." She turned on her heel and went to her room. Aleene latched the door, sat in her father's chair, and contemplated her defeat. She had spent months trying to gain the respect of her people after Tosig's death. They had resisted her. They whispered terrible things about her: that she had killed Tosig, that she was a hated foreigner, that she had no heart. But still she had worked, and at least gotten them to obey her, though she trembled inside with each order, sure it would be at that moment one of them would defy her.

And now she would have to start from the

beginning, even before the beginning. For this time her people were not even trying to hide their disrespect. Aleene bowed her head. She did not think she had the strength to try anymore.

She stayed in her room for three days, refusing the baths Berthilde tried to bring her and ordering her food brought to her on a tray. On the third day, as she sat in the gloom of the oncoming night with no candles to light, she heard a knock at her door.

"Aleene."

It was him. The traitor.

"Aleene, I wish to speak with you."

"If you think to share my bed, Norman, you invite maiming."

There was a long silence, and Aleene relaxed her tense shoulders. A tremendous crash made her jump backwards as the wooden latch on her door splintered. The leather hinges squealed a protest as Robert threw open her door.

"How dare you!"

Without answering, Robert closed the door, then turned toward her, his blue eyes dark with anger. "You try my patience."

Aleene sputtered, her resolve to maintain her indifference toward her husband melting before the fiery anger that raced through her. "I try your patience?" She clenched her hands so tight, her nails dug into her palms. "I try *your* patience?" Her voice grew louder as she felt every ounce of her self-control seep from her body.

Grabbing the first thing her hand touched, Aleene heaved an empty candlestick at her husband's head. He ducked and it clattered against the door then dropped to the floor, the sound an insulting and inferior mimicry of the great show of force Robert had just made. An exasperated, frustrated huff of air escaped Aleene's lips as she searched the room for another weapon.

"Cease this childish tantrum, woman. Let us speak as adults."

"Childish tantrum?" Her voice deceptively low, Aleene grabbed one of her father's treasured Spanish vases. "You wait, Norman, I shall strive to make this tantrum more adult for you." She hurled the vase. It thudded against Robert's shoulder as he turned out of the way, and it crashed to the floor. A good loud crash that made Aleene smile. "Do not think to come near me. I will not speak with you, pig Norman, ever!"

"How very adult."

"Shut up!" Giving up on missiles, Aleene went at Robert with her fists, hitting as hard as she could. "You took everything! Everything! You control my castle." She clawed at his face, then hit out again. "My people!" She opened one fist and slapped, connecting with bare skin somewhere for she heard a satisfying smack and felt a fiery sting in her palm. "They shall never accept me now that I am a traitor. I hate you!" She continued to hit and scream until finally she realized that her face was wet with tears and her punches had become mere taps.

Turning away, Aleene pushed her fists against her eyes and cried great gulping sobs. When she felt Robert's large hands on her shoulders, she didn't even stiffen. She turned into his arms and put her head against his chest. "I do hate you," she cried, her fingers clenching in his tunic. "I do."

"I know." He held her tightly.

"I cannot do this yet again. I vowed not to." Aleene tried to dredge up the strength that had kept her cold to Robert's warmth and love, but it would not come. She wished only to keep her head against his chest and feel his arms about her. She wished nothing else existed, not William, not England, not the need to fight.

Her sobs subsided and she only took deep shuddering breaths now and then.

"It is nearly Christmas."

"Yes," Robert answered her.

"There should be laughter and festivity."

"Yes."

Aleene sighed. She wondered if Christmas would ever be the same again. "When my father was alive, I loved Christmas." She took another hiccuping breath.

"My brother loves Christmas. His eyes light

up as they do at no other time of year." Robert stroked her hair. "He doesn't show much emotion."

"We would probably get along well," Aleene said derisively.

"Yes, John is like Cyne."

The name sent a shiver through Aleene, and she pushed away from Robert. "Cyne?"

"John is simple." Robert held onto one of her hands, refusing to let go. "A horse kicked him in the head when he was eight."

"And your father did not make him leave?"

Robert shook his head, a small smile tilting his lips. "No. My family is very different than most. My mother is full of love, my father full of wisdom. It is a strange household I come from."

Something that might have been jealousy stung Aleene's heart. "It sounds wonderful." She hadn't meant to say that out loud, and when the words sounded in the darkening room, she winced.

"It is." Robert pulled her towards him. She resisted, but not strongly. "I never realized how wonderful until lately." He kissed her, a light, feathery kiss against her brow. "I want to have that here, with you. Please, Aleene, it can be so."

"It can't." Despair, so deep she didn't think she could breathe, clenched her stomach.

He kissed her again, his lips against her tem-

ple, her cheek, her lips. "I promise we shall
have it right here." His lips caressed hers, his
tongue lightly touched her mouth. "We can
have it now if we but work together." He deepened the kiss.

The despair did not go away for Aleene could
not believe that anything could ever be wonderful again, but still she returned her husband's kiss. Through the despair came need,
and with the need came lust.

She deepened their kiss, urgency lending her
courage. To purge the conflicting emotions and
thoughts from her head became all that mattered. Robert could do that to her. Remembering the night before Hastings, Aleene pulled at
the strings to Robert's tunic.

She wanted only to feel physical satisfaction.
She wanted to forget everything else but the
racking convulsions of release. Aleene broke
their kiss only long enough to help Robert from
his clothes. Her hands shook as she tugged at
ties and ripped material.

He did the same for her, his fingers catching
in her chemise and ripping the soft linen. Her
body was on fire.

They fell as one upon her bed, hands roaming
over bodies, lips roaming over faces, tongue
twining with tongue.

And then he was inside of her, hot, hard, and
full. Aleene gasped, grabbing at the coverlet
above her head. She bucked against her hus-

band, taking him fully within her. He kissed her hard, then bent and took her nipple into his mouth. A tremor shook her entire body, and she closed her eyes, centering her entire attention on the tightness of her womanhood and the growing tension low in her belly. Robert sucked hard, and Aleene groaned, the tension moving lower, growing more intense. "Yes," she cried, "yes." And then the release came. Crashing through her senses, making her collapse on the bed, breathing hard, experiencing it with all of her soul, trying to keep it, savor it.

He moved within her, and she grasped his arms. It was gone, her release, her sweet agony, gone. Robert pumped into her, his teeth biting his bottom lip, his eyes closed. Aleene watched, feeling him hard inside of her. She knew he was close, she could feel it at her core, and then he gasped and she felt him gush within her. His eyes opened, and he stared at her. They stayed silent for a long time, still joined, but so far apart.

"I am inside of you, and yet still I do not touch you." Robert shook his head then rolled off of her.

She turned away from him, tucking her knees to her chest.

She could feel Robert beside her, feel his confusion, his hurt. But she could not care. Finally he cupped his body around her and laid his arm around her waist. "It can be wonderful, Aleene. It can."

Aleene did not answer. She closed her eyes and slept.

The servants bustled around him, bringing everything he asked for and keeping their eyes averted as Robert broke his fast in the great hall the next morning. No one said an unkind word, no one balked at serving him, but he could feel their animosity. They ran to do his bidding, but Robert could see their resentment in the set of a jaw and the stiffness of a shoulder. It was beyond tiring. He would have to win their trust, and was not entirely sure it could be done.

Robert glanced at Aleene with that thought. He had made love to her. That should have broken through her barriers, and yet it hadn't. It had brought up new ones, different ones, ones Robert did not understand. He watched his wife eat her food, the motions slow and ponderous. Her gaze stayed on the trencher before her, never straying about the room or at him. It was as if she were dead, and yet her body still went on with the motions of life.

Pushing back his bench, Robert stood abruptly. He needed to get away. The hatred from his servants and apathy from his wife frustrated him to no end. "Jon," he called striding away from the table. "Bring me my hunting gear." Jon jumped forward from his post by the door blinking quickly. Obviously the boy had begun to nod off in the quiet of the great hall. The only noise that echoed through the room was an occasional cough or crunch of shoes on rushes. Frustration was not the only thing haunting Robert's emotions; insanity flirted with his mind also. "Now, boy. I shall meet you outside."

The boy turned and ran to do Robert's bidding. "I will use a falcon from the mews, also," Robert said to no one in particular.

"No!" His wife stood quickly.

Robert stared at her in surprise.

Aleene glared back at him for a moment, life finally stirring within her eyes. But then, just as quickly, her dark eyes dulled and she bowed her head. "The falcons were my father's."

"And so not worthy of me?" Anger made his voice shake. Aleene did not even look at him as she sat again at the table. With a disgusted sigh, Robert stalked from the hall.

Berthilde smiled at him as he stepped outside. She had a steaming loaf of bread in her hands. "Done already, are you?" She hefted the bread. "I was just bringing some fresh, hot bread to fill your stomach."

Robert eyed the curl of steam escaping from the loaf. It looked tempting with the chill winter air already making his fingers feel like ice. "I thought I'd go out and bring us back some meat for dinner."

"Ah," she nodded, her eyes showing sadness. " 'Tis warmer out here than it is inside, is it not."

"Aye." Robert smiled slightly.

"I don't blame ye for trying to find a respite." She broke the bread in half and wrapped it in a cloth she was carrying. "Take this with you. And not to worry, milord, the people will soon see ye're not to be feared or hated."

Jon came out then with his bow and arrow. Robert took the wrapped bread from Berthilde, smiled his thanks, then accepted his hunting gear from Jon. "I'll be back soon," he said to no one, then left, not truly wanting to be back too soon.

The sun had started to peek through the fog that hung over the harbor as Robert left Seabreeze and turned toward the forests that bordered the keep. Slinging his bow over his shoulder, he took a deep breath of the cold air and rubbed his hands together quickly. He should have brought his gloves. He would catch nothing with numb fingers, but he'd left so quickly, he had forgotten to retrieve them from the trunk that sat in an alcove of the great hall. Robert hadn't had the courage to take it to Aleene's chamber that first day when William had landed.

He could probably have it hauled to the room now. He could probably move his entire garrison into Aleene's room, and she would not even frown. Robert sighed, stuck his hands in the folds of his tunic, and watched his warm breath turn the air in front of him white. He would rather Aleene yell and throw things at him than act the beaten creature as she had this morning.

Robert heard a shout in the distance and looked up. One of William's men waved from the fortress that still stood within the Roman ruins on the cliff. Robert waved back half-heartedly. He wished William would call his men away. They were not needed since Robert had Seabreeze well in hand. He laughed aloud at that thought. Well, he had more control than the men at the fortress. Perhaps he would send a message to William.

He entered the forest then, the tall trees blocking out the weak rays of the sun and sending a shiver down Robert's spine. It hadn't snowed yet. He wasn't at all sure if it did snow here. But it seemed cold enough that he expected white flakes to fall from the heavens at any moment. Robert shivered again and buried his hands in his tunic once more.

He spent nearly an hour without spotting a single creature among the trees. He was sure his stomping probably scared them all into their burrows. He had to keep jumping up and down to keep the blood flowing through his body. Finally, he spotted a nice fat hare and brought it down with one arrow. He had a small inkling of hope in the back of his mind that he could find and bring down a deer. Robert could just imagine the look on the faces of the people of Seabreeze if he brought back such a prize. They would have to stop hating him completely then. To have their bellies full because of the marauding Norman would perhaps make them hate him a little less.

Robert chuckled derisively as he twined string around the hare's back feet and hung the creature on his quiver. As he straightened from his task, he saw a flash of white out of the corner of his eye. Turning quickly, he caught a quick glimpse of blond hair as someone ducked behind a bush.

Pulling an arrow from his quiver, Robert placed it against his bow and walked slowly toward the spot. "Who goes there?"

A twig snapped beneath his feet, but no other sound broke the forest silence. He stopped, fearing a trap. "Show thyself!" he yelled.

He heard a whimper that cut off abruptly. Robert frowned. He had never known assassins or soldiers to whimper. "Who is it?" he asked again, this time a bit more gently.

Quiet. And then, slowly, a small face peeped from around the bush.

" 'Tis only I, Meg, sir." A young girl stood before him, her blond hair ragged and dirty, her face streaked with mud, her bare feet peeking from beneath the hem of her thin gown. She held greens in her hands, a big bunch of them.

Robert quickly put his arrow away and shouldered his bow. "Are you picking greens, child?"

She looked down at her hands, then back up at him, her eyes wide with fear. "I didn't know I shouldn't, sir, really I didn't." She dropped the offending branches and boughs.

"No, Meg, 'tis quite all right." He smiled and inched forward. "Are you picking them for the Christmas season perhaps?" Mayhap he should bring some back to Seabreeze? A bit of Christmas cheer to go along with the rabbit for the peoples' stew, they would hate him even less, he was sure.

Meg looked at him, the fear in her eyes turning to confusion. "Christmas?" She said the word like she had never heard it before.

Robert wracked his brains. Had he used the wrong English word for the celebration of Christ's birth. He shook his head, no, Aleene had used the word only the day before.

Meg bowed her small head before him, wringing her fingers together. "Nay, sir, not for Christmas. I was picking them to eat."

"Eat?" Meg jumped, and he softened his tone. "You were going to eat those?" He looked at the leaves in the small heap at Meg's feet.

She tilted her head back, and bright blue eyes met his. "Yes, sir."

Robert was fairly sure one didn't usually eat

the types of greens the child before him had gathered. "Did your mother send you?"

"No, sir." She looked away again. "She is dead."

Before Robert could continue with his questions, the child took a hasty step forward and looked at him again. "I will sell my favors, sir."

Robert choked, then coughed and tried to breathe.

"For the rabbit." She pointed to the hare that hung from his back. "I have been tried before, sir, I can pleasure you." She did not smile, she did not frown, her face stayed a blank, unemotional palate of white skin and large blue eyes.

Robert felt as if he were to be sick. Swallowing back bile, he asked, "Who? Who has been with one so young?"

"I have twelve summers, sir. I am not young."

"Who?" He could barely speak for the churning of his stomach and the shaking of his limbs.

A tiny furrow formed between her brows, her only concession to emotion. She pointed back toward where Robert had come from. "The soldiers, sir, at the fort. I ventured near one day and they saw me."

He was to be sick. Turning quickly, Robert dropped his bow and quiver, ran for a tree, and lost the breakfast he had so hastily bolted that morning. Leaning against the tree, Robert tried to get his breathing under control. When he turned, finally, he saw Meg eyeing the rabbit. She looked up at him then, a crestfallen expression finally giving life to her face. Obviously the child had contemplated thievery, but she had hesitated too long.

With a sigh, Robert pulled the wrapped loaf of bread from under his cloak. As he walked toward Meg, she backed away from him. Robert stopped and held the bread out. "Here."

Her gaze narrowed.

"It is bread." He gestured with the loaf. "Take it. 'Tis yours."

Her gaze on him, Meg moved forward, grabbed the bread and retreated. Breaking the bread, the girl bit into half the loaf and chewed, her eyes closing as she savored the taste. She took only three bites, then bundled the rest up in a pocket of her skirt. "I shall pay you now," she said quietly and sat on the ground.

"No!" Robert strode forward and pulled the girl up. "No, there is no need for that."

She only stared at him.

"Have you no family?"

"No, sir."

Turning, Robert took up his bow and quiver. "Come with me."

"To the fort?"

He could hear the fear that laced her words, and he wanted to kill every man of William's who sat in the fort on the cliff of Pevensey.

"No." Robert sighed and looked into Meg's large eyes. "No, I shall take you to the lady at Seabreeze Castle. She is English. She will find work for you and clothe you."

She did not believe him. With hands clasped in front of her, Meg shook her head. "I will give you back the bread, sir, but please don't take me away."

"Believe me, Meg." Robert bent down on one knee so that he was on her level. "I shall not harm you. I will take you to a place where you will be warm and have food to fill your belly."

He could tell this tempted her. The small girl bit at her bottom lip and the furrow between her brows returned.

"Come, I'll carry you."

Her brows met abruptly over her nose, and she backed away quickly.

With a sigh Robert gestured to her poor bare feet. "Your feet must be nigh unto frozen, child. I will not hurt you."

She blinked at him, then slowly looked down at her naked toes. Robert stood and carefully moved toward her, asking for her trust with his eyes as he bent slowly to pick her up. Meg stiffened at his touch and stayed like a collection of fragile sticks within his arms as they made their way to the edge of the forest. When they reached the open, and saw the fortress on the cliff, little Meg started breathing faster, her gaze shifting nervously from the bread in her hands to the wooden Norman fort.

"We go to Seabreeze, child. 'Tis an English lady that lives there."

Meg obviously didn't believe him. She bowed her head and ate some more of the bread, her body shaking in his arms. Robert shrugged his cloak more fully around them to shield Meg from anyone watching and, in his mind, he cursed the men in the fort.

When they finally reached Seabreeze, Robert took his small companion to the kitchens where he knew he would find Berthilde. The old woman stood over a wooden block kneading dough with the strength of a lion.

Robert put Meg down and called, "Berthilde, I have brought you a helper."

The woman looked up.

Robert put his hand lightly on Meg's shoulder and felt her small frame stiffen. "I found her in the forest. She needs a hot bath, warm clothes, and food. You have said you need another helper in the kitchen. I think Meg here would be just the person."

Berthilde bustled forward clucking under her breath like a mother hen. "Darling girl, you are like ice, you are." She took the girl's hands between hers. "Goodness and you must have been out in them trees for many a cold day. It's a wonder you are still alive!" She looked up at Robert and spied the rabbit. "Take the hare to Gwen." Then she turned and yelled, "Nan! Nan!"

A plump young girl came running in from somewhere outside. "Yes, Berthilde?"

"Heat water for a bath, and tell Wat to bring the tub to the curtained-off area of the hall." Berthilde took Meg's little hand in hers. "Not to worry, dear, we'll have you warm soon. Come with Berthilde, when you are warm we shall put you to bed with a hot broth and some bread."

Her words trailed off in the crisp air as she hurried the small girl across the bailey and into the hall. Robert watched them, the anger he had kept at bay so as not to scare Meg, rushing through his veins and making him clench his fists at his side. "Nan," he turned toward the girl boiling water over the fire.

The poor thing jumped, her face going white. "When you are done, gather five or six women and meet me in Cuthebert's chambers."

Nan blinked, her eyes going round in horror.

Robert sighed in exasperation. "I am not going to harm you, nor am I going to rut with all six of you. I have a project that only women can do." He turned. "Only English women." He left, knowing that Nan was probably more scared now than before. But he knew she would do his bidding, so he made his way quickly to the keep, calling three of his men as he went.

They followed him through the hall to Cuthebert's chambers.

Cuthebert sat hunched over his ledgers, scratching in numbers with the tip of a quill. He looked up in surprise as Robert and his men intruded on his sanctum. The surprise in his eyes immediately changed to fear. The little man jumped from his chair and backed away. "What goes here?"

Robert cocked a brow at the man. "What goes *here*, man?" He had proven in the last week that he was not going to hurt anyone. Why, then, did the steward seem ready to piss in his pants? Robert looked behind him at his men. A rather formidable group, but still . . .

"I . . . I am but doing my work." Cuthebert sputtered and nervously fingered the quill in his hand, not realizing that with his anxious movements he managed to get ink all over his tunic.

"Well, then, you should not be so nervous." Robert eyed the man steadily. "I need to make use of this room."

The fear did not fully leave Cuthebert's eyes. "Yes, milord." He backed up even further so that Robert and his men could enter, but Robert could see that the man was not going to leave the room entirely without a fight.

Robert shrugged and turned to his men. "In the forest I found a girl, a hungry and cold child. She had been abused by the men at the fort. I want you to go out and see if there are more people hiding in our forests."

Robert heard a strangled sound and looked over at the steward. Cuthebert's thin lips clamped together.

"I am not going to hurt them. I wish to help them." He shook his head and turned back to his men. "I will send English women with you. The people will trust them and listen to them. I want to have anyone you find brought back here. I do not want people dying whom we can help."

The men nodded their understanding.

"You are going in order to protect the women. You will frighten the people, so don't get too close to them."

At that moment there was a timid knock at the door. Robert gestured toward the exit. "You may leave, but stay close and be ready to escort the women. I wish you to be on your way after dinner."

The men filed solemnly out.

Nan peeked around the door, her gaze immediately going to the man who still stood behind Robert. She seemed a tiny bit pacified that there was an Englishman there, and she moved slowly into the room, with the other women following her closely. They all stared first at him, then Cuthebert. Their gazes asked questions of the steward and warred between anger and fear when they fell upon him.

Robert could not help himself from saying, "I am not going to eat you all now that you are in my lair."

Each of the women blinked, the fear overtaking the anger in their eyes.

Robert rolled his eyes. "I only wish you to go into the forests. There are people there, children, hungry and cold. I want them brought here."

The women still eyed him warily and Robert suddenly felt very weary of constantly being the object of fear and animosity.

Nan finally swallowed audibly and said, "You will not hurt them?"

"No, I wish to make sure they do not die of starvation or freeze to death out there. I wish to find them homes."

Nan looked over at the woman next to her and they exchanged glances. They were not entirely sure Robert spoke the truth, he could see.

Frustration made him move abruptly to the door and open it. "You will leave after dinner, but be home before dark. Make sure you wear heavy, warm clothing. Go now, I have work to do."

They left quickly, muttering to each other once they got outside the door.

Robert turned toward the desk, remembering Cuthebert when he saw the man staring at him from across the room. "I must write a letter, Cuthebert. I need a quill and parchment."

Cuthebert stared for a moment, then nodded reluctantly, suspicion still darkening his gaze.

"Thank you, Cuthebert." Robert sat on the rickety chair at the table, wondering for a moment if it would take his weight.

Without acknowledging Robert's thank you, Cuthebert dropped a rolled parchment on the table and stepped back.

Robert glanced at him. "I'll only be a moment."

Resentment and hatred flashed through the steward's eyes before he bowed slightly and left.

It was hard to be feared by all of the people who had once smiled at him and led him about as if he were a child. Robert laughed as he dipped the quill. When he thought about it, it was probably just as hard for them. All of a sudden the half-wit poacher was a Norman knight who had helped ravage their land. The laugh died on Robert's tongue as the last of his thoughts flitted through his head. With a sigh, he bent to his work, penning a note to William. Hopefully, Robert would be able to persuade his liege that Seabreeze was the only defense needed at Pevensey. Robert wanted the fort and William's men gone.

Chapter 16

Aleene left her chamber to take dinner in the great hall. Heads turned as she entered, but she shut her mind to the reaction of those present.

As she washed her hands at the table, a servant brought a trencher for her. Seabreeze seemed to be running smoothly without her. Obviously, Berthilde and Robert had all well in hand. She glanced at the men that broke bread at the lower tables, their Norman haircuts and dress proclaiming them foreigners. And yet they were the rulers of this household.

Another servant ladled a heaping spoonful of steaming broth into her trencher. The tantalizing smell wafted up to Aleene, causing her stomach to rumble in anticipation. Tearing off a piece of bread, Aleene bent to eat. She did not care that Normans ruled her castle as well as the land. It no longer mattered. She had let down her king, her people, herself. She finally realized that she was not strong enough to fight the forces that controlled her life any longer. That she had tried for so long made her want to laugh. Laugh strong and hard forever.

She had always known that she had no control over her life. She had tried to refute it, tried to change it, but inside she had always known it was impossible. And yet she had tried and ended a humiliated failure.

Robert did not come to sit by her, and she wondered for a moment where he could be. She glanced around, noted his complete absence from the room, then took another bite of stew. Wherever he was, he was missing a very fine stew. Aleene looked up to take some cheese and bread from the platter before her and noticed five women talking at one of the lower tables. They seemed quite excited about something. The knights, too, it seemed had something of great importance to discuss. Aleene then noticed that the servants also seemed to be interested in some topic. Conversation buzzed about the room. Silence had been the norm since she had come back to Seabreeze. Aleene wondered what could have excited her people so thoroughly.

With a sigh, she bent to her food again, banishing from her mind her slight interest in the topic of conversation.

"Your husband is a good man, milady." Berthilde laid another loaf of bread on the table.

"He saved a poor girl today from certain death in the forest."

Aleene looked up at her maid, then shrugged. "You no longer help me at my bath, Berthilde. I assume you have too much to do?"

"Nan will do well enough, I should think."

"No she will not." Aleene sat back on her bench. Truly, it did not seem to matter anymore. She had insisted upon Berthilde's assistance before because the old woman knew Aleene's secrets. Berthilde knew that since her stepfather had begun visiting her at night, Aleene could barely stand to look at herself, much less show herself to another. That fear had dissipated, though, with all that had happened to her. Aleene could have accepted another's help, she was sure. But she did not want anyone else to help her.

Aleene stared up at Berthilde. Her gaze took in the old woman's familiar brown eyes, the gray hair that crinkled just so at her temples. They had been through much together, this woman who had been more of a mother than Aleene's true parent. "I shall have no one if you cannot help me."

"That may be difficult."

"It does not matter." Aleene shrugged.

"He is sending the women out with an escort of soldiers to find others who may be hungry or cold."

Aleene tore off a piece of bread and dunked

it in her stew. "Who?" she asked, not really caring.

"Robert, of course."

"This stew is wonderful." Aleene sopped up some more of the steaming broth with her bread. "Did someone go hunting? It tastes like fresh meat."

"Robert brought home a hare. He said he would get more tomorrow, but today he found the girl."

"The girl?"

Berthilde huffed and rested her fists on her hips. "I do not like this way of yours at all, Lady Aleene, you are acting the part of a spoiled child!"

A tiny spark of some emotion penetrated her apathy for a moment, and Aleene stiffened. "I don't remember how to act the spoiled child, Berthilde, the opportunity was taken away from me rather early in life."

"Well, you seem to be remembering well enough. You are needed, milady, I have work enough to do without having to take on your responsibilities also." She turned, her skirts throwing up a breath of dusty rushes and stalked toward the door that led out to the cooking area.

Aleene's flare of defiance sputtered to nothing, and she turned back to her food. She just did not care, could not make herself care. Without looking about her again, she ate the rest of her dinner and left the table.

"Milord, a message for you." A young boy came running through the bailey, a man on horseback coming up behind him. Robert looked up from the young girl to whom he was speaking. Nan and her companions had found three children, one with her mother, in the forests the day before. He had sent them out again today, and meanwhile was trying to learn from each of the children if they had any family living. He patted the girl on the head and told her to run in to Berthilde.

"What is it, Peter?" Robert turned, knowing he had gotten the boy's name right when the boy beamed.

"A messenger from William!" Peter announced triumphantly. Robert had given him the duty of standing at the gate and bringing any news.

Robert nodded. "Thank you, lad, 'tis good work you do."

The boy grinned and went running back to the gate and his post. The messenger dismounted as he reached the bailey, handing the reigns to another boy who came running from the stables.

"Robert de Guise, of Seabreeze Castle?" The messenger asked, walking up to Robert.

Flinching at the name, Robert nodded. He

recognized the young man as Frederick, one of William's squires.

"I'm to await an answer," Frederick said as he handed over a rolled parchment.

Robert eyed the young man. He had always joked and kidded with the boys of William's company, but Frederick did not smile, or even offer a friendly hello. Obviously, Robert was persona non grata in William's ranks now. Of course, he did not fear outright hostility. Robert had risked his life to bring William's amazing feat of landing an entire military force on English soil to fruition, not to mention fighting valiantly at Hastings.

Still, Robert was obviously not rising higher in his liege's esteem. With a sigh, he unrolled the parchment and read, scanning the neatly penned message quickly.

Christmas Day was to be William's coronation. Relief surged through Robert. At least the fighting was over, he hoped. He looked back up at Frederick. "This does not give me much time to get to London," he said.

"He wishes you to attend, sir." The boy gripped his hands together in front of him. "May I tell him to expect you?"

"If I do not come myself, I will be sure to send a representative." Robert gazed toward the direction of the fort. "Or perhaps representatives."

"He will be disappointed if it is not you, sir."

Robert detected the warning in Frederick's young voice. "I shall do my best."

The boy stared for a moment into Robert's eyes, as if unsure of whether to press for a more affirmative answer.

"Go, tell William I am happy for him. He has succeeded where many thought he would fail," Robert said sincerely.

Frederick hesitated a moment, then nodded. "May I quench my thirst before I go?"

"Of course!" Robert pointed to the door of the great hall. "We have food and ale, boy. I shall send someone in to serve you."

Frederick relaxed a bit. "Thank you, sir." He went to the hall.

Robert was probably going to catch hell from William for what he planned, but at least the rambunctious men with nothing to do at the fort would finally be gone. He went and told Berthilde of their visitor, then headed for the fort.

The men were drunk and lying about in their own filth. Robert was sorely tempted to plug his nose when the leader came barreling up to him, breathing heavily in his face.

"Lord Robert! Have you come to celebrate with us?"

"You've heard the news then?" Robert backed away quickly. "Are you not going to the coronation?"

"Weren't given orders to leave our post, sir."
The man slurred his words so horribly, Robert
was hard pressed to understand him.

"But surely you and your men would enjoy
such a great event?"

"Aha!" The man let out a great belly laugh.
"And that we would, sir!"

"I'll tell you true, man, I have already written
to William telling him that there is no need for
this fort to stay intact. I have an entire garrison
of men at Seabreeze who will keep order here.
I also just told William's personal messenger
that I would send you and your men as representatives for me at his coronation."

The man's eyes widened in surprise and excitement. "Really? What a fine thing!"

"Yes, so, if you think to make it before Christmas Day, I suggest you form ranks and get
moving!" Robert ended his enthusiastic suggestion with a hard thwack on the garrison leader's
back. He coughed and stumbled forward,
nearly landing face first in the dirt.

Robert wished he could hit him harder, this
time somewhere it would be terribly painful,
but he stayed his hand.

"Yes, sir." The man finally managed to stand
upright. "We will do just that!"

Robert smiled, nodded, and went on his way.
He would write another message to William as-
suring him that the garrison at Seabreeze was
quite capable of defending Pevensey and keep-

ing order. Whatever happened, Robert would not accept a garrison of William's men back in Pevensey. None of the people who now looked to Robert for protection would be hurt ever again.

Aleene sat in her father's chair tracing one of the stars carved into the dark wooden arm. She heard the knock at the door, but did not acknowledge it. When Robert walked into the room, she glanced up, then away from the sight of his large, imposing form in the doorway. His shoulders nearly touched either side of the frame, and, again, Aleene wondered how she could have mistaken him for a half-wit poacher.

Aleene quickly shut her mind to those devastating memories. She stared hard at the carvings on her father's old chair and set herself to tracing them again. Over and over, her finger never left the smooth wood.

"I have ordered you a bath," Robert stated.

Aleene said nothing.

"I have set some men to building crofts for the people left homeless."

Aleene bent her head to her task. People left homeless because of her failure, she thought, closing her eyes and willing the guilt to oblivion.

She heard another knock, then the sound of bustling about the room. She did not look, tried not to care.

"Get in the tub, Aleene."

A tiny shiver of alarm shook her. Bathe? In front of Robert?

His large hands curled about her upper arms and hauled her from the chair. It took all of her willpower not to fight, and all of her strength to blank her mind to what was happening.

Robert set her down and began undoing the ties at her throat. "I think back to only a few days ago when you threw things at me, and I would give anything to have that Aleene back with me now." Robert's voice was low as if he spoke only to himself. "And I tried to halt the tirade." He chuckled without humor. The old, dirty gown she wore dropped to her feet. "I would allow it now, exalt in it." His fingers curled about the bottom edge of her chemise and pulled upward.

Willing her soul into a very small, dark corner of her body, Aleene allowed herself to be undressed. She stared at one spot on the wall and thought of nothing. The steam rising from the tub caressed her legs, licking up toward her belly when Robert put her into the tub. He pushed her gently down so that she sat.

Aleene kept to her corner. Still, she could feel his hands against her skin as he rubbed soap into her back. She had lost the knack to separate from herself. Before, when she had done this, she had ceased to feel as well as care.

With that thought, the memories began to

trickle into her mind. The footsteps coming toward her small chamber, the putrid smell of an
unwashed body, the hands touching her
roughly, hurting her.

Aleene clenched her hands, drew up her
knees and hugged them. She was that person
again, the small, helpless girl, controlled by
everything but her own will. She was dark,
ugly, unlike the golden-haired people around
her. She was different. She was bad. She lived
without love.

She shivered and bent her head forward to
cradle it on her knees. No. She could not let it
happen again.

She stood, water sluicing from her body,
splashing to the floor. "Get away from me," she
yelled and stumbled from the tub. "Don't touch
me!" She backed away from the man who stood
watching her with a frown. The image of Tosig
danced before her eyes, and she hit out at it.
"You can't do this to me again, never again. I
will not let you!"

"Aleene!"

"No!" She hit out again. "I can't stand it any
longer." She closed her eyes then, putting her
arms about herself and crouching down to the
floor. "I don't want to be different." She
dropped her head to her knees again.

"Aleene." She flinched as his hands touched
her shoulders, but didn't move away. The
memories had receded and she knew it was

Robert, not Tosig who touched her. He would not hurt her.

She sighed, knowing that she was no longer the small girl vulnerable to everyone and everything. And yet, she still felt ugly and bad. She was different from those around her. She was dark, not of English blood, and she had betrayed the people she had so wanted to accept her. She had hurt them by doing stupid things. She *was* bad.

Aleene began to tremble. She felt Robert's arms about her, but they provided no warmth, her teeth chattered together, and she felt goose bumps rise on her arms.

"Come, Aleene, we must get you warm." Robert picked her up and took her to the bed. He wrapped her in a blanket and laid her down, curling up behind her. "Shh." He rubbed her through the cover, then brushed the wet tendrils of hair from her face. "It will be all right, everything will be all right."

Aleene shook her head, knowing nothing would ever be all right again. "It cannot be all right."

"It can."

"I failed, in everything I failed. I was a traitor, and now my people hate me. They have a foreign king and I am a foreign lady." Aleene felt a tear finally drop down her cheek. "Oh, how I failed in everything."

"You, Aleene, are no traitor. Were there any

other landowners in London trying to rally troops against William?"

"There was a soldier who had fought with Harold."

"Were there any other women?"

That quieted her. "But I did it from guilt. I brought William here with my treachery. I opposed Harold's will. I would not marry the one he chose for me."

"The one he chose was the traitor, Aleene. I saw him, Aethregard, with William while we camped outside London."

Fury shot through Aleene's body, chasing the chill from her with its heat. "Aethregard! He came to the meetings with the archbishops proclaiming William's right to the throne." She sat up, hugging the blanket to her body. "I shall kill him."

Robert sat next to her, wrapping a large arm about her shoulders. "He was not worthy of you, Aleene."

She turned to her husband. "I would never have married that spineless bastard."

A smile lit Robert's face. "Do I hear my Aleene?"

She frowned. "What nonsense do you speak, Robert? Who else is here in this room?"

Robert laughed outright. "When I entered there was a timid mouse sitting in that chair." He pointed to the large chair in the corner.

"Afraid of everything, shutting it all from her mind, she was."

Aleene stared at the chair a moment, her hate for Aethregard withering before the memories of her own traitorous activity. "She is still here, Robert."

"Why?" Robert gripped her shoulders and turned her toward him. "Why is she here? What are you afraid of?"

"I am afraid of myself. I hurt the people I only ever wished to make love me."

"Aleene." Robert shook her, not roughly but gently. "You hurt no one. If anyone here should make recompense 'tis I. You did not bring William here. He would have come even if you had tortured and killed me in your dungeon."

Aleene could only gaze into her husband's eyes. Those beautiful sky-blue eyes that had made her trust him, love him. "I know." She hung her head. "I know. But now we crown a foreign king, and we shall all suffer for it. I wish I could have stopped it somehow. And I didn't." She looked back at Robert. "I didn't stop it, and while it was happening, I loved you. I loved an enemy. I prayed for you on the day of battle, not my people, not my king, you!"

Robert pulled her toward him, crushing her in his arms. "You loved a person, Aleene. That did not make your king die. And now, I am not your enemy. I do not wish ill upon these people, our people, I wish to help you rebuild."

"Heal," Aleene said into his shoulder, remembering his words when he had come to her in London.

"Yes, heal. We cannot change what has happened. We can only move forward. If you still feel guilt, mend yourself by helping your people heal."

Aleene sagged against Robert, shaking her head. "I can't, Robert, I can't. I have not the strength or the ability."

"What?" He pushed away from her. "What happened to the Aleene who married me, a half-wit poacher, so that she would control her own castle?"

"That was not strength, it was fear. I was weak, Robert, I could not stand to be at another's mercy. I was never the person I showed to everyone. I trembled at even the thought of giving orders to the servants."

"But you gave them. That is strength."

Aleene blinked. "I . . . I, no, Robert, I was afraid."

"Everyone is afraid of something. It is those who go forward despite the fears who have strength."

Aleene searched her husband's face, wanting to believe him. Wanting so desperately to believe in herself. "But I was not strong with Tosig."

"That I will not hear! You were a child,

Aleene. A victim of violence from a man ten times your size. I will not have you demean yourself because of that."

Pressing the back of her hand to her mouth, Aleene tried to ingest everything Robert had told her. She was not a failure? She had strength? The memories of Tosig automatically began filtering through her. "He would come at night. My mother didn't protect me. She barely knew life about her still happened." Aleene closed her eyes. "She sat in my father's chair day in and day out, living only in her mind, living in another time. He hurt me. He hit me and took my innocence until I thought I should die. I felt ugly and dirty. I would go out into the sunshine and see the children playing, their golden hair like rays from the sun, and I felt so dark and dirty next to them. I felt so apart from them. I felt so bad."

"But you were not, Aleene." She felt her husband's hand pushing the hair back from her shoulders. "You were beautiful, a dark-haired, dark-eyed beauty. You radiate goodness and love."

Aleene lifted her eyes to her husband. "Goodness?"

"You care for your people, you make sure that none go hungry."

"Love?"

"Me, you love me. As a half-wit mute you loved me. My brother, John, is just as I pretended to be, and people shun him. They think him possessed by Satan. But you cared for me, protected me, loved me.

"You are beautiful, Aleene. I cannot take my eyes from you when I see you. Your beauty is like no other I have ever encountered."

With a sigh, Aleene breathed out all the hurt inside of her and melted against her husband. His arms came about her, bringing strength to her, and warmth. Oh, so much warmth. Aleene turned her face, so that her cheek lay against his chest.

"Take off your tunic, Robert, I need to feel you," she said, wanting the warmth of him to seep through her skin and into her soul.

He stripped off his tunic and took her into his arms again. "And I need to feel you, Aleene. I cannot function without you."

Aleene ran her hands up his arms, the muscles contracting beneath her touch, and threaded her fingers in his long hair. "I feel strong, Robert, your warmth makes me strong."

His head dipped and his lips lightly touched hers. "No, Aleene, we make each other strong." He kissed her again, harder this time.

"Healing," she whispered against his lips as his tongue swept into her mouth. They did not speak again, only touched. Robert's hands caressing her breasts, his leg sliding between hers to open her.

She felt no vulnerability as she lay open to

her husband, and then felt only fullness when he entered her. He moved within her, kissing her mouth, smoothing his hands over her breasts, bringing her to the ultimate edge of wanting, then coming with her into the complete perfection of satisfied love.

"It will be all right, Aleene," he whispered to her as they lay in the aftermath of their love. Robert tucked her head beneath his chin and held her close to his body. "We will make it all right together."

Chapter 17

〜◯◯〜

Peter again came running from his station at the watchtower. "My lord!" he cried, his face alight with childish joy. "They are leaving!"

Robert laughed and held up his hand as Peter stopped before him, panting. "Ho, son, you shall lose all the breath in your body running and shouting so."

"They leave, milord!" he said again once he had caught his breath. "The soldiers at the fort march past even as we speak!"

"Ah, it will be good see their backs." Robert put a hand on Peter's shoulder. "Let us go watch this wonderful thing happen."

Peter jumped with excitement, then ran ahead. Robert followed, joy edged with trepidation making his heart hammer against his breast. William would not be happy, but the people of Pevensey would.

Robert went up the ladder after Peter, then

stood in the watchtower as the troops that had
sat at the fort for nearly three months marched
past. Pevensey looked deserted. Probably the
people hid in their homes, scared at what the
march of the soldiers meant for them. Robert
smiled. It meant no ill, he knew. Keeping an eye
on the soldiers, Robert ruffled Peter's hair. "It
will be a good morning, indeed, lad, with this
as its beginning."

"Aye sir. Where do they go, sir?"

Robert waited until the last man had left the
village and taken the tract bound for London.
"To London to see their liege crowned king."
He looked down at Peter.

The boy took in a quick breath of air, his eyes
going wide. "William? He shall be king?"

"Aye."

Peter worried his bottom lip with small white
teeth. "Will they come back? Will they hurt us
now that they rule over us?"

"No, lad, not as long as I am lord of Seabreeze Castle." Robert turned and looked toward the cooking area where Aleene helped
with the preparations for the Christmas celebration. "And not as long as Aleene is your lady.
She would not suffer her people to be hurt."

Peter nodded, his eyes serious. Robert could
almost see the wheels working in the boy's
head as he thought on all he had heard.

"She fought for your people, you know, in
London," Robert said, hoping the lad would

carry the news to others. "She went before the witan, she argued with the archbishops. She did everything within her power to put an Englishman on the throne."

Peter's eyes widened and a look of awe came over him.

"She is a heroine to the English, really. She actually entered William's camp, risked her life, to take information back to Harold."

Peter's mouth hung open.

Robert knew Pevensey would soon be buzzing with the information that their lady was a heroine. He smiled. "Now, I must return to my work if we are to have the entire village here for Christmas only two days hence." Robert started down the ladder.

"Sir." Peter's call stopped him.

"Aye, lad?"

"Did you tell the men at the fort to leave?"

Robert nodded, a smile curving his lips. "That I did. And we shall pray now they do not return."

Peter smiled back. "I will, sir!"

Robert laughed and continued down the ladder. He passed people going about their business. There were no smiles as when he had been Cyne, but at least they no longer looked at him with pure hatred. The blacksmith even called out a greeting.

"How does it go?" Robert asked as he came upon Aleene.

She handed the stirring spoon she wielded over to a young woman beside her. When Aleene turned, her entire face was lit from within, her white teeth a breathtaking contrast to her dark skin. Robert's blood ran a bit faster in his veins, and he could not help dipping his gaze to see her full breasts outlined against her tunic. Ah, the woman fired his blood.

"All goes very well, my lord. I am so excited for Christmas now. What fun it will be to share it with all the people in the village."

"But what hard work, also."

Aleene shrugged, the motion pulling the cloth of her dress tighter across her bosom.

Robert swallowed hard.

"It is an enjoyable work." She took a step toward him, placing one of her hands over his heart. "The people are very excited for it. There are more smiles than frowns this morning."

Her voice, low and husky, made Robert's heart beat unevenly beneath her hand. He wanted to pick her up and take her to their room right then, but he knew he had to tell her something that would banish that dazzling smile of hers. He only hoped it would not banish it forever. "Aleene," Robert said, putting his hand over hers and wrapping his fingers around it. "Come with me."

"Robert, I am busy, could it not wait?"

Robert only shook his head. She looked at

him, her mouth open as if to protest more, but then she closed it and nodded.

Robert led her away from the bustling kitchen and around to the deserted herb garden, now empty of greens. "Aleene," Robert said, turning to look at her, and putting his hands on her shoulders. "William is to be crowned king of the English this very Christmas day."

She made a small sound of distress and seemed to crumple. Robert caught her, holding her close to him. "We knew it would happen, Aleene, when we left London." He could only hope that this news would not make her retreat back into her shell once again. "It will be all right, darling love, I will make sure that no harm comes to the people of Pevensey."

Aleene wrapped her hands in his tunic, clenching her fists until her knuckles showed white. "I know, Robert, but what of those people in London? What of the people outside Pevensey?"

Robert sighed, his heart nearly breaking at the sound of complete devastation in Aleene's voice. "I am sorry, Aleene." He pushed her head against his chest. "I am sorry." They stood silently for a long time, and then Robert said, "I know that William has hopes that there will be no more fighting. That the Norman people and the English people will coexist and find peace. He does not wish to subjugate your people, Aleene."

"That is a wish that will never come true, Robert." Aleene pushed away from his chest, her eyes large and dark in her face. "The English people will fight him."

Robert was struck in that moment by Aleene's exotic beauty. Even at this terrible moment, he wanted nothing more than to spend the rest of his life looking into this woman's face. He leaned forward and kissed her hard. "I am not exactly one of William's favorite people right now, but I will go to him after his coronation and woo him."

He smiled at the confusion that brought Aleene's brows together over her slim nose. "I will get on his good side again, then use my power to help the English people."

Aleene bit at her bottom lip, her eyes going suspiciously moist. "I want to help you."

"Of course!" He hugged her tightly to him. "We will have to be discreet, love, and probably work in roundabout ways, but we will alleviate the plight of your people, that I promise."

"Lord Robert!" Robert recognized Peter's voice calling him and smiled.

"My trusty news gatherer calls."

Aleene sighed, then called out. "Peter, we are here in the herb garden."

The boy bounded through the wooden gate. "Two villagers await you, Lord Robert. They have a problem that needs mediating."

Robert blinked. "They have brought their problem to me?"

"Of course, milord." Peter looked non-plussed.

Aleene squeezed his hand. "It seems your people trust your judgment, my lord."

"They shall trust yours, also, my love."

Aleene dipped her head. "I fear that day shall never come."

Robert slid his finger along her jaw, tilting her face toward him. "Hold your head high, Aleene. They shall realize the gift they have in you, I am sure."

Aleene stared up at him for a moment, her face a window to her emotions: hope, fear, yearning.

"Let us go, Aleene. I need you to sit at my side and advise me."

She swallowed and her eyes misted. "I should like that, Robert, very much." She kissed him.

"Ah, geez," Peter mumbled, turning away from them. "They await you in the bailey." The poor boy ran from the frozen garden.

"Come, wife." Robert broke away from Aleene and took her hand. "We have work to do." He led the way toward the bailey.

Aleene smoothed the front of her kirtle with nervous fingers. She had worked hard to make this Christmas celebration a wonderful event, but now that it was upon her, she wished nothing more then to shut herself away in her room.

She stared at herself in the wavy glass on the wall for a long moment, then took a deep breath and closed her eyes. If only her hair weren't quite so dark. If only her skin were a bit more pale. If only she hadn't married Robert, invited the enemy onto their soil.

Aleene dropped onto the edge of her bed and buried her head in her hands. If only she hadn't married Robert? She really could not sincerely wish that treacherous act away. Robert made the mess of her life tolerable.

But would her life be such a mess if he were not there?

"Nervous?"

Aleene jumped and looked up into the sparkling blue eyes of her husband. Guilt made her wince.

"There is nothing to be nervous about. The hall looks marvelous hung with boughs and the smell from the kitchens is making me drool." He held out his arm to her. "Shall we? Your people await, my lady."

Aleene only stared at his arm. Even in the dim light she could make out lean muscles and the golden hair that dusted his forearm. She let her gaze travel up to Robert's chest, then to his face. Oh, what a beautiful man. "I'm afraid," she said.

Robert let his arm fall to his side and sat quickly beside her. "My love." He reached out and took her hand in his. The familiar warmth seemed to seep right into her blood and pulse into every part of her body. "I shall be with you."

Aleene looked away. How hard it was to accept such a statement as good after so many years of fearing closeness.

"And, anyway, I think you might find this night easier than you believe it will be." He smiled, his teeth bright in the shadowy room. "Come." He pulled her up and started for the door.

She hesitated, but then took a deep breath and followed. She shook as they entered the hall. Always before the small tremor in her hands was hidden from all, but now Robert turned and looked into her eyes. He had felt her fear.

"I'm here."

They entered the hall and all noise ceased. People turned in their seats to watch as she and Robert made their way to the head table. Candles flickered on every table and from every sconce. Boughs of green draped the tables, filling the air with the scent of pine. They had not had such a celebration since the time of her father, and even then there had been tension. She had never realized it as a child, but now as she remembered back she knew the people had not celebrated with her family. They resented the dark Spaniard that ruled them.

Aleene stared at the ground before her feet as she walked. And, still, they resented the dark lady who ruled them.

She sat, tears burning the back of her throat. Her life was so full of questions now. Always, before, she had not questioned, she had just moved forward in her goal to rule Seabreeze for it was the only place her heart had ever been happy.

Now she questioned. Would these people do better under the rule of Aethregard? Her stepbrother was a weasel of a man, but his father had been able to unite the people behind him. And they all seemed to relish the thought of Aethregard as the lord of Seabreeze.

The thought brought an acid taste to Aleene's tongue and she grimaced as she sat. Robert still held her hand as she finally lifted her eyes and met the gazes of her people.

No! Aleene raised her chin. She could not question. She knew that Aethregard would make no kind of a leader. And she knew with a certainty that she could. She would just have to prove it, as she had set out to do when Tosig had died.

A man at one of the tables toward the back of the hall rose and for a heart-stopping moment Aleene thought he was going to walk out. Perhaps they would all leave in defiance of her.

Instead, the man came up between the rows of tables to stand before her. He bowed solemnly.

"We have heard, my lady, how you fought to keep an Englishman as our king. We know you were favored by Harold, may God rest his soul, and we know that you mourn him as we do." The man held out a small bundle and placed it before her. "For you." He bowed again, then turned and made his way back to his seat.

Perplexed, Aleene stared at the small bundle.

"Open it," Robert whispered from beside her.

Tentatively, Aleene reached out and unwrapped the gift. A simple necklace of seashells fell to her lap and she held it up for everyone to see. " 'Tis beautiful!" She smiled out at the man at the back of the hall. "Thank you so very much."

He bowed and sat as Aleene had Robert tie the necklace around her throat. She caressed the shells at her throat that seemed more beautiful to her than all the jewels in the world.

Aleene looked up again as another man came to the head table and laid a gift in front of her. She bit back tears as he, also, expressed thanks for her courage. Part of her wanted to reject their praise. She had been anything but brave, but she stayed her tongue and only smiled.

By the end of the Christmas celebration, Aleene had a great collection of small trinkets given to her by the people of Pevensey.

That night, as she and Robert settled into bed, Aleene lay on her side and could not think of a more happy moment in all her life.

Robert curled up behind her, and Aleene turned around to burrow into his warmth. They stayed that way for a moment before Aleene's body began to react to Robert's closeness. She stretched languidly, then pressed herself against him.

"You're insatiable," he whispered against her ear, causing goose bumps to raise along her arms. She laughed softly, kissing his neck and arching her body into his.

His hands moved down her arms and cradled her hips, pulling her against his hard manhood.

"Insatiable," she agreed, kissing a line down his throat and over his chest before she used her legs to push him over onto his back. She climbed on top of him, straddling his hips and kissing his mouth. He groaned as she brought him into herself, his hands on her hips helping her find their rhythm. She smiled in the darkness, tilting her head back and feeling him inside her.

One of his hands left her hip and ran up her side to cup her breast. Aleene sucked in a quick breath, then bit her lip when Robert's thumb flicked at her nipple. She quickened their rhythm, her eyes fluttering closed as the intensity within her grew. She felt her insides tighten, tense, and then fall apart in a great release, and she gasped.

"Insatiable," he laughed against her temple when she crumpled against him, replete.

"I love you," she said, "my Cyne."

The next morning it was as if the night before had been a beautiful dream and she had awoken to a nightmare.

Chapter 18

The moment his men marched Cuthebert through the gates of Seabreeze Castle at the points of their spears, Robert knew he had made a great strategic error. The people of Seabreeze stared at him with renewed animosity, and Aleene lifted her chin even higher.

When he had ordered the treacherous steward run down, Robert had only been thinking of the look in his lady wife's eyes when she awoke the morning after their Christmas celebration. The terrible rumors that buzzed about the castle were almost more than she could bear.

Robert looked at the stooped old man surrounded by strong warriors and rethought his first instinct, which was to throw the pitiful Cuthebert in the dungeons. "Take him into the hall. Don't let him from your sight!" he said roughly.

A low murmur of disapproval followed him

as he stalked toward Aleene. She stood at the entrance to the kitchens supervising the women. They did not need her there, truly, but Robert knew that Aleene was trying desperately to keep her authority in the face of catastrophe. He took her hand when he reached her and felt her flinch.

"I shall never hurt you, Aleene," he said softly. Words for her ears only.

Her lids flickered shut for a moment before she squeezed his hand. "You should have let him go."

"I could not!" Robert stopped himself and took a deep breath. "He must answer for the lies he has spread."

"Lies?" Brows arched over dark eyes. "You do not believe I pushed my stepfather to his death? Cuthebert says he saw me do it."

Robert cupped her cheek in his hand. "Do not play this game with me, Aleene. I know you could not have done such a thing."

They stood silently for a moment, Aleene's gaze full of such agony Robert wished only to spin around and kill the foul little steward who had crushed his wife's burgeoning happiness.

Aleene was shaking her head. "I will not hurt Cuthebert. I don't want you to hurt him, either." She closed her eyes. "I only wish my people would take my word as truth."

Robert cursed. "I shall not hurt him." He turned and went to the hall. One of the serving maids skittered out of his way as he entered, and he knew his look gave away the anger that ran through his veins like fire.

"Cuthebert!" Robert yelled, causing the man who sat hunched at one of the tables to jump. "What cause have ye to defame the name of your lady, my wife?"

Robert stalked toward the man and stopped, his hands in fists at his hips.

"You were not here before!" Cuthebert whined. "She hated Tosig. She killed him, and I saw it with my very eyes." He darted glances about the room, catching the eyes of a few servants. "And now you . . ." Cuthebert looked up at him, then quickly averted his gaze. "You stand behind her in her perfidy." The man had begun his accusation with a loud voice as if to make it carry to those working in the hall, but he ended in a squeak as Robert grabbed the front of his tunic.

"I stand behind the lady of this castle, a lady who saved your rotten hide."

Cuthebert gulped so hard Robert felt the man's Adam's apple slide against his fingers. "She killed our lord."

"Your *lord* was a disgusting excuse for a man." Robert hissed into Cuthebert's ear, then flung the man back onto his seat. With a deep breath, Robert furrowed his fingers through his hair. "Why do you make these ridiculous accusations now, Cuthebert? Why did you not come forward with this information when Tosig died?"

The man sat up straighter as if, finally, he was sure of what he said. "I did." He nodded to punctuate the sentence. "I told Aethregard."

Robert scowled when he heard the name.

Cuthebert lifted his pointy chin. "He wished me to keep what I had seen to myself because he did not want Lady Aleene's reputation damaged." The man slitted his gaze and sneered. "She *was* to be his wife, after all."

"The day Aethregard thinks of another with no thought to himself is the day men live upon the moon."

"Aethregard was to be our lord. A good man of English blood!"

"A swine no matter what blood runs in his veins." Robert shook his head and turned away. Servants had begun spreading fresh rushes. They stood staring at him, baskets of dried herbs forgotten in their hands.

"Go!" Robert yelled to them, gesturing toward the door. "I am conducting business, not a play for your amusement."

One of the women snorted, then laid her basket on the ground and turned with a swish of her skirts. The others followed. Another mistake if he were ever to salvage his and Aleene's authority among the people of Seabreeze Castle. Robert sighed loudly.

"Let him go."

Robert rubbed at a spot just above his nose and turned to see his wife.

She looked at Robert. "You should never have brought him back here." Aleene went to stand near Cuthebert. "Let him run away." She stared disdainfully at the steward. "If it was truth he spews, he would not have run."

Cuthebert did not answer, which made his lying all the more blatant to Robert's way of seeing it.

"You will not defend yourself to the lady, I see."

" 'Tis not I who need defend myself," the man said, never looking up from his toes.

"Oh, and are you not the courageous one, talking to your feet . . ."

"Cease!" Aleene slammed her hand down on the table before Cuthebert. The steward slid quickly away from her. "Go, Cuthebert."

The steward eyed the swords of the men who still watched over him.

"I do not think . . ."

"Please, Robert." Aleene lifted pleading dark eyes to him. "Let him be gone from here."

Robert held his breath for a moment. His morning had been filled with one mistake after another; would this be yet another? He let out the air in his lungs and gestured for the two guards to stand down.

"Go," Aleene said.

Cuthebert stood slowly, took a few steps to-

ward the door, then began running. He heaved
raspy breaths that echoed in the high-ceilinged
hall and his feet spit up stray herbs the servants
had left behind.

Robert sank down on the bench Cuthebert
had just vacated. "I wanted to prove him wrong
before your people."

"That will not work, Robert." Aleene
smoothed her gown with shaking hands. "I do
not want their trust because they are shown that
another lies. If I am to ever be one of them, if I
shall ever be the true lady of this castle, they
must trust *my* word."

Aleene sat at the head table that night and
looked out over the people gathered for supper.
With a yearning pain she remembered the
Christmas celebration only a few nights before.
It had been the most wondrous night of her life,
and she had actually let herself believe that
things would be different.

Closing her eyes, Aleene dredged up all the
courage she could find and stood. The low murmur of voices receded until silence echoed in
the hall.

"You have all heard the accusations of the
steward, Cuthebert," she said, her voice breaking on the man's name. Aleene cleared her
throat and continued. "I cannot prove them
false."

Soft gasps followed her words. "I can only

tell you that I did not kill Tosig. 'Tis my word against Cuthebert's, and I can only hope that you will believe me."

Clenching her fingers in her kirtle to stop them from shaking, Aleene looked about the room, her gaze lingering upon Nan, then Peter, and finally the old priest. She felt a warmth on her shoulder and reached up to cover Robert's hand with her own. They sat then and ate in the silent hall.

Two days later Aleene awoke as her husband readied to go out hunting. The sun had not yet shown its face, and Aleene was not at all ready to quit her bed.

"I love you," Robert murmured in the dark of the room and kissed her.

Aleene smiled and stretched as Robert opened the door to leave. "Take one of the falcons, Robert."

Her husband hesitated. "Are you sure, Aleene?"

Aleene laughed. "Of course. The poor birds have probably forgotten how to hunt."

"Well, there shall be no more lazy birds about this place. Except, perhaps, my wife." He left as Aleene pulled the coverlet up over her head. She wished away the world and reveled in the smell of Robert that clung to everything around her. She must have fallen asleep then, for when she opened her eyes again, the dim-ness of dawn had become bright. Still, the sky showed gray and dismal through her small window. With a groan, Aleene left her bed and washed. The water had turned cold. She shivered and had to jump back beneath the covers for a moment before she could stand to brave the chill once again and dress.

Rubbing her hands together furiously, Aleene went to chapel and knelt to say her prayers. 'Twas with relief she finished and moved again, trying to keep the blood flowing through her chilled body. She sniffed the air as she ran to the hall. It smelled of snow.

Aleene saw Berthilde as she entered the hall and summoned her maid. "Do you know where Robert is this morning?"

"Hunting with the men, milady."

"His men?"

"No, milady, the lad Peter and a few others from Seabreeze."

Aleene blinked, a small hope stirring within her. "Seabreeze men? They all went out together?"

"Aye." Berthilde nodded, one side of her mouth lifting in a tiny smile. "I even heard one of the men laugh as they went out."

Aleene made herself breathe slowly. Turning she went to the door and looked out at the slate-gray sky. She rubbed her hands together to ward off the chill.

"Snow is coming," Berthilde said.

Aleene nodded. She stared at where Robert must have walked, the men following him as they went out to hunt. Oh please, she thought, let them begin to believe in us.

"Do you remember, as a child, going sledding behind Old Man Rigdon's hut?" Berthilde asked from behind her.

Aleene frowned as she faced her maid. "Sledding?"

With a smile and a sigh Berthilde shrugged. " 'Tis been many a gray winter since children played in the snow behind Old Man Rigdon's."

Aleene furrowed her brow. "Why do you speak of this, Berthilde?"

"My old mind was just wandering."

Aleene laughed lightly. "Your old mind never wanders."

"You would come home and have hot mead, your eyes lit from inside like a Christmas candle."

Aleene stared at Berthilde. "I do remember," she said finally. "When father was still alive, it made winter much more bearable."

Berthilde nodded. "That it did."

Aleene returned her gaze to the bailey beyond the door. "If it does snow, I think I'll take Robert . . ." she stopped, thinking of something else. She peeked at Berthilde. "Ah, I see what you are getting at. Do you think they will come?"

"You will not know unless you ask."

"I shall take everyone, then. We will go sliding on the hill and have hot mead. We shall make a winter party of it!"

"A good party that will be, milady, a very good party indeed." With a smile Berthilde nodded and brushed past Aleene.

Aleene watched the maid make her way across the room and out toward the kitchens. The day didn't seem quite as dismal as it had only moments before. Taking a deep breath, Aleene went to the head table and sat. One of the women brought her a bowl of rosewater for her hands.

"Thank you," Aleene said.

The woman blinked and smiled cautiously.

The doors heaved open at that moment, bringing in a rush of bitter cold air and the first swirl of snowflakes.

"Take him to his chamber," Berthilde ordered as men stormed through the open door.

Aleene squinted in confusion at the chaotic mass of humanity that swarmed into the great hall. The men carried someone, another man, a large man. A breath hitched in her throat and she stood quickly. She moved forward, but her feet felt like lead as she tried to go toward the people.

"What has happened?" Her small question was not heard. The men moved quickly, others followed asking their own questions, and above it all Berthilde yelled orders.

She reached them finally and saw her husband, his face pale, his chest covered in blood. "Cyne!" she cried, running toward them. Pushing people aside, she shoved her way to Robert's prone body.

"Milady!" someone took hold of her arm, but she shook free.

"Cyne, oh, no, Cyne." She took his face between her hands, kissing his cold lips. "No!" She felt as if her own blood drained away with Robert's.

"Milady." Berthilde took her arm forcefully. "Let the men take him to your chamber. We must clean the wound and stop the bleeding."

Aleene could not seem to translate Berthilde's words for her own grasp. She stared at the woman, then looked back at the men taking her husband toward their chamber. She pulled away from Berthilde's grip and hurried after them.

They laid him gently on the bed, then stepped back as one. Aleene pushed through the men and went down on her knees at the side of the bed, taking her husband's limp hand in hers. "What happened?" She looked at the faces surrounding her. "What?"

"An arrow." One of the men pointed to just below Robert's heart. "It came out of the woods. Someone shot him with an arrow."

Aleene felt as if a fist had hit her in the belly.

She gulped in air. "Who?" she finally managed to ask.

The men shook their heads.

Peter stepped forward, his face nearly as pale as Robert's. "I took the arrow from his body and he fainted." The boy wrung his hands. "Will he die, milady?"

Aleene swallowed hard.

"Out with you now." Berthilde bustled in carrying water, bandages, and a jug of wine. "We'll need room to work."

Peter looked from Berthilde to Aleene, then to his silent lord. "We shall find the one who did this!" he said with boyish fervor. The other men just backed out of the chamber never meeting her gaze.

Aleene watched them leave, gripping her husband's hand.

"Strength, Aleene, have strength," Berthilde said, handing her the jug of wine.

Aleene grabbed the neck of the bottle in one hand, not letting go of her husband. *Be steady, Aleene.* The words ran through her mind, and Aleene swallowed. Oh, God, she could not. Not now.

Be steady, Aleene.

With a deep breath, Aleene let go of her husband's hand and placed the back of her palm against Robert's forehead.

"We must remove this tunic," Berthilde said.

Aleene put down the bottle of wine and

helped the maid as they struggled with Robert's clothes. He groaned once when they had to peel the cloth away from the open wound.

Berthilde leaned close to Robert's chest, picking out pieces of cloth from where the arrow had entered. "I wish those numbskull men had brought the arrow. I would like to see it and know that none of it remains within Lord Robert. But we can only hope now." She straightened. "Clean the wound with the wine, milady."

Aleene took a deep breath to steady her hands, then grabbed the bottle at her side and uncorked it.

Berthilde held cloths, ready to wipe the wine that would run down Robert's chest.

Swallowing against the panic that edged her mind, Aleene slowly poured a portion of the wine over the wound.

They worked for what seemed forever, packing the bloody hole in Robert's chest and binding it with tight bandages. Then Aleene knelt back down at the side of the bed to pray as Berthilde left to inform the people of Robert's condition.

Aleene wished with all of her heart she knew his condition. She could only watch his chest move up and down, and hope with everything she was that it would not stop.

Robert had still not stirred when darkness stole through the chamber. Berthilde brought a lighted candle and placed it beside the bed, resting her hand on Aleene's head for a moment before she left again.

Shouts roused Aleene from her vigil a while later. She jerked her gaze toward the closed door, wanting to know what happened beyond, but not daring to leave Robert even for a moment.

The door heaved open. "Milady," Berthilde said breathlessly, "there are people here from Pevensey." She frowned. "They have brought Cuthebert."

"Cuthebert? Why?"

"Come, milady, you must listen to them yourself."

Aleene bit at her bottom lip and looked down at her husband.

"I will sit with him." Berthilde picked up her skirts and went to stand at the other side of the bed. "Go now."

Aleene nodded then and forced herself to leave Robert's side. She heard anger as she entered the hall. People shouted at each other. She even saw one push another. As she got closer she realized that the person being pushed around was Cuthebert.

"What do you here?" she asked, staring at the steward.

The man jerked his head toward her. The words that he had been about to yell back at the people died on his lips.

One of the burgesses from the village stepped forward, his dark, bushy brows drawn angrily over his eyes. "This man here, your steward, has been in the village saying many bad things about you and the Lord Robert. When we heard of this terrible thing that happened, we decided to bring him here."

The people around the burgess murmured their agreement.

"We think perhaps he would know something of the killing of Lord Robert."

"He is not dead!" Aleene said quickly, her heart hammering against her breast.

The man blinked and nodded. "Of course, milady, my apologies. The reports have been confused."

"Very." Aleene forced herself to breathe. "I am sure you meant no harm."

"No, in fact, we wish to help." The burgess cleared his throat. "As the lord and lady of Seabreeze, you two have helped us greatly. We have heard of your courage, milady. And we know of Lord Robert's kindness to those who have been left with nothing." The man turned a darkened gaze on Cuthebert. "We fear this man means you harm."

Under any other circumstances Aleene would have rejoiced at the burgess's words. Now she could only bite her lip to keep back bitter tears.

"Harm?" Cuthebert interrupted. "She is the one who means harm." He pointed an accusing finger at Aleene. "She killed Tosig. She ran off Aethregard." He shook his finger in emphasis. "She brought in the enemy!"

Silence followed the tirade.

"Why do you fight her, sir?"

Aleene could not see who had asked the question. It was a small female voice emanating from the mass of people.

"Yes," the burgess turned on Cuthebert. "How does defaming Lady Aleene profit you?"

"I *saw* her kill Tosig." The steward whirled around, holding his hands out as if in supplication. "She pushed him from the cliff."

"And you said nothing then?" asked a young man in the crowd.

Cuthebert huffed a frustrated sigh. "You will take her word over mine?"

Again silence hung over the assembly.

"Yes," someone finally said.

"Lady Aleene," the burgess caught her attention. "I ask you this for all of us. Did you know of the money we have been demanded to send to you these months since Tosig died?"

"Money?" Aleene shook her head, caught off guard from the question. "Of what do you speak?"

"We have been told by this man," he pointed to Cuthebert, "that you demanded payments for your protection."

"I told you before and it is true!" Cuthebert

yelled angrily. " 'Tis all her fault: the death of Tosig, the demands of payment."

Aleene looked from the burgess to her frenzied steward. She wanted nothing more than to return to Robert's side and the argument happening around her was only making her confused and frustrated. She settled her gaze on Cuthebert. "I know not what you speak of, man. I did not kill Tosig, and I have never asked for more than the rents due this estate." Aleene's hands began to shake as she asked, "Do you know something of the attempt on my husband's life? For if you do, I would have that information from you." She took a step toward the man. "Now!"

"I . . ." Cuthebert fidgeted and shook his head. "I know nothing of that." He took a deep breath and whirled around. "But of what matter is that? He is a Norman, Lord Robert. He has no right to rule over this castle, or these people."

Before anyone could answer the doors to the hall burst open.

"He has been found, milady." Peter pushed his way through the mass of people. "The one who tried to kill our lord has been found!"

Aleene rushed forward as a whirl of frigid wind and snow heralded the entrance of the Seabreeze men. "Who?" she stopped Peter with a hand on his arm.

" 'Tis Aethregard, milady, your stepbrother."

Chapter 19

The men laid their burden roughly on the ground. Aleene ran forward to see Aethregard, his eyes closed and his lifeblood seeping into the rushes.

"I would have what is mine," he sputtered as Aleene entered his line of vision.

"You will have hell, brother, in answer to your wish."

He closed his eyes and coughed. Blood trickled from his mouth.

"Why did you do this? You would not have Seabreeze only by killing Robert."

"I would," he managed to say, keeping his eyes closed. He opened them then, staring at her, his gray orbs dull. "William said if anything were to happen to Robert I should have Seabreeze."

Aleene let out a distressed gasp. "He sent you to kill Robert?"

Aethregard laughed, sputtered blood, and

choked. She thought him dead when he went silent, but he opened his eyes once again. "Never that. William would never say outright that he wanted his precious Robert dead."

Aleene felt relief wash over her. "But . . ."

"Shut up!" Aethregard yelled, clutching at the wound that poured blood from his chest. "I cannot speak of this now, not now!" His body spasmed and another spurt of blood came from his lips.

Aleene swallowed against the bile that rose in her throat.

The people around her stood silently watching.

"I hate you." His voice was so soft, Aleene didn't think she had heard right at first. "I hate you. You have everything I ever wanted. Beauty, wealth . . ." he stopped, his throat working as he tried to continue. "My father."

Aleene stiffened.

"He loved you more than he loved me. He looked at you, touched you, loved you." A sickening laugh echoed in the hall. "He even threatened to annul our betrothal. He could not stand the thought of me having you instead of him."

Aleene felt she might be sick. "He did not love me."

"He did, so much that he risked my inheritance." Aethregard sputtered up more blood and closed his eyes. "And so I killed him."

A collective gasp came from those who stood

around the dying figure they had once wanted as their lord. Another sound drew Aleene's attention, and she looked up to see Cuthebert push through the gathering. The man pointed a gnarled finger at Aethregard. "You shall rot in hell! You had us believe the Lady Aleene to have killed your father and all along you were the murderer."

Aethregard opened his eyes for a moment, then closed them again. "That is right, Cuthebert, try to save your own weathered hide now as I lay dying." He laughed roughly and blood gurgled in his throat.

"The ramblings of death!" Cuthebert yelled desperately.

"Since the day Tosig went over the cliff, I have set Cuthebert to the task of undermining you, Aleene." Aethregard closed his eyes. "You think I will go without taking you to hell with me, Cuthebert?"

The steward searched the room with terrified eyes. "I never . . . he knows not what he says."

Aleene stared at her steward. "Go, now, Cuthebert. If you are ever seen within the walls of this castle or the boundaries of Pevensey, you will be killed."

The man's jaw dropped. "But . . ." He looked about as if asking for support.

The village people turned away from him.

Cuthebert blinked and then nodded. "So be it." With shoulders hunched, he left the hall.

Aleene watched until the door closed behind her former steward, then returned her attention to her stepbrother. The pathetic tableau he created only made her wish even more pain on him. She walked forward slowly and dropped to her knees at his side.

"You are sick, Aethregard," Aleene bent low next to his ear and whispered, "if you think what your father gave me was love."

He opened his eyes and turned his face to hers. "Bitch." He spat in her face, but she did not even flinch. "You have everything and still you whine."

"I have everything now," she said finally. "And I will not let you take it away from me." She wiped her face with the back of her hand and stood.

Aleene looked about her and spied Nan. "Clean his wounds."

"But . . ."

"He will die this night, I am sure. But God would not have even his filthiest creature die thus. Clean him and come to me with the news of his last breath." She stared at her stepbrother then turned on her heel and went to Robert.

Beyond his closed lids, Robert could see red. It seared his brain. He winced and tried to turn his head. Soothing words were whispered in his ear and a cool hand touched his forehead. Ah, that it would stay and seep away the pain.

"Robert?"

When he finally recognized the word, he realized someone had been saying it over and over. He tried to respond, but couldn't.

The hand left his forehead, and he tried to reach for it. He needed it back. "Please." He said it in his mind, but wasn't sure it had made it through his lips.

"Robert?"

He opened his eyes, the brightness making him close them again.

"He opened his eyes. I know he did. I saw it."

Someone seemed rather excited over something so trivial. Robert squinted against the bright light and peered around him. At the movement, his head put up a new clamor of protest. "Ahhhh," he groaned.

"Oh, Robert, finally, you awake!" The hand rested again on his forehead and he sighed. If only it would stay there.

The figure at the side of his bed slowly focused. Aleene. "Aleene." The sound that came from him resembled not a voice but perhaps the bleat of a sheep.

"You're going to be all right, Robert!"

He winced.

"There is no fever, and your wound is healing nicely. 'Tis just that you have been asleep these six days."

Six days? He had slept six days? He tried to

sit up, but a slicing pain ripped through his chest.

"No, Robert, don't move. You don't have the strength."

He blinked his eyes open again. "What happened?"

"You were run through by an arrow."

"Who?" He moved his head, cringing against the pain, and saw Berthilde standing at the other side of the bed.

"Aethregard."

Robert groaned. "I should not have broken his nose."

"You broke his nose?"

He moved his head again to see Aleene. "I'll tell you later. How do you know it was Aethregard? Where is he?"

Aleene's smile spread across her face and lit up her eyes. "He is dead, my lord. Your people found him and killed him. They were very upset that someone had tried to kill their lord."

Robert closed his mouth in stunned silence. "Their lord?"

"We heal, Robert, we are a people healing and we are in need of you."

He closed his eyes. "It will be all right."

Aleene's soft lips caressed his forehead. Ah, even better than her fingers. "Yes, my lord, we will be all right."

"I love you, Lady Aleene," he said, feeling sleep tugging at his diminished strength.

"And I you, my lord Cyne."

Epilogue

Berthilde sat on a weathered chair in the cobbled yard just off the newly finished stone hall. Sunlight dappled the ground and the children who played there as she slowly pulled the silk thread she worked with through the cloth on her lap.

"Berteede!"

"Yes, dearest?" She glanced up and smiled at Aleene's youngest daughter as the girl came flying at her, a jumble of big feet, long legs, and raven hair.

"Harry poked me with the stick!" Bertie pointed a grimy finger at her older brother and narrowed huge blue eyes on her nemesis. The girl's other brother, Edward, melted away from the scene of the crime as Harry opened his mouth to protest.

"Harold!"

The boy's mouth snapped shut at Berthilde's admonishment.

"But . . ."

Berthilde gave a small shake of her head and the boy stopped. He sighed heavily, his thin shoulders caving inward.

"What do you say, Harold?"

The boy scuffed the ground with his toe, then turned his woeful dark eyes on his sister. "I'm sorry."

"Very nice, Harold." Berthilde turned to the four-year-old at her knee. "And now you, Bertie."

The girl's small hands fisted, and she plunked them against her waist. "I didn' do anyfing!"

Berthilde had to bite the side of her cheek to keep from laughing as Bertie glowered from beneath beetled brows. "Bertie, I heard you teasing your brother. 'Tis why he came after you with the stick." Berthilde softened her chastisement by stroking Bertie's soft hair. "If you are nice to your brothers they will be nice to you."

"Hummmph." Bertie obviously did not believe older brothers *could* be nice.

"Darlings!" A singsong voice rang out over the yard and all arguments were forgotten as the children ran pell-mell toward their mother.

"Mummy!"

Grubby hands wrapped around Aleene's knees, long arms grabbed her waist, and tiny fingers twined with hers. Berthilde watched the scene and smiled with complete joy.

"I have a surprise, little ones!" Aleene laughed and tucked Edward's golden hair away from his face. The boy shrugged her hand away. He had just turned ten and was trying desperately to be thought of as a big boy like fourteen-year-old John. "Your father is home early with your brother John!"

"Aha!" Robert burst through the doors from the hall, a smile stretched across his face as the children transferred their boisterous attention on their father. "Presents for everyone!" he laughed, then fell to the ground and allowed himself to be used as a climbing toy.

John arrived a bit more sedately, although his smile matched his father's. "Berthilde," he said and came to her. The boy was fast turning into a man, his shoulders nearly double the width of her own. Berthilde had to crane her neck at the dark-haired, light-eyed boy.

"Did you do well, John, on your first trip to court?"

He bit his bottom lip with the cocky humility he had perfected. "Of course, Bert, but miss you, I did!"

Berthilde had to roll her eyes. "Yes, I will just bet you did. When you were not batting your long eyelashes at all the girls."

John laughed and gave her a quick kiss on her cheek. The tiny show of affection made her heart quicken with happiness. The boy went to pick up his little sister then, as Aleene came over.

Her former charge took Berthilde's hand and squeezed.

"All went well?"

"Robert said the trip was successful. He managed to get the restrictions on English ale-brewers lifted."

"Wonderful!"

"Yes."

The two women stood quietly for a moment watching their family cavort about the small yard.

"Of course he brought home some strays," Aleene said as an afterthought.

Berthilde chuckled. "Of course, how many?"

"Two boys: ten and thirteen. He found them on the streets in London."

"Perfect." Berthilde patted Aleene's hand. "Tom the fisherman is in need of some good boys to help him now that his youngest is married." Berthilde took her hand from Aleene's. "And Tom's wife is wonderful with children."

Aleene turned and smiled down at her. Berthilde noticed that the wrinkles at the corner of her eyes were deepening, but they only added more character to a beautiful face. She reached up and cupped Aleene's face in her gnarled hands. It was good to see wrinkles caused by laughter on her child's face. "Such a smart one you've become, Aleene."

"You sound surprised, Bert."

"Well, milady, there were times I thought you would never learn."

Dear Reader,

If you loved the book you've just finished, then make sure you look for more terrific love stories coming next month from Avon Books. First, there's Connie Mason's TO TAME A RENEGADE. In this sassy, sexy love story a tender-hearted bad boy returns to a Wyoming town, and his life is turned upside down when he meets a falsely disreputable single mother.

There's nothing quite like a sexy hero in a kilt, so don't miss the latest in Lois Greiman's *Highland Brides* series, HIGHLAND SCOUNDREL. Pretty, pert Shonna has vowed to never marry, but her parents have other ideas. They invite all the handsome highlanders from miles around to court her. But only one—Dugald—catches her eye...

Rachelle Morgan creates western romances filled with love and laughter, and in WILD CAT CAIT you'll meet an unforgettable heroine who learns to love again when a sexy mountainman rescues her from danger.

ABSOLUTE TROUBLE, September's contemporary romance, is an exciting debut from Michelle Jerott. Stunning sensuality and taut romantic tension are hallmarks of Michelle's writing, and in this sultry love story a strong-yet-vulnerable heroine meets a dynamic man bent on revenge. Can she show him that the best choice in life...is love?

Until next month, happy reading!

Lucia Macro

Lucia Macro

Senior Editor

AEL 0898